# DEADLY LIES

## and

# STOLEN MOMENTS

*by John Preston*

The Alex Kane Missions
Books 3 & 4

**ReQueered Tales**
Los Angeles • Toronto
2022

# Deadly Lies
# Stolen Moments

## by John Preston

The Alex Kane Missions, Books 3 & 4



*For more information about current and future releases,*
*please contact us:*
E-mail: *requeeredtales@gmail.com*
Facebook (Like us!): www.facebook.com/ReQueeredTales
Twitter: @ReQueered
Instagram: www.instagram.com/requeered
Web: www.ReQueeredTales.com
Blog: www.ReQueeredTales.com/blog
Mailing list (Subscribe for latest news): https://bit.ly/RQTJoin

# Praise for the
# Alex Kane Missions

"The Alex Kane adventure novels expand the boundaries of family constructions. Alex, his young lover Danny, and Joseph Farmdale, his late lover James's father, unite to exact justice for hate crimes directed toward gay men. A precursor of Queer Nation's activists, superhero Alex Kane does not sit idly by as terrorists and bigots extort and kill factions of the gay male community: he pulls out an Uzi. Preston's theme in these works is literature's most enduring: the conflict of good and evil – this time with homosexuals being the good guys."

— Jane D. Troxell,
*Contemporary Gay American Novelists*

"John Preston published six cases, collectively entitled The Mission of Alex Kane (1984–1987). They have the quality of comic books, and the dynamics between Alex and his young lover, Danny Fortelli, resemble a sexualization of the Batman-Robin myth ... The books provide pleasure on several levels. They acknowledge the harsh world in which we live, and they appeal to our need to think someone is standing up for our rights. They embody a set of values that we can emulate: [a] heady sense of individualism is firmly coupled with the need to participate in a partnership and in the community to work for the common good. A prominent message throughout the series is that the closet kills. Out people are not only happier but also become positive role models for other gays as well as ambassadors to the straight community ... Though the superheroes are unbelievably good-looking and impossibly skilled, the cases are particularly notable for portraits that are missing from much of gay literature. In a vision of the way things could be, gays and straights thus work together to make a better world."

— Drewey Wayne Gunn,
*The Gay Male Sleuth in Print and Film*

# By JOHN PRESTON

## THE ALEX KANE MISSION NOVELS

*Sweet Dreams (1984)*

*Golden Years (1984)*

*Deadly Lies (1985)*

*Stolen Moments (1986)*

*Secret Dangers (1986)*

*Lethal Silence (1987)*

# DEADLY LIES

## and

# STOLEN MOMENTS

*by John Preston*

The Alex Kane Missions,
Books 3 & 4

# Table of Contents

# DEADLY LIES

**by John Preston**

# Author's Note

*No, no, I can't swim!* Charles Howard's last words.

On July 7, 1984, after this novel was begun, a young man was thrown from a bridge in Bangor, Maine. He had been beaten by three teen-aged men for only one reason: He was gay. Charles Howard died, drowned in the Kenduskeag Stream. His assailants, tried as juveniles on the reduced charge of manslaughter will spend as little as forty-one months in a juvenile detention center.

The fantasies of Alex Kane, the escapism into the story of a gay vigilante, may be fun entertainment, but they shouldn't allow us to overlook the real world, the world where there must be constant struggle for gay rights and a concrete affirmation of gay dignity.

At the time of publication, the University of Southern Maine had instituted a memorial scholarship fund in the memory of Charles Howard. It has since been discontinued.

Those interested in supporting Maine LGBTQ+ issues are encouraged to contact Equality Maine at:

> www.equalitymaine.org
> 511 Congress Street, Suite 107
> Equality Community Center,
> Portland, ME 04101

# I

"I don't like it," Mike Ahern said.

"What don't you like?" Tim Ranson looked over to his co-pilot with hardly any interest. Tim had learned long ago that Ahern was one big bellyache. Here they had one of the most plush jobs in private aviation, and Ahern was always carrying on as though they were slaving in salt mines.

"Having that guy in the plane."

*That guy!* Tim had recognized the man who was their only passenger. Not that he could ever have forgotten anyone who looked like that. Those green eyes had been so striking that anyone would have to remember them after even the briefest encounter.

Tim had had more than a few jobs piloting the man. He had often wanted to reach out and touch him, just touch him. Partly to see if he was real – there was something about the sharp facial features and the obvious musculature that made the guy look as though he were a Greek statue brought to life by some forgotten ancient god. There was also something ob-viously sexual about the man – something that Tim couldn't have denied, even if he had wanted to.

"Nothing wrong with him. The job order said pick him up in Chicago and take him to Boston. What's your beef? We're even getting some overtime out of it." Getting overtime on top of their regular salary from Farmdale Industries was no small consideration.

"Someone like that shouldn't be in the old man's seat, that's all." Ahern's jaw was set with his bravado determination. He was playing his usual game, the one that went: *You should know what I'm thinking. You figure it out.*

Normally Tim would ignore the whole thing. He'd gotten pretty good at ignoring Ahern over the last six months they'd been working together. But the subject of the man in the back of the plane was one he had more interest in than usual.

"Look, I don't know what you mean. He's obviously a friend of Farmdale's. I've ferried him around before, so have the other pilots in the fleet. So you might as well get used to it."

"I'll never get used to piloting a faggot." Ahern spat out the words.

So, that was it. Tim's grasp on the controls tightened and he looked down to see the skin around his knuckles turn white with exertion. He was so fucking tired of this game. Damn Ralph and his fucking closet!

Tim relaxed, forcing himself to take a deep breath and get a hold of himself. He glanced one more time at Ahern who seemed to have been satisfied to get his bigoted words out and into the air. Did he know? Did Ahern know that Tim was gay? Was this just a way to needle the pilot he had to work with? Or was it possible he was really that ignorant?

The 727 kept on its course to Boston. Damn Ralph! Tim had to smile though. His lover, Ralph, was the most important person in his life. Tim could picture him walking into their bedroom straight from work, still in his conservative business suit but undressing as quickly as possible so he could join Tim in their big double bed and begin their passionate lovemaking.

He felt a constriction in his underwear just at the thought of it. His whole life was built around Ralph. Their sex was a part of it, but other things came with it. They enjoyed life together, had a fine apartment, good friends, wonderful vacations ... and an airtight closet.

Ralph was a lawyer with one of the prestigious firms in downtown Minneapolis, the same city where Farmdale Industries kept its fleet of corporate planes in order to take advantage of the Twin Cities' central location. Ralph was constantly concerned that the other partners in his law firm would discover his sexuality and that they would ruin his career if they did ever find out about him and Tim. They had to go through complicated charades because of Ralph's paranoia.

Some things were just ridiculous. Ralph would mess up Tim's bed before the maid came three times a week to clean. He would insist that they brag about their conquests of women whenever they were around any of Ralph's attorney friends. They even had to rehearse their stories before Ralph would dare to venture out in public. They couldn't go to gay bars in Minneapolis together; only in other cities when they were on vacation would Ralph dare to enter one of those "forbidden places." Nor could they ever have any but the straightest looking friends in their apartment. Ralph was too concerned that a nosy neighbor might happen to pass someone he deemed "too blatant" in the corridor and report him to some kind of imagined thought police.

Usually Tim could handle it all. If it was the price he had to pay for the relationship then it was worth it. But there were so many moments like this one where he had to listen to an idiot like Ahern that made his teeth grind in frustrated anger. There was no avoiding another fact: Those moments were increasing.

Tim just wanted to scream at Ahern: *I'm a cocksucker too!* He wanted to yell: *I get fucked in the ass by my lover and I like it!* At times like this he wanted to march in parades and sing in choruses; he wanted to hold hands in public and live on Castro Street. He was fed up with the bullshit that he had to go through.

But I can't blame Ralph.

Or could he? Ralph was possibly right about losing his job if the partners found out that he was gay. But someone was going to have to do it sometime. Everything was moving, everything was changing. Why couldn't Ralph have the balls to be the first one instead of hiding behind his conservative façade and letting everyone else do all the work and get all the glory?

Tim was sitting at the controls of a Farmdale Industries private jet. It was no surprise that Mike had figured out that the passenger they were carrying was gay. The man was a perfect clone. His leather jacket and his tight jeans, his black leather boots and his white t-shirt, all of it amounted to a uniform. This was someone that the old man knew very well. There had been other hints that Farmdale Industries wasn't going to have any problem hiring a gay man. There were rumors that the oldest son – the one who had died in Vietnam – had been gay. Tim could probably come out in his job and not lose it. He could support Ralph while he built up another career, one that didn't involve hiding and lying about who he was.

Then Tim wouldn't have to be silent in the face of bigots like Ahern. He could just tell him to shut up and be quiet or find another job himself. He could walk down the street with some dignity. He could live without fear and without constant worry that the wrong person was going to walk into the wrong room at the wrong time.

But now, really, he had to be quiet. Silent. He had to sit at the controls and wonder about the man in the back and what kind of life he led. His silence was going to let people like Ahern keep on going, thinking they had more allies than they did.

With immediate regret Tim realized he was helping people like Ahern. For a moment, he realized he was as guilty as the rest of them.

*Damn Ralph!*

# II

The 727 was making its final approach to Boston's Logan International Airport. Alex Kane looked out the window at the familiar skyline without any real interest. He just wanted the plane to be on the ground and he wanted to be moving.

He had to find Danny.

There was always an air of sadness around Alex Kane. There had been too much in his life, it seemed, too much to make him sad. There had been James, his first and, until recently, only lover. James had ripped away the shreds of self-deceipt and forced Alex into the self-awareness that he loved other men.

He had met James in Vietnam, during the war, the war that had been so good at destroying so many illusions. Alex Kane and James Farmdale had been passionate lovers once James had completed Alex's initiation. They had been a team – The Lieutenant and His Sergeant everyone had called them. Then James had been murdered by another American for just that reason: The Lieutenant and His Sergeant had gotten too close. The image of the two men in love with one another had been too disgusting for a beer-bellied NCO from North Dakota who took advantage of a firefight to frag James, to shoot him from the back.

That had begun it. When Alex had turned around and wreaked his revenge on the killer by performing an immediate execution he had committed himself to a life that he could never have foreseen.

He had tried to avoid it. He had tried by drowning himself in the cheap booze and the faceless bodies of San Francisco's Tenderloin district. But it hadn't worked. Even that one day when Alex had woken up and discovered there was no one in his bed and no money in his pocket and no future that he could see, his avoidance was impossible.

While he had lain there thinking, *So this is the end of the line,* his door was broken down and the goons hired by Joseph Farmdale had captured him. Captured him and taken him unconscious to the Farmdale mansion on the coast of California where the father of his lover was waiting, waiting with his orders and his instructions. Alex Kane had perhaps avenged one death with his actions in Vietnam. But vengeance was not complete. Vengeance would never be done so long as gay men remained the underclass, their fights, dreams, and hopes all brutalized by a society that could no more stand their existence than that NCO had been able to stand Alex and James' lives being intertwined with love.

It had begun: The endless campaigns, the countless battles, the ongoing struggle to secure something for gay men against the overwhelming odds. They had trained Alex Kane's body until it approached mechanical perfection. Farmdale had turned his awesome computers into a weapon of their own. They tracked crime figures, social reports and economic analyses in ways that had never been thought of before, ways that saw the patterns of discrimination and oppression in the gay world.

They hadn't worked.

They hadn't worked enough so far as Alex Kane was concerned at this moment of his life. There was no reason for it all to have happened. He was a failure. The Farmdale operation was a sham. It was for no good reason.

The plane touched the runway. He felt the familiar tug of the resisting jet engines roaring as they brought the craft to a slow motion that allowed a turn towards the terminal.

He had to find Danny and beg forgiveness. He had failed.

•   •   •

As soon as the plane had stopped, the steward had run to the back and had lowered the steps for Kane's exit. He just nodded unsmilingly at the man and waved away his and a ground attendant's offer of help with Alex's bags. There was only one piece of carry-on luggage. He didn't have time to indulge in the luxury that came with riding the Farmdale private jet. Not that he ever would. Alex Kane wasn't one to indulge in much luxury in any place at any time.

He walked quickly into the terminal and found a bank of coin telephones. He punched a number into the set and waited while the connections were made to California. Farmdale himself answered: "Yes."

This was their private line; Kane was the only person in the world who had the number. "What more do you know?"

"Nothing." The voice at the other end was flat, as though Farmdale felt the same desperate sense of failure as Alex. *"Nothing?"* It was an unacceptable answer to Alex right now. All those goddamned computers should have been able to tell them something.

"Only the police reports that we had earlier. I've had men on the case in Boston from the beginning. There's nothing more to say. The culprits have been caught. They're in jail. The evidence is clear and they ..."

"Danny? What about Danny?" Alex demanded.

"I know nothing."

Alex Kane slammed down the receiver.

# III

Alex Kane had checked into his usual hotel in Copley Square. He didn't really care about the supposed elegance of the place. He was more interested in the fact that the staff knew him, knew not to bother him. A hotel was just a place to sleep and make phone calls to him. Especially this time.

He'd dropped off his bags and made a few inquiries, but none gave him any idea where Danny might be. There was no answer at the college dormitory. His parents hadn't heard from him in days. There were no other friends that Alex knew well enough to ask for information.

As he'd done before, Alex began his search in the city's gay bars. He went from disco to raunch, from LaCoste to leather; none of them gave him the first clue.

At ten o'clock that night he stopped short. He was walking down Cambridge Street on the way to still another bar hoping someone would know something about Danny. But now he had suddenly realized that he knew precisely where lie should be looking.

Of course.

He closed his eyes and rubbed a hand over his forehead. That's where Danny would be. He sighed and turned around, walking back towards the Charles River.

There was no need to rush now. Danny would be there.

Danny wouldn't leave there for a while. Alex followed

the winding paths along the banks of the Charles until, after passing Massachusetts General Hospital, he came to the approach to the Longfellow Bridge.

The bridge spanned the Charles just over the locks that protected Boston's riverfront from the effects of the ocean tide. A subway line rose up on the same structure, coming up from its underground tunnel to take an easy route over the water. Alex climbed up the sidewalk parallel to the transit line and ignored the loud rumble of the passing cars.

Danny Fortelli stood on the bridge, halfway between Boston and Cambridge. He was staring down at the black water. The lights of Boston and Cambridge reflected off the surface, bright neon against ebony. Danny wasn't noticing any of the special effects of the urban illumination. The expression on his face clearly was concentrating on the darkness; the bottomless appearance of the river seemed to be seducing him.

"Danny?"

The younger man slowly looked up when he heard Alex speak his name. It seemed as though he had expected Alex all along. He just nodded his head without speaking.

Danny Fortelli was a handsome young man. While Alex Kane was someone you always remembered – those eyes, the chiseled features and his air of sadness were all memorable characteristics – he was not picture perfect. There were lines that were too hard in his facial features. His appearance was striking and sexual, but didn't have the appeal of a commercial model.

Danny did. His hair was nearly as dark as Alex's and it was more curly. His shoulders were more noticeably wide, the proportions more in line with the ideal of American manhood that Madison Avenue was giving out. His cheeks were dimpled, a slight hint of his boyishness showing through there. His complexion was unflawed. He was a gymnast, and his taunt torso's sleek lines weren't hidden beneath the simple jeans and flannel shirt that he wore.

He was, in fact, the gay man that every gay man dreams about. There might be some idiosyncracy somewhere that would make him unattractive to someone, but that person would have to look awfully hard to find it. Even now, in his obvious mourning, he was beautiful, so handsome that Alex found himself automatically responding to him, even though this obviously wasn't a time or place to act on it.

"I've been looking for you. All over the city. I got here as fast as I could."

Danny nodded once more. He had turned back to study the surface of the Charles again. A tear slipped out of one eye and tracked down his right cheek.

There wasn't any more that Alex could say. He needed some opening, Danny had to say something to give him a clue. Did Danny want to be alone? Did he want to go home? Did he want to go back to the hotel? Alex would have done anything, but he had to know what Danny wanted.

After a few moments of excruciating silence, the other man started to talk. "This is where they did it." His hand moved out over the edge of the bridge, pointing down toward the water. "This is where they threw him out into the river."

Another tear followed the first. Alex watched helplessly as Danny's throat moved with small convulsions, fighting back his sobs.

"He'd never learned how to swim. I was going to teach him this summer. I made him promise he'd go with me to the beach so I could teach him." His battle with the tears was a losing one. They were streaking down Danny's cheek faster now.

"Danny, I ..." Alex was at a loss. He wanted to touch this man he loved; he didn't dare. He wanted to comfort him; he didn't know how.

"They say they didn't know Sy couldn't swim. They say it was supposed to be just a prank. The subway was going by. He was screaming, but they thought he was just acting like a queen, just screaming for the sake of screaming, so they went ahead, thinking – they *say* – he'd just get to the shore.

"He didn't. He didn't get two feet. He thrashed around, there were witnesses who saw that, then he went under. He never came up again."

Danny finally looked towards Alex. He had delivered his description of the murder of his best friend with a controlled monotone. But now, looking at Alex's face, no longer able to keep in the pain, he screamed at the top of his lungs.

*"Why?! Why?!"*

Then the sobs were overwhelming. Danny's hands went to cover his face and his knees seemed to buckle underneath him. Alex quickly took the few steps between them and clutched Danny to his own chest, his hands tried to give comfort, his lips softly touched Danny's face.

Through the wails Danny kept on asking, "Why, why, why?"

Anger and grief, fury and sorrow battled inside Alex as he held Danny tightly. Wrath and sorrow fought for his attention. He didn't know which was going to win.

The subway careened up out of its tunnel and passed them, its loud noise momentarily blanketing the noises of Danny's lament. But Alex Kane knew this was an anguish that wouldn't be easily dismissed. This was a desolation that would stay for a long, long time.

# IV

Danny was finally asleep on the big bed in Alex's hotel room, his mouth was open, his breath was softly audible adding to an impression of youthfulness. *He's only nineteen years old,* Alex reminded himself. Nineteen years old. It seemed impossible.

Danny had the wisdom of a much older person. It had come to him through his willingness to always listen, to never play-act being older than he was. He went through life absorbing things that people said and observing how they acted. Only when all his information was complete would Danny act.

The wisdom came from other places too. Alex sat on one of the big overstuffed chairs in the room and continued to watch his lover as he thought back to their meeting. Kane had come to Boston after the Farmdale computers had discovered a pattern of personal destruction in the city's young men. There was a cause to anything that devastating, there had to be. It was Kane's job to discover that cause and to eliminate it.

He found the poisoned web that was entrapping some of the best and brightest gay youth in Massachusetts. It had been a blackmail ring. Handsome young men would be seduced by operatives not knowing that their activities were being videotaped and photographed. Then the evidence was used to force them into a vile and erosive prostitution.

Danny had been one of the victims. At the age of eighteen he had been forced to serve up a series of perverse sexual acts to paying customers who dealt with him and the others as oddities. Prostitution itself wasn't such a bad thing, it was often a means of survival for men and for women who had no other economic option. Some of them gave decent human services to decent human beings who needed their companionship. But the use of blackmail was unavoidably negative, its effect was unconscionable.

Alex had broken up the ring through a tip from Sy, Danny's best friend, and a remarkable young man in his own right. Sy was one of the thousands of gay men who had found their freedom on the streets. Viciously abused by his father, Sy had left his home and made his own life, financing his adventure with occasional prostitution. It was his street smarts and his willingness to talk to Alex Kane that had delivered the information necessary to destroy the evil kingpin who had been responsible for the destruction of so many young men – until Alex Kane had sent him flying out of a skyscraper window and into the waiting arms of Storrow Drive.

Sy. Tall, skinny, effeminate, strong Sy. The one who wore his gayness with abandon, who organized street kids and the spark that kept the Gay Youth Discussion Group going. Sy. Vibrant, courageous, dead Sy.

Kane picked up the copy of the Boston *Globe* and read the story for still another time. It seemed so easy to read the cold type of the newspaper. It was so distant.

### GAY YOUTH MURDERED BY TOUGHS

Boston Police reported today that Sy Mestrell, 23, of Boston drowned last night when a gang of local youths known as The Angels threw him from the Longfellow Bridge.

Mestrell, originally from Somerville, evidently could not swim. He died only a few hundred feet from the banks of the Charles River.

Indicted for second degree murder in Suffolk County District Court were ...

Kane put down the paper and closed his eyes. He wouldn't even have the satisfaction of catching the ones who did it. The police had moved in quickly and effectively for once. The gang had been under surveillance for a while. There was an undercover agent in their midst when they'd taken Sy and tossed him into the river. The arrests had been quick, the prosecution was going to be effective.

Not so for Sy, but because the police wanted the group off the streets. Sy was just their excuse. Kane tried to get his anger stoked up over that reality. But he couldn't. He couldn't feel it while he looked at Danny and realized the hurt and loss that Danny Fortelli felt. His best friend was dead. There was nothing anyone could do.

*What's the use of this life if I can't even protect my lover from this pain?* The thought ravaged Kane's mind. That was the reason he judged himself a failure. For years he'd dedicated himself to this battle against anyone who would dare to attack the vulnerable lives of gay men. James had been the beginning, the beginning of his vow that gay men should live decent lives free from the constant fear of hatred.

He had had some successes. There were young gay men roaming the streets who had never tasted heroin's poison because of Alex Kane's work. There were old gay men who were living in respectful comfort in adequate retirement homes because he had stopped the leeches who would have eaten their savings and their precious last years.

But he couldn't stop Sy from being murdered.

*What's the use?*

# V

The waiter in the hotel restaurant watched the two men as they ate their breakfast. *Why should they look so sad?* he wondered. *If I had one or the other I'd be in heaven.*

His name was Eric Appel. He'd been serving up food to travelers and tourists for five years now. The hotel might be four-star rated in the guide books, but he was just slinging hash so far as he was concerned. It was all just a scam to earn the money to keep up his own quest for the lust of his life, a man he was determined to find in one of Boston's gay bars. His determination was immense. He kept up his search every night of the week, supplementing his constant wanderings with regular visits to a local gym.

He had the looks, he had the pecs and he had the desire. But somehow his goal had always avoided him. He had the right to be sad, not them. *Look at them,* he thought.

The young one was too good looking for words, so attractive Eric wondered if he hadn't seen him in one of the gay magazines. Eric would have killed for hair as naturally thick and curly as that. He could only have been twenty or so, but there was ample evidence that there was a matching rug on the guy's chest, little wiffs of hair were creeping up over his shirt collar. He was the kind of guy who could wear any clothes and all those assets of his would still show up. Eric had watched him when he'd walked in. That was a *significant*

29

ass.

The other one was weird. He was easily ten years older. That didn't faze Eric. Ten years older, ten years younger, his lover-to-be could be either one. The man's eyes were strange. That was where the weirdness came in. They seemed to change in intensity with the man's moods. He'd certainly gone through some moods in a short time this morning. Anger had flashed for a while; so had a look of love that Eric had always wanted to have directed toward himself. It had been an expression of sheer adoration that had come over the guy. Then the sadness had crept in. Deep, deep sadness, like the guy was going to cry.

*They must be breaking up*, Eric thought. It was the only excuse for that look that he could imagine. *But why would they ever break up? he questioned. If you had that in bed every night, how could you leave it!*

He went over and poured coffee in the two half-empty cups, hoping that one or the other man would notice him. If there was a divorce going on here, he was perfectly willing to pick up any pieces that were available. But they ignored him, continuing to study the white linen tablecloth.

Well, maybe they'd be in the bars alone later tonight. Eric wondered which ones they'd go to and revised his schedule to make sure he was present in those he guessed the most likely.

*Either one would do me fine,* Eric thought.

• • •

Neither Danny or Alex had noticed the waiter. They were startled to discover their coffee cups full. Each grabbed at his cup, glad to have the distraction.

After more painful silence, Alex finally spoke. "What would you like to do?" It seemed a pitiful question. Kane hated this feeling of inadequacy.

Danny seemed to think for a while. "I want to go away." It was delivered that simply. Alex felt his stomach tighten. Did that mean Danny wanted to go away from him? Was he going to get thrown out with the rest it?

"Where can we go?"

Alex sighed with relief. "Anywhere you want. Really. Anywhere."

"Away from people. I just want to be alone. I just want to be with you."

"Danny, I don't know if ..."

"Alex, I just want to go away." Danny had cut Kane off before he had a chance to try to present anything that could masquerade as another option. "I want to get away from all this shit." His hands tightened around his coffee cup. "I don't want to deal with it any more."

"Then we won't, Danny. We don't have to." Kane reached across and massaged one of Danny's hands. "I have plenty of money. More than enough. We'll just go. Wherever you want."

Danny leaned back in his chair and saw the crowds walking busily through Copley Square. "The mountains. It's summer. I don't want to stay in the city in the summer."

"Fine," Alex said quickly. "We'll go to the mountains for the summer. Then you can come back when school starts again ..."

"I don't know about that, Alex." Danny was still looking out the window. "I don't know what I'm going to do when the summer's over." He sipped more coffee. "I don't want to plan."

"You don't have to." Kane knew he was speaking too quickly. His concern about staying with Danny and somehow soothing the pain his lover felt was too pressing on him. He tried to calm himself. "Is your car here?"

Danny nodded. "Not far, it's in a garage."

"Good, let's get our stuff and check out. We'll just drive north. We'll find something for the night and then look around for something more permanent."

"Permanent ..." Danny almost whispered the words. He finally looked at Alex. "You want that, don't you, permanent?"

Alex was stunned. "Of course I do. We've talked about that before. I've always wanted something that would last with you."

"No you didn't. You didn't at all in the beginning. You played all kinds of games about it."

"Danny, please. We've been through that. Yeah, it was difficult for me in the beginning. But for the last six months it's been obvious that I want to stay with you, hasn't it?"

Danny nodded. It was hardly a major affirmation, but Alex wasn't going to argue about it. Danny went back staring out the window and Alex realized suddenly that he had that same expression as he had last night, when he was looking down into the black water of the Charles, studying Sy's grave. A chill went through Alex's body. *Permanent.* Was Danny worrying about Alex meeting the same fate? Was that the problem? Was he afraid he would find love only to have it snatched away?

It had happened to Alex Kane when James had died. He could never be the cause of it happening to Danny Fortelli. But what else could Danny be thinking of? Look at the life Alex led, the constant danger, the seeking out of possibly mortal battles.

Permanent.

At least with reason, Alex supposed. Why shouldn't Danny want that? Why shouldn't Danny have that? If all of Alex Kane's struggles abandoned Danny this way, what was the use? None.

Alex Kane was making some decisions that he didn't dare investigate.

# VI

"What's the use of all this bullshit I've been doing?!" State Representative Andrew Marston threw his sheaf of paper down on the big conference table that dominated the meeting room. Around it sat his campaign advisers. "You assholes have told me for years that I had to get a good record going. So I did it. I did all the crap you wanted me to do.

"I should have divorced the alcoholic bitch you call my wife ten years ago. But, oh no, you said I had to have the image of a good family man. So I kept her. You've made me go to feminist meetings with a bunch of dykes who'd like to cut off my pecker, you've forced me to march in gay pride parades, you made me go against every value I hold and act as though I love and support fucking labor unions, you ..."

"It was the right thing to do," insisted Marty O'Brien, Marston's top aide.

"The right thing to do isn't going to get me elected dogcatcher in Minnesota any more." Marston was furious and disgusted. He picked up the papers once more and flipped through them. But the figures weren't going to change and the conclusions weren't going to alter. "The damn thing's all for shit. All of it. The field's so crowded with left-wing candidates now that there's no way in hell I'm going to get the governor's seat."

"Who could have anticipated the change in the electorate? Minnesota was supposed to be the most liberal state in the country. Anyone looking at your chances ten years ago would have told you what we all did – establish yourself on the left. Things changed in ways that we could never have thought. Abortion, national pride, stupid mistakes by other Democrats, all of it was unforeseeable." O'Brien was getting red in the face as he defended the counsel he'd given Marston.

But the would-be candidate wasn't buying any. "For Christ's sake, the field of liberal candidates is overcrowded. We're all going to knock each other off, spend huge amounts of money doing it, and then whoever is unlucky enough to win is going to get the shit beaten out of him by the Republicans. It's clear as day.

"These last ten years have been wasted, absolutely wasted. The master plan is a farce. We're all going to look like assholes."

No one could argue with Marston. He was speaking the obvious truth, and they all knew it. There he was, tall, thick-haired, perfect teeth and an athletic body, the perfect candidate. He had the right background: good middle-class family, football star in college, law school, never a hint of scandal in his personal or his public life.

That last part was important, because the group that sat around the table where he was presiding sure did have more than a few scandals among them.

Marty O'Brien was the cleanest, but that was only because he had never been caught. O'Brien was from the old school of politics. He knew every dirty trick in the books. He knew how to get people who had been dead for fifteen years to vote for his candidates. He knew which ballot boxes could be bought for how much in which precincts. He had a dossier on every major and minor political figure in the state that told him where the mistresses were hidden, how the illegal money was kept away from inquiring eyes, and just when which politician had been caught drunk driving in what state. He was the perfect campaign manager for Andrew Marston.

He had no morals and he wouldn't even know what they looked like if he happened to find some wandering around in his soul. He only knew how to win.

Not winning was going to be much more of a bother to Luther Angstrom. The head of the Minneapolis drug trade had to have a man he could trust in the governor's mansion. He'd invested millions of dollars in Marston. If it didn't produce the desired result then there were some very painful investigations going on in the state police department that could have even more painful results for him. He studied Marston and O'Brien carefully, picking at his nails with a letter opener. No one had to say the obvious: Something awfully similar to that letter opener could be used to pay back anyone that Angstrom thought was doing him wrong.

Angstrom usually did make sure he collected on those kinds of debts. He'd learned the hard way that being tough was the only way to succeed in his business. It was a lucrative operation, so lucrative that some guys down in Chicago had once thought it might be a good thing to move in on it. The result had been one of the bloodiest gang wars in recent history, one that left dead bodies of Angstrom's friends and foes all over the corn and wheat fields that surrounded Minneapolis. Once he'd been blooded and seen the good effect that the sight of a dead man can have, Angstrom was like a wild animal who'd been unleashed for the first time.

Martin Martello was one of the only men at the table who wasn't too concerned with the implied threat of Angstrom's paper opener. He had his own scam, one more than successful enough to keep him from coveting the other gangster's. Martello ran one of the largest and most profitable prostitution rings in the country. It was national in scope. He moved women around with the efficiency of Avis or Hertz. Need more product in Florida during the winter? Charter a plane and ship your surplus from the Northeast down to where the demand was. Was Atlantic City low on stock? There was extra inventory in Buffalo. Hire a bus and right the balance.

Martello even had computers working on those problems. But so did the FBI have computers working on the problem that was Martin Martello. And if those computers kept on getting helpful hints from the Minnesota Attorney General's office, Martello was going to discover himself as the prize in one hell of a big bingo game.

The rest of the group had similar investments in Marston's long march to the governor's office. They were desperate for his victory and just as desperately opposed to any other man or woman sitting in that chair.

But they had all taken part in the miscalculation. It had sounded so good, so obvious. In a liberal state, elect a liberal man. Take over the state government and use it like real men had used it in the past. They all had dreams of a return to the days of politicians who had understood the value of a dollar – at least a dollar that had been deposited in a secret bank account.

When the left wing of the Democratic Party had begun to take over they had all been caught in a wave of self-righteous crusading that was led by people who didn't give a damn about their own private wealth and who were too happy to subvert the time-honored way things were done.

The only option seemed to be to co-opt that movement. That's when they'd set up Marston. He had been well on his way to victory when the electorate had taken a sharp turn to the right. Law and order was the big issue now. Abortion undercut much of the feminist movement's appeal to middleclass women who had once been their major support. Gay rights had turned off many of the religious moderates. Unions were getting a worse name and their membership was drastically declining.

And they were stuck with Marston.

Andrew Marston looked over the room and studied the faces of the men who were sitting in wait for some answer. He knew perfectly well what was going through their minds. He was a liability now. A nothing so far as they were concerned. His access to their funds and their resources was about to be cut off and with it would go his dreams of ultimate power.

They thought they were going to use him once he's gotten to the governor's mansion. They were wrong. Once he was there his plan had always been to turn the tables on them. They were stuck in old-fashioned modes. Oh, Martello may have finally discovered the values of computers, but he was an exception. These men were stereotypes of old-fashioned gangsters.

They held their fiefs through sheer brute force. What they didn't realize was that if the power of the state was really directed toward them, directed by someone like himself who understood just how they worked, they would all be knocked off in a matter of days.

If he could grasp hold of the sophisticated resources of the Minnesota State Police and direct it at organized crime, he could wipe it out in a matter of days. But, of course, he didn't intend for the crimes to be destroyed, just these kingpins. Use him? He was going to use them. Nature abhors a vacuum; remove the natural parasites who lived off people's vices and you only created the situation where a new parasite would thrive. And the next one was going to be named Andrew Marston.

If he could ever get to the governor's mansion, that was.

"So we change priorities," O'Brien said.

"After ten years I'm supposed to stop loving Teddy Kennedy and start wanting to stand proud with the John Birch Society? Don't you think that's a little much for people to swallow? We've invested everything to make me look like the good clean, conscientious citizen. How can I justify the turnabout?"

Angstrom was cleaning his fingernails still. He stopped and looked up at Marston. "So find a reason to change that people can buy."

Marston stopped short for a moment. A change that people can buy? If it existed, it should be right here in this room. The men here represented everything that an honest person would hate. Violence, drugs, prostitution, illegal gambling ...

*No, no,* he thought, *they're too expected.* You can't start a crusade against something that people expect. Nor could you suddenly turn around on an issue like abortion. It was too tricky, there was as much support for it as there was feeling against it. Then what? What would get people so pissed off that they would understand a candidate ...

"Fags!" Andrew Marston shouted. "Everyone hates fags! What if the faggots in Minnesota started to do things that got everyone really upset, really angry and disgusted. What if I was the one who started the movement against them? I could do that with the radio program.

"I could introduce bills in the state legislature. I could begin a new crusade!" Marston's eyes were glassy with the thought.

Martin Martello, Luther Angstrom and the rest of the crew went through their mental files. Martello was the first to draw the obvious conclusion: "They don't do anything that other people don't do." Martello had once been amazed at some of the specific sexual acts his clientele requested from his women. But that had been a long time ago, so long ago that now he was incapable of responding to any sexual preference with anything but a yawn.

"But we can make them do things that will shock the hell out of the public." Marston was on a roll now. He had his answer. "Think of everything that the suburban mother thinks fags might do. Think of every possible thing that would turn a liberal minister's stomach, make an ACLU lawyer throw up. Think! Think! Think! We'll stage it all."

Martello was the first to sit up in his chair. Sure, he was used to anything on the possible menu, but if his wife knew what ... "It could work."

"We'll make it work," Marston insisted.

"How?" Angstrom stopped picking at his nails. This was getting interesting.

"Sure, fags do lots of things in private that would upset people. But it's all hushed up. Well, we just make sure it gets very public and very messy. You guys must be able to help me on this. You know what's going on here in the city and in

St. Paul."

"Sure, there's leather stuff, and some guys like teenagers," Martello admitted. He'd gotten some requests from clients that proved that.

"Okay, there's the start. Leather. People hate that. What if it turned really dangerous and really dirty? I mean, what if it got *sick?*"

"They play games," Martello swept his arms open. "Big deal."

"What if their games got out of hand? Say their games got real bloody."

Martello looked on with interest. "Yeah, I mean, you take risks, sometimes you fall on your face."

"And those guys that like boys ..."

"No big deal," Martello dismissed that idea. "Look, you want a young piece of skirt, there's skirt out there waiting for you. You want it with a pecker, it's there too."

"But if it was violent? If there was evidence that it was organized? If it was something that we could smear all over the papers? Come on, come on, don't you see? We'll create reality from the public's worst fantasies. It's perfect. It's fucking perfect.

"I can even make it so some of the fags come over to us. You know the type, the ones that want to be married in churches and have you think they're just like real men. Well, we'll make it look like there's someone attacking the gays. We'll make it so bad we'll get them to lead the crusade to close the gay bars."

"Hold it a minute!" Sonny LeBec wasn't buying any of that. He'd been silent during the whole meeting. But Sonny's many holdings included a couple of very lucrative gay bars. He didn't want to give those up.

"For the short run. Of course the bars will open up again. There'll always be places for the fags to meet."

"We'll make it up to you, Sonny." Angstrom had put away his letter opener. "Let's talk some specifics. I think our boy here has an answer to our problems."

Andrew Marston broke into a big grin. He was going to have another chance to win.

# VII

Alex Kane tried to let his senses take over. If he could only just let the bright, warm sun and the cool water overwhelm his thoughts, then, perhaps, they could be shut off.

He was on a float in the middle of a small, isolated lake in the White Mountains of New Hampshire. He was naked, there were no people around. The sunlight that was heating his skin was erotic. *Think about that,* Alex commanded himself.

His legs were spread far apart, each one hanging over a side of the plastic float. The water was just able to reach his testicles as they hung down. It was also cooling his buttocks. *Think about that,* he said to himself again. This time he smiled.

He could still feel the afterglow of his sex with Danny there, between his legs. The younger man had gone at it with abandon last night and again this morning. He was driven with sexuality it seemed. Maybe he was using it to escape ...

Don't think about that.

*Sex with Danny, just think about sex with Danny.* The smile returned. For years Alex Kane had only used sex as another one of his tools. It was something he used to barter with, to gain entrance to closed circles or to collect information. Very occasionally he used it as a form of recreation. When he had found another man who was as independent and as anxious to avoid emotional entanglements as he had been, then Alex could jump into the arena of recreational sex.

But from the beginning, sex had been different with Danny. Alex sometimes felt as though Danny had a strange power of his own, one that he could use to rip through Alex's defenses. The intense physical training that Kane had gone through had had a side effect. He had become a sexual athlete, one who could provoke the most intense and almost spiritual reactions from his partners. Over and over again men would stop in the middle of sex and ask him, "How did you do that?" He would only reply, "It's just something you learn."

It had been that to him, just something that he had learned. Something you did to achieve an orgasm. He had never had any kind of relationship with another man after James Farmdale, perhaps because he couldn't imagine suffering that kind of loss again. Perhaps ...

But Danny had made him lose it all. From the beginning, sex with Danny had been disarming. Alex couldn't use his skills against him. They were useless. Danny made Alex respond like an overanxious teenager himself. He longed for the feel of Danny's skin, he dreamed of his mouth covering Danny's cock, the same cock he loved to have driven inside him.

Now his face was breaking into a huge smile. His buttock muscles tensed as he thought of Danny fucking him. The guy had been a gymnast when Alex had met him. His torso was a perfect sight, covered with a soft pelt of dark body hair. His stomach was chiseled, his thighs tight as most men's biceps. And when he decided to fuck, he used all his own physical expertise to drive his body into Alex's.

Alex almost never got fucked. At least, he hadn't until Danny came along two years ago. But it was the guy's preference and Alex certainly wasn't going to deny him. Usually when Alex met a man the other male would assume that Kane was going to be "on top." It was the harsh way he came on, he supposed; he knew his appearance was one that fed a lot of people's fantasies about a "real man."

So Alex had gotten used to doing the fucking. Then comes

Danny and he wants the situation reversed. It had taken Kane a little bit to get used to the idea, but once he did, he wasn't in any mood to argue.

His cock was ramrod hard now, bouncing off his belly as it jerked with the thoughts of his excitement. Alex rolled over; he liked the feel of the cool lake water on his erection, and he rubbed it slightly against the plastic. He couldn't help but think of masturbating this way. The pleasure was consuming him.

"That was a mistake."

Alex turned and looked over his shoulder towards the shore. There was Danny, his body also naked, his hands playing with his naked crotch. They were only a couple hundred feet apart. Their mutual admiration didn't have much distance to hide it.

"Why mistake?" Alex teased.

"It was going to be fun to watch you get hard, but I can't hold back if you're going to show off your ass that way."

"Don't you have any self-discipline?"

"Not where that's concerned."

"Well, what are you going to do about it? If you think I'm going to just swim in every time you throw a boner, you're crazy."

"Then I'll have to come and get you."

Danny stretched his arms over his head and leapt into the water and swam right over to the plastic raft. Alex was able to turn back over before Danny got to him. The young man grabbed the raft and half climbed up it, right at the apex of Alex's legs. He smiled, then pulled on the legs, bringing Alex toward him and his waiting mouth.

Alex moaned as Danny took in his erection and used his tongue to send sensations from the tip of Alex's cock to the furthest extremes of his body. An unwilling groan of pleasure escaped from Alex's mouth.

Danny stopped suddenly. He smiled at his lover. "Well, do you want to come back up to the cottage where we could get a little more ... sophisticated?"

"I didn't think you were that big on sophistication," Alex responded.

"I'm a good learner. I have a good teacher." Danny reached up and cupped Alex's testicles in one palm. "Quick and easy right here, or long and slow up there?"

"Up there." Alex slipped off the float and the two men swam back to the shore.

• • •

Even though it was June, this part of New Hampshire was high in the mountains and the evenings still had enough crispness to justify a fire. Alex watched the flames grow in the stone hearth. They were mesmerizing. That was good; it meant another thing to take his mind away from his thoughts.

Not that Danny wasn't doing a good job of that.

They were on the floor, their bodies sprawled on the thick carpet. Danny seemed to be napping. He deserved it. He'd worked hard all day, hard at staying hard. When Danny had offered "long and slow" he'd meant just that. Long and slow for hours.

The opening between Alex's legs wasn't just warm now, it was heated, even a little raw from the use Danny had given it. *Time to do a little role-switching,* Alex thought. That wasn't going to be any problem. He could see the twin mounds of hair-covered muscles right now. Danny was lying on his stomach, his head on Alex's chest. It would be a pleasure to do nothing but switch roles back and forth. Fuck, get fucked. Suck, get sucked. With Danny, it would be pure bliss, in fact.

*All we need is one another,* Alex thought. *We could be so happy with just one another.*

# VIII

Tim Ranson was tired. He'd just finished a long flight, a round trip from Minneapolis to Kansas City with a big layover. He was sitting in the cab, grateful not to have to drive his own car home. The taxi was speeding up Interstate 35 toward downtown.

Tim had a copy of the *Minneapolis Tribune* in his hands. However fatigued he might have been, the headlines in the paper were enough to wake him up.

### GAY SEX RING UNCOVERED

What the hell was going on that a liberal paper like the *Tribune* was leading with that kind of scare? It wasn't like the newspaper to feed lines of yellow journalism to the public.

But the story answered the question clearly enough.

Minneapolis Police, following an anonymous tip, discovered today that a ring of professional men, all evidently homosexual, have been involved in the buying and selling of young immigrant boys.

The youths, who police say were imported from various Caribbean countries, were all between the ages of fourteen and seventeen. They were kept in virtual slavery by their supposed employers who threatened them with arrest and extradition if their sexual demands weren't fulfilled ...

The story went on. The *Tribune* was a family newspaper

and didn't pander to lust-hungry readers with unnecessary gory details. But Tim could read between the lines. The kids had been recruited in poverty-stricken villages, promised a decent life and, instead, discovered themselves misused and maltreated by a set of middle-class gays.

The story sickened Tim. He read carefully over the list of men implicated in the scheme. A doctor, a couple of engineers, a dentist whose name was familiar to Tim, it must have been someone Tim had met. Allen Chisle. He thought for a while. Allen Chisle. Hell, the guy had been at the same Christmas party as Tim and Ralph.

Tim stared out the window and watched the freeway traffic speed by. Who would ever have guessed that Chisle was someone who would have been caught up in a scam like that? He had seemed a really nice guy, interested in Tim and his career. He's been interested in more than that until Tim had made it clear he had a lover. Allen had even seemed to respect the fact of the relationship.

Tim had liked the man a great deal. He had even played with the fantasy that Chisle would certainly be a great candidate for an affair if Tim was ever going to take up something on the side.

But that hadn't gone far. Ralph was adamant about their monogamy and Tim respected his lover's wishes. But how could Tim have been so far off about Allen? If someone was going to be so clearly interested in a 35-year old man like Tim, how could he go off the deep end and wind up treating a young boy like a piece of chattel?

The cab driver turned off the freeway and wound the car through the streets of Minneapolis. Tim and Ralph lived in a highrise on the banks of the Mississippi River which bisected the city. By the time the driver had pulled up to the entrance, Tim had nearly forgotten about Allen Chisle's indiscretions. So he had made a miscalculation? It was just further proof that it wouldn't be a good idea for him to play around on Ralph. Jesus, he could have been caught up in that mess himself.

Tim paid the driver and dragged his bag from the back seat of the taxi. He nodded to the doorman as he entered the imposing lobby of his building. He whistled softly as he waited for the elevator to arrive. He was smiling when it did. Ralph would be waiting. It was late, too late for dinner. But not too late for sex.

The elevator seemed to take forever to rise up to the fifteenth floor where the two men had their apartment. Tim walked swiftly down the corridor to their door and opened it with his key. He was still whistling when he walked in and heard the music.

It was a Bach fugue, something Ralph usually wouldn't have had playing. Tim didn't think much about it. There was a strange smell though, as though Ralph had burnt a late dinner. In fact, it stank. Tim called out. "Hey, Ralph, where are you?" He didn't get a reply. He walked into the bedroom, wondering if Ralph was planning a surprise for him.

There was a surprise, all right, but it wasn't one that Ralph had planned. Someone else had done the honors. There, spreadeagled on their bed, was Tim's lover. He was dead. He had to be. His genitals weren't attached to his torso. They were cut off, on the ground at the foot of the bed. Where they had been was only a gaping hole – a hole where nearly all of Ralph's blood had spilled out.

Tim didn't have time to think. He stood straight up as he vomited.

•   •   •

Tim felt as though it was all some bad dream, some horrible joke that had been played on him. All around him the police and their technicians thronged, picking through the evidence. Unbelieving, he watched as two men from the coroner's office carried out a large plastic bag that Tim knew contained his lover's body.

"Mr. Ranson, I'm afraid I have to talk to you."

Tim looked up and tried to remember the name of the

police detective. Carlson, that was it, Lieutenant Carlson from the homicide division.

"Yeah, of course. Can I get you some coffee?" What a ludicrous thing to ask. Coffee during a murder investigation

"No thank you." The officer didn't seem to think Tim's reaction was strange. He sat down on a sofa across from Tim's chair. "We know you were in Kansas City tonight. We know what time your plane returned to the airport."

*Of course*, Tim thought, *I would be a suspect.*

"So, obviously, since the time of death was determined as about six this evening, you are totally in the clear." Carlson must have been through this many times, but he still seemed uncomfortable delivering the judgment to Tim. He averted his eyes for a moment, as though he felt guilty even thinking that Tim would have murdered Ralph ... especially that way.

Tim just nodded.

"Can you give us any idea about your ... roommate's friends?"

"He wasn't just my roommate, he was my lover." Tim felt some strange and great relief to finally be able to say that. It was a minor victory in the middle of all the rest, but it still felt god-damned good. *My lover ...*

"*I* ... assumed so. I still have to ask about his other friends."

Tim hesitated. "Mainly people from his office. He worked at a firm here in Minneapolis." The detective nodded, indicating he already had that information. "Then, well, a few friends of mine knew him." Tim rattled off the short list of gay men that he and Ralph used to see. *Used to see ...*

"Do you know," Carlson stopped short for a moment. Then he began again, apparently forcing himself to go through with this unpleasant conversation. "Do you know if any of them were also interested in the kinks that your friend enjoyed?"

"My *friend* didn't enjoy any kinks." Tim sat up straight. He stared into the policeman's eyes. "My *friend* never got into any kink at all." It was true. Ralph had been a good lover and a hot bed partner, but he had been straight vanilla for the years he and Tim had lived together.

The way Carlson reacted infuriated Tim further. The detective obviously didn't believe Tim's judgment. "Well, but perhaps some of his other gay friends were ... inclined that way. Maybe they experimented every so often with one another."

"They did not." Tim would know. If there was any experimenting to be done, he would have done it. He was always vaguely interested, Ralph had always rebuffed his hints with a trace of disgust.

"Mr. Ranson, someone entered this apartment with your friend's permission. There's no sign of forced entry. He tied your friend to the bed. There's no sign of a struggle. Your friend enjoyed – or endured – at least an hour's worth of physical activity from our reports. There's no sign of drugs to indicate any unfair play. Then your friend's companion went too far. Obviously, he went way too far. Now, we're grown ups in the police department, Mr. Ranson. I'm not going to make any moral judgments about what activities you and the rest of you take part in. But I have some experience in these things and I knowed damned well that what went on in that bedroom wasn't in any way a little experimentation. Those men knew what they were doing, they did it with finesse and knowledge ... up to the end.

"Mr. Ranson, your pal was no amateur. He was playing in the big leagues. I want to know all about his activities. I want to know where he learned his lessons."

Carlson sat there waiting. Tim couldn't help but cry. He covered his face with his hand. "I honest to god don't know."

# IX

Joseph Farmdale knew that he should be impressed with the New England countryside that sped by his car window. His rented limousine was climbing up the White Mountains. There was still snow occasionally visible on the top of Mt. Washington. That, his memory reminded him, was not unusual. It was still June.

He sighed at the labor involved in trying to find comfort in things aesthetically pleasing. It wasn't his forte. Farmdale had truly given up that direction of life's pleasures decades ago. His were now found in the maintenance of what he called a sense of propriety. He did enjoy the results of good breeding, the kind he could see clearly in his thoroughbred horses back on his California ranch. He only wished that good breeding had shown in his children. It had, actually, and the evidence of it in his first son, James, had been the greatest pleasure of his life, for as long as that pleasure lasted. But the other illustrations of breeding in his own family line had been just as distinctly disappointing.

Farmdale sneered at the remembrance of the rest of his children. James had been such a Farmdale! He had had the dignity and the intelligence that good breeding and the finest educational opportunities should have produced. But the rest ...

He was simply thankful that the rest were narrowminded enough to be satisfied with their trust funds, their well-stocked bars and their endless lines of spouses.

It was only fitting that James would have been the one child of Joseph Farmdale to choose an adequate mate. Joseph had foolishly dismissed James's search for a male lover as a passing phase that his eldest son would leave behind. When he hadn't, when it had become obvious that James was determined to remain homosexual, Farmdale had gone into one of the only deep depressions of his life.

It was his son's final accomplishment of a relationship that had brought Joseph out of it. James had written from Vietnam that he had discovered the man he wanted as a life companion. Joseph had been aghast. The existence of the lover had meant some final statement about his son's sexuality that the father had difficulty accepting.

He was sure that his son's lover must be some kind of gold digger. He had ordered extensive investigations of this new person's past. He had discovered, much to his amazement, that James had made a tremendously admirable choice.

The new man was named Alex Kane. "Kane" was an anglicization of a Greek name that an immigration officer at Ellis Island had decided was too unAmerican. "Kane" would do. The family had lived and prospered in one village in Greece for centuries. They had been honorable and proud people, adamantly opposed to the alien Turkish rule that held a stranglehold on their country. That opposition had forced their exile.

They'd come here, to New Hampshire, and settled in Portsmouth where they were fishermen. They had maintained their pride and they had persevered against tremendous odds to establish themselves in the Yankee seaport. This young man, Alex, was the last of their long line. He was the beneficiary of all their heritage.

Brought up by his grandparents after his own father and mother had died in an accident, Alex Kane had been a top student in public schools. He had refused the easy way out of this military service that a college scholarhip offered, instead deciding to enlist in the Marine Corps.

That's where he'd met James. Farmdale remembered his son's glowing letters. There was an enthusiasm in them that could not be denied. That, and an insistence in Alex's rightful place in the family that demanded a response from his father.

Slowly, with the luxury of letters being sent over great distances which allowed Joseph Farmdale to absorb the shock of his son's revelations, Joseph had come to accept his son's position.

He supposed that none of the radicals in the country would have appreciated the precise process he had gone through. Joseph Farmdale simply realized that if his son were, indeed, the repository of all that was decent in the Farmdale tradition – and Joseph did not doubt it to be true – it would have to follow that James could not make a totally foolish decision.

If the scion of the Farmdale line decided that it was good to be homosexual, then it was good to be homosexual. The question was resolved as soon as Joseph Farmdale had defined his correct line of reasoning.

It was his son's murder which had led him on from that starting point. Joseph Farmdale seemed to be studying the green foilage of the New Hampshire mountains now. But the memory of that death was one that he had never truly accommodated himself to. It was painful even now.

If a totally ignorant person could take it upon himself to murder James Farmdale only because he was a homosexual, then the bigotry that was directed towards homosexuals was unacceptable. Utterly, totally and eternally, it had to be wiped out.

That had been Joseph Farmdale's conclusion. It was James who gave him the vehicle to achieve that goal: His lover, the young man, Alex Kane, who had acted to erase the murderer of his son.

Farmdale had found him in the sleaziest part of San Francisco. He had rescued him. He had given him all that James had requested that he have. Kane had the money that a Farmdale's spouse was entitled to, a great deal of money. He had entry to any office, any home in the country that he desired.

Joseph Farmdale would not have it any other way. Most people assumed that Joseph was incapable of emotions, and indeed he very rarely showed them. Nor did he display passion. His wives would certainly attest to that. But there were things important to Joseph Farmdale, there were things that one simply did not forget. Those things made up a short list. But at the top of the list was his son's memory.

The car pulled to the side of the road. The chauffeur pressed a button to roll down the window that separated the passenger from the driver and the bodyguard who sat in the front seat.

"I think this is the place, Mr. Farmdale," the man said. "As I told you ..."

"Yes, yes, you told me. I read your report." Joseph Farmdale looked at the narrow dirt road that was immediately in front of them. "Well, drive on. We'll see if they're here."

The huge limousine could only barely make it over the five miles that they had to travel from the highway. But eventually, to the driver's great relief, they came to a large clearing. There was at least an acre of rough lawn here. The brush had all been cut down, and it allowed them a sudden vista of a large lake. Between the entrance to the carefully cared for property and the water was a log cabin. Smoke drifted up its chimney.

There was a Mercedes coupe parked near the house. Farmdale recognized it as the gift he had given Danny Fortelli as a graduation present. "They are here," he announced. Both the driver and the other passenger took revolvers from the shoulder holsters. "Oh, put those away!" Farmdale commanded. "He's not going to harm *me!*"

The two men looked at one another in obvious distress "Mr. Farmdale, sir ..."

Joseph Farmdale cut off his chauffeur. "I'll have none of that. You're in my employ. He's hardly dangerous to me. Now just wait here."

The driver jumped out of the front door and opened Farmdale's. He still had the revolver in his hand. "Put it away." The driver shrugged and complied. "Wait here," Farmdale repeated.

Using his cane, the necessity for which was a constant annoyance these days, Farmdale walked the rest of the distance to the cabin, carrying only a briefcase.

He didn't knock. He simply opened the door. He wasn't surprised at the sight that was waiting there. Just as he knew he was supposed to be excited by the vistas of the White Mountains, so Joseph Farmdale also knew he should be affected by the image of these two males. They were exercising; Farmdale thought that Alex Kane was always exercising. He and Danny Fortelli were wearing only those silly things that athletes wore – supporters, he remembered the name. He must have had one on himself at some point in his life, perhaps when he'd played polo as a younger man. But he was thankful he didn't recall the indecency of it now.

The supporters were their only covering. The rest of their bodies were exposed. Sweat glistened on their skins. They had obviously been at it for hours again. *Don't they ever tire of all this!* he wondered.

He waited for them to stop; they apparently hadn't noticed him yet, though there was a breeze coming through the doorway. Farmdale decided that Alex was pulling one of his irritating stunts, purposely ignoring him. He would play the same game. He took a chair and continued to watch them.

They were doing those things where you tortured your stomach. Somehow they had crossed their legs together, for leverage, Farmdale assumed. One would sit up, the other stay on his back. As one descended, the other ascended. Foolishness.

He realized that there were many men and women who would give a fortune to watch this display. Some would be attracted to the youthfulness of Danny's body. Others would appreciate the lines in Kane's torso that were etched so starkly that he appeared to be a medical textbook illustration.

Farmdale, of course, didn't respond to either in any sexual fashion. He simply watched, waiting for them to get over their self-inflicted torture. He had to wait a good fifteen more minutes.

The two men sprawled on their backs on the floor. Their breath was labored, but not nearly so much as it would have been on another man after this kind of workout. Only after their chests had begun to assume a more tolerable cycle of expansion and contraction did they sit up, then stand and face Farmdale.

Danny, the old man was pleased to note, at least had the sense to seem slightly embarrassed by his nearly naked state. He bent down and retrieved a pair of elastic-waisted shorts to cover himself.

Alex Kane was scowling at Farmdale. "We're retired."

Farmdale lifted a single eyebrow. "You were never employed. How could you be retired?"

Danny seemed surprised. "I thought he worked for you."

Joseph smirked. He had thought that Alex had given that impression. "I don't know that many men who are worth as much as Alex Kane bother with things such as working for a salary."

Alex crossed his arms over his bare chest. "I worked with you."

"If you, in fact, have been in partnership with me for that long a period of time, I would have hoped some sense of graciousness would have been passed on to you, perhaps enough to allow you the taste to offer a visitor a bit of refreshment."

"I'll get it," Danny offered. "What would you like? We don't have much. Herbal teas, some wine ..."

"Wine would be appreciated."

"I don't want visitors," Kane hadn't relaxed his arms.

Farmdale waited a moment before answering, "For all my years I have had to tolerate unexpected, unappreciated, unwanted, inconvenient, unannounced visits from my relatives. It is a great pleasure to finally be in the other position. I am visiting my family. I expected to be treated with courtesy."

The word "family" hit Alex Kane. He closed his fists in anger. Danny watched, puzzled. His curiosity wasn't assauged when Alex announced, "Give him some wine."

Danny delivered a full glass to Joseph Farmdale in a short time. "Alex," he turned to his lover, "we shouldn't stand around all sweaty like this."

"The odor is not the most enjoyable," Farmdale said as he sipped the wine, gratified to discover that it was one of his favorite St. Emilions. Kane had learned some things.

"We're not worried about the smell, Farmdale," Alex said gruffly. "But it's not healthy to work out and then stand around this way."

"It is certainly not enjoyable for me to have to witness you in such embarrassingly scanty clothing."

"I know," Alex kept his same tone of voice, "it must upset your sense of propriety."

Farmdale sipped more of his wine. "Danny, would you mind bringing the bottle over here. I may need more of this to fortify myself while you two clean off."

• • •

Farmdale had gotten halfway through the wine by the time the pair had come back from the second floor of their house. The sounds of the shower had at least meant that they had running water.

Danny was obviously still reacting to Farmdale's presence. He had put on a quite reasonable set of clothes, a pair of khaki trousers, loafers, a polo shirt. His hair was still damp from the shower. Kane, probably in defiance, had only put on a pair of gym shorts.

No one made any attempt at civil conversation. Farmdale immediately went into the business at hand. "I've some papers for you to sign. Some are simple forms for the maintenance of your trust. I must assume since you've not been in contact with me for the past few weeks that you no longer wish me to handle your affairs."

He opened his briefcase and brought out a folder. "This is a series of documents which transfer responsibility – including a power of attorney – to a bank in Boston. I assume you'll find it a worthy institution for your needs. This," he brought out another set of papers, "is necessary for your estate to be transferred from my own bank in California. You should also, it's always advisable at times such as this, renew your will. It's enclosed. The bank will want to review it with you."

"I don't want to talk to any fucking bank."

"I've told them what a difficult customer they should expect you to be. They're prepared to do all the necessary transactions by mail."

Farmdale poured himself still more wine. "My doctors would have a fit if they knew I was imbibing this much."

Danny and Alex stared at the piled documents as though they contained some kind of time bomb. Farmdale watched the effect of his little scheme and was delighted to see its apparent success.

"Don't you have something else to say to us?" Danny asked.

"Why bother? You are an adult in the eyes of this state, also in Massachusetts. You have the right to make your own decisions. This other one," he waved at Alex Kane, "is so pig-headed that discussion is seldom worthwhile with him. He most certainly is an adult in any event. From the tone of your question I have to assume you've practiced your lines and perfected your defenses. You have the right to your own lives."

Farmdale finished the wine with a loud appreciative smack of his lips. "You've also done me a great favor. When I was in school we often came up to this part of the country I think it must have been that some of my mates skiied." Farmdale was obviously announcing that he would never have done anything that foolish.

"We had a favorite inn. The Red Crow. It's only a few miles from here. Having flown all the way from California, I've determined to enjoy the place anew. I'll be there for a few days if you'd like to reach me. Perhaps we could have dinner?"

"No." Alex Kane stood up. "We don't want to go to dinner."

Farmdale stood as well. "If you change your mind." He held out a hand. Kane reluctantly came across the room and shook it. Danny followed suit. "You can find the inn in the phone book."

"We don't have a phone."

"I do think you must have a dime for a pay phone, Alex." Then Farmdale smiled and made his way back to the car.

• • •

Alex was still sitting in the same chair he had taken when Farmdale left. Danny finally broke their brooding silence. "What's wrong?"

Alex wouldn't look him in the eye. "I don't dare move. I know he left it here. I know the bastard left it somewhere we'd find it and I can't ..."

"Left what?"

"The book."

"What book? Alex, you're not talking sense."

"There's always a book, Danny. It always has a red leather binding. He could never just leave a report or have a manila folder. There had to be a book. He had to have it bound. He had to have it all neat and tidy the way the goddamned Farm-dales always had everything."

"What's in the book, Alex?"

"Don't you remember? When we were in Boston, when we met? When I told you all I knew about you?" Danny nod-ded his head yes; he certainly did remember that frightening encounter with the power of information. When Alex was investigating Danny's case he had confronted Danny with his own life story in a matter of a few hours. Now Danny remem-bered: Alex had read it to him from a book with red leather binding.

"But, what difference does a book make? We can just ignore it."

"Can we? Can we really?" Alex looked at Danny. His lover had known the broad outlines of Alex's work. He had always talked about perhaps joining Alex in his labor once he had finished college. But Alex had always assumed that Danny knew enough, he had gone through enough. There was no need to burden the kid with more. Once you'd been black-mailed, attacked on the streets of your home city and forced into prostitution, you had more than enough experience for a nineteen-year-old.

Danny didn't know the power of those books. The way their computer printouts made sense of random acts, the manner in which they produced patterns where no one else had even seen connections. When one did see that power ...

Danny stood up and walked over to the chair where Farmdale had sat. He didn't see a thing. Then he felt under the cushion. There it was. A red leather book, carefully bound in a fine old Spanish fashion.

"Don't open it, Danny," Alex said.

But Danny had already begun reading the first page.

# X

Tim Ranson stood in a bar off Hennepin Avenue. It was early, but he was taking good advantage of happy hour and was well on his way to being drunk.

He looked around at the crowd of men that had gathered, most of them in their office clothes. *Bunch of perverts.* What else could he think after what had happened to Ralph? And after what else had been reported in this morning's newspaper. The *Tribune* had the story on the front page. There was lots of gay news on the front page nowadays in Minneapolis. All of it was bad.

The director of one of the big gay community organizations had left town. That wouldn't have been news. But he'd left town with the entire annual budget of the group. *Rip their own off.* It was to be expected, Tim decided. Not one of them had any respect for the others.

There was another story as well. Another of the gay bars, one of those that proudly announced itself as gay owned – implying that others were part of some mafia conspiracy – had been closed when it was discovered that the fire exits had been purposely blocked. The owner had claimed he had nothing to do with it, but the files of the city safety office showed he'd been warned for the same infraction numerous times before.

*What a bunch of scum.*
*Who just happened to be gay.*
Tim thought that one was worth another double Vodka on the rocks. What an efficient drink it was, nearly pure alcohol that could knock you out faster than anything else in the bar.

The bartender filled the glass without comment. He was obviously used to the ones who came in at this time of day and tried to anaesthetize themselves with the half-price drinks the boss used to lure them in. They'd get so drunk so quickly that they wouldn't stop when the place reverted to full prices for watered-down drinks in another hour.

Actually, it wasn't going to work too well for Tim. He wasn't used to drinking this much. He'd tried these past few days. He'd taken a leave of absence from Farmdale Industries. There hadn't been any hassle about that. He'd spent the time moving; he couldn't stand the idea of staying in the same apartment, not even in the same building. He'd spent a small fortune from his savings on the necessary deposits for a new one-bedroom place.

He'd refused to keep any of the things he and Ralph had purchased together. That had meant a lot of shopping. He'd gotten new furniture for his small living room today at Dayton's. Thank god for the savings he'd accumulated and the fat check he had been collecting from his job.

He downed half his drink. He should go back to work soon. The schedule would do him good, make some sense out of the hours of the day. He didn't have that now. He'd find himself sleeping in the afternoon and then, at night, reading endless numbers of paperback books to keep his mind occupied.

Actually, there was something here that could do that for him awfully well. A new man had walked into the bar. He looked tough, real tough. He had a bodybuilder's muscles and a kind of bravado about him that appealed to Tim. It was the same kind of surface masculinity that Mike Ahern, his copilot, had.

Rough Trade. That's what the guy was. God, Tim hadn't thought of that term in years. But it sure sounded appealing to him now. A straight man who only wanted a blow job, someone who might even throw in a few threatening, demeaning remarks about cocksuckers. *We deserve those.* Tim was getting hard at the thought. Straight man, using a gay man, no emotional entanglements, no fantasies about a life together, that made a lot of sense these days in Minneapolis. Who in his right mind would trust another faggot in this city after what's been going on?

But someone else made a move before Tim even had a chance to cross the bar. The other guy was older and less attractive than Tim, but the score didn't seem to mind. He smiled in a gloating way when the bar patron had introduced himself. They talked and, after only a few words, left their unfinished drinks on the counter and walked out.

*I'll get him next time*, Tim vowed. *Him or someone like him. No more faggots.*

No one else in the bar appealed to Tim. He didn't really like the tipsy sensations that were coming over him; it was time to leave. He left a tip and walked out. He found his car where he had left it only a block or so away. When he got in he turned on the radio. Any kind of noise was welcome company at this point.

There was some kind of talk program on the air, but Tim wasn't paying much attention to it until some words slipped into his consciousness and he began to listen.

"... While we've all been insistent upon the civil rights of all our people, there comes a time when decent people must say stop. That time has come in Minnesota. I have been in the forefront of the battle for gay rights. I have done so believing that gay people should have the same opportunities for fair housing, fair employment and fair treatment before the law.

"But rights bring with them responsibilities. It's become clear that the gay community of the Twin Cities has not been willing to bear those responsibilities. Until they do, we, the family people of our state, must protect our children and ourselves from their capricious, unfeeling behavior ..."

The guy was right. Tim Ranson wasn't going to argue with him, that much was for sure. The voice droned on.

"... It's time for all of us to re-examine the priorities with which we live. Yes, the First Amendment has played an important part in our civil liberties. But now feminists are showing that the protection of free speech is something that hurts. Yes, we thought that gay rights were the correct thing and we tried to do right by advocating them. But giving gay people free rein has only provided their most predatory members with the license to kill, corrupt and misuse one another. For their own protection, we have to look at just what it is that we have loosened on society.

"These are painful things for a man with my reputation to have to acknowledge. But there is no doubt about the dangers that are threatening our families and our moral values.

"Every thinking mother and father, brother and sister, knows that it's true. The endless stories that have been reported in the press have proven it. We can't deny that gay rights have backfired."

*I sure as hell can't*, Tim agreed.

"That's been this week's program from State Representative Andrew Marston. Mr. Marston's position tonight has represented a drastic change in his political agenda. He invites you to respond to his observations. For a transcript of this speech, simply write this station. Mr. Marston thinks that this topic is so important, you needn't enclose the usual fee for that transcript. Just send your name and address on a post card."

# XI

Now Joseph Farmdale remembered the attraction of the Red Crow Inn. The breakfast was remarkable. Really homemade bread, homemade sausages as well. The coffee was strong and fresh. The jams were probably made right here in this kitchen. He was delighted with the meal. He was also delighted when he saw Alex Kane and Danny Fortelli walk into the dining room. There was no doubt that his strategy had worked.

The sadness wasn't there. Farmdale saw it immediately. Instead there was anger, great anger. Alex's eyes glistened with it. It was always remarkable to see how the green in his eyes shone when this particular emotion had taken over Alex's person. There was an iridescence about him. He was like some kind of beacon.

The two men took their seats without a word. Farmdale waved toward the proprietor of the inn who smiled and brought coffee to the table. "We've eaten," Alex said to her when she offered menus.

Only when she'd left them alone did Kane speak again. "You're a bastard."

"There's a plane at Logan waiting for you. At the usual terminal. On it you'll find further briefing papers. There's more data than you'd normally expect. The case is more complicated and more dangerous."

Kane didn't respond. Farmdale looked over to Danny. "Are you sure you're ready to begin this now? I know that Alex has ... sheltered you in the past."

Danny smiled vaguely. "Have I really been sheltered?" It seemed a personal joke to him. "Have I really?" No one spoke for a moment. Danny continued, "I guess I *better* be ready, Mr. Farmdale. Like you said, I'm an adult now. Mommy and daddy can't protect me any longer." Danny's smile disappeared. "Yes, I'm ready."

"There's money on the plane as well. I trust you have more than enough in any event. But ..."

"Fine," Alex stopped Farmdale's speech. "I burnt all the papers you brought. Nothing's changed."

Farmdale nodded. He had expected nothing else.

The two men stood. "You're a bastard," Alex Kane repeated.

Farmdale met his glare. "One should learn not to blame the messenger for tragedy. That's all I am, Alex, a messenger. You don't have to read my messages and you don't have to trust my dispatches. You don't have to believe my facts, nor do you have to act on them. You choose to do that. You choose to do that ... for Danny."

Alex closed his eyes. He'd heard the speech or one like it many times before. But the ending had changed. It had always used to be, "... for James." Now it was "... for Danny." But it was still Joseph Farmdale and it was still Alex Kane.

# XII

The campaign advisors were meeting again. This time Andrew Marston wasn't complaining. Not at all. "It's a fucking dream come true."

He waved at the huge pile of mail that filled the center of the conference table. "It's all from a single radio broadcast. The media's eating it up. I have all three networks and Cable Network News all lined up for interviews tomorrow. The *New York Times* is coming to cover the moral revolution in Minnesota. The *Washington Post* is sending a top reporter to interview me."

"Watch out for all them," Luther Angstrom warned. The big Swede was glowering. "Those pinkos aren't going to give up their crusades that easy."

"You're wrong, Luther, wrong. I tell you, we've pulled it off. We have more crime in the gay community here than in any other segment of the population. It's working wonders! The plan to have lots of it directed at other gays is doing the trick perfectly. Not one of them's talking against me."

"That crazy one is," Luther insisted. "The one that runs that center."

"Oh ..." Andrew dismissed the objection. "He's pissing in the wind. No one's paying attention to him. Not even the real lefties. You know, I don't think they ever really did like the gays, the way they're back peddling on this issue."

"How can you blame them?" Marty O'Brien asked with a grin. "We got child molesters, murderers, sex fiends gone mad, bar owners caught for breaking every rule in the books, everything we could ever have dreamed of."

"Hasn't been a bad scam," Sonny LeBec agreed. He'd had a good time getting at all his competition. Only his own bars had escaped any notice in the press recently. And there was much more to come. He'd seen to it.

"You're set for the next act?" Andrew asked.

LeBec smiled. "It's begun. Real easy. Real expensive, but real easy." He hesitated, waiting either for an acknowledgement of his accomplishment or else an offer to help pay the price. But they all knew how much more he was taking in these days and no one felt a need to underwrite his success. He shrugged. "It'll start in the papers tomorrow, I bet. What about your plans?"

Sonny had turned to Martin Martello. "Oh, on schedule. It's going to really cost me too." Again no one responded. "But I got some set-ups you won't believe. You don't have to worry about that Anderson kid." Martin was referring to Mike Anderson, the gay activist that Luther Angstrom had been concerned with. "He'll get his."

"All of them," Andrew Marston smiled, "they're all going to get theirs. I'm taking another turn to the right tonight. It'll be in the papers tomorrow. This little bit of magic we're pulling has given us the perfect opportunity to justify the change in my positions. I'm going to out-family the Republicans on this one and no one's going to question my motives in the least. Hell, they're all going to be cheering by the time I'm done. Cheering."

*The way they will when I get elected to the governor's mansion.* Marston didn't have to verbalize that. They all knew he was thinking it; they all were thinking the same thing and liking the sound of it very, very much.

# XIII

"I tell you, he couldn't have done it. Dr. Chisle never would have done anything like that." Mike Anderson was pleading with his compatriot, Charlie Tile. Usually Mike was clear, concise and spoke with an air of authority. But the recent events in Minnesota had eroded that strength.

Charlie didn't dislike Mike, but he'd been secretly bristling at all the attention the leader of the community center had been getting. It was too good a shot to pass up, getting at Mike when he was this vulnerable and when he was backing such a stupid cause.

"You've got to be kidding, Anderson. Look, just because you've tumbled with *Dr.* Chisle doesn't mean he's a saint. Your politically correct behavior isn't a communicable disease, you know. He's a typical closeted middle-class queer who only thinks of sex. The way he got into your pants was to talk the right line, that's all. You fell for it.

"The guy's a sex fiend. Hiring kids from poor countries and then using coercion to get them to do what he wants. Get over it, Anderson. He's a lost cause."

"Look, I went and talked to him at the jail. He promised me he's been framed ..."

"Mike, stop it! Can't you see you're letting your emotions get in the way of your best judgment? He's a classist, ageist, sexist pig and he's getting what he's got coming. You should be happy to have him out of the way."

"He's not." Anderson's voice sounded feeble now. It was hard for him to react to the litany of anti-gay liberation charges when they were directed at a man he was in love with.

"Mike, you're only twenty-five years old. What's a man of nearly forty doing going after you?" There was a distinct and vicious edge to Charlie's voice.

"He's ... Charlie, he's not like that. I swear. Look, you know damn well he's given the center money, a lot of money. He's closeted to some extent, sure, but he's not like the rest. He at least makes sure that we all have something to work with. He's had fundraisers for our causes in his home, and as for me, well, sure he's older. But he's never used that in any oppressive way."

"He didn't have to," Charlie Tile was studying his finger-nails in a faint imitation of a fading movie star. "You never made him work for his little piece."

Mike stood up and made a move toward Charlie. But stopped himself. Violence, he had long ago decided, would never be a part of his life.

"Face it, Mike, he pays for the dinners, he chooses the restaurants, he pays for the airplane tickets for your little vacations, and you put out. He's using you, buying you the same way he bought those starving kids. You just don't want to see how he's oppressing you."

Mike sat back down again. The words sounded right, but somehow the logic didn't. He'd been living on a subsistence income for years while he worked in gay activism. Somehow the chances to have a big meal out and a week in the Flori-da sun with Allen Chisle just hadn't seemed all that horrible when the dentist had offered them to him.

"He's eroding your politics." With that damning state-ment, Charlie stood up. "Besides, this is hardly the time for any of us to be backing one of them. For Christ's sake, we have gay murders going on, there are a hundred and one things wrong in this city. We don't have the time or the luxury of appearing to be on the side of one of the guys that have been grabbing the headlines. They've been ruining the reputation of all of us. All of our work is going down the tube.

"You can bring it up to the steering committee if you want to, Mike. But they're going to be on my side on this one for a change. There's no way in hell we're going to go and defend someone like Allen Chisle with the way things are happening in Minneapolis now."

Charlie had stood up and walked out the room. Mike sat stunned in the chair behind his desk. There were the sounds of people chattering in the other offices in the building. He was torn, desperately torn. Right here were the fruits of his years of labors. There was a housing group, an organization that coordinated a whole series of support groups for gay fathers, lesbian mothers, gay and lesbian alcoholics ... the list went on. It had taken long hard work to get the funding for it all. Mike knew perfectly well that the coalition of church and fraternal organizations and foundations that he had put together was already starting to fall apart. A conservative Lutheran committee was the first to withdraw, citing conflicting priorities, but Mike knew that the wave of gay scandals throughout Minneapolis and its twin city, St. Paul, were the real reason.

All that got mixed up with his even more personal feelings about Allen Chisle's possible connections. He'd been dating Allen for over three years. All Allen's requests for a commitment had been fended off by Mike. He had been the one to insist on an "open relationship" – even though he actually hadn't had sex with anyone else in over a year. It had been a matter of principle to Mike, or so he had thought. Where his principles actually were was becoming less clear to him.

As the head of the center, he had to defend the community against these incredible attacks. As the man who loved Allen Chisle, he couldn't abandon the dentist for political expediency. If Allen needed him during this crisis – and it was obvious he did – then Mike wanted to stand by him.

But what if Allen were part of the reason for the crisis?

That part hurt. Not just because it meant that Mike had misjudged Allen politically; it meant that his vision of their relationship with one another had been false, that Mike had been had. It wasn't a good thought.

"Are you Mike Anderson?" Mike looked up when he heard his name spoken. Two men stood in his doorway. One of them appeared to be younger than himself, but not much. He was about 5'10" and had a beautiful face and that loose shirt he was wearing wasn't covering up the build he had underneath. The other was older, maybe thirty. He was cleanshaven. He was wearing only a strapped t-shirt and a pair of jeans. There was smooth skin showing, very smooth skin, the type that usually meant a guy hardly had any body hair. But he certainly had strange green eyes. They were slightly hypnotic, it seemed.

He also had a body, an incredible body with etched muscles apparent on his arms. Everything said that the rest of his torso would be the same.

"Yeah, I'm Mike." He stood up and offered a hand to each of the two visitors, then waved toward empty chairs that sat facing his desk.

He sat down as they did, then realized they hadn't introduced themselves. Before he could ask their names, the older guy had opened up an obviously expensive book, one with deep red binding. He had begun to read.

"You've been seeing a Dr. Allen Chisle for quite some time. Pretty friendly it seems. Dr. Chisle's taken you to Key West a couple of times, to Provincetown one ..."

"Hold it right there," Mike said sharply. "You guys must be cops if you have that kind of data. Well, if you think you're going to get me involved in Dr. Chisle's trial ..."

"You already are involved." The younger man spoke now. "You're in love with him."

"How do you know that?" Mike was stunned by the stark statement.

"It's all over that book. All over your life. I can tell. I know what love looks like."

Mike spat back a response, "Oh, you do?" The guy nodded yes. Mike looked at the handsome youth and suddenly, for some reason he'd never understand, he said, "You do." Then he looked over at the other man. He took a deep breath. "Look, let's get out of here. The phone's going to start ringing, there'll be lots of interruptions. I'm hungry anyway. There's a restaurant down the street."

"You're on," Alex Kane replied.

•　•　•

"It just doesn't make sense." Mike had listened while Alex Kane had finished reading the dossier on Allen Chisle. There hadn't been anything new in the report. Oh, a couple tricks Allen had had, but they'd been with men close to his own age. It was Mike's own fault if there was any "infidelity" – he'd been the one, he had reminded himself, who'd wanted that open relationship.

"I've seen the evidence the police have. It looks open and shut. There are signed agreements, there's the testimony of the kids, including the one he had in his apartment. He didn't do anything outlandish with them on the surface of it, but there was the definite element of coercion. He made them give him blow jobs and let him fuck them."

Danny studied Mike for a second. "Does that make sense to you?"

"What do you mean?"

"That he'd want to fuck them. Was that what you and he ..."

"Well ..." Mike blushed a bit, "No it doesn't make sense. Sure, we would switch around, but, well, I ... he'd rather I was doing that. No big deal, I mean it's not a part of my macho self or something, it's just that ..."

Danny put up a hand. "Look, I understand." He smirked at Alex. "I understand perfectly. People have preferences. But if Dr. Chisle's preference was to have you do it, why would he all of a sudden be going to these lengths to start doing the fucking himself?"

"It's typical." Mike gathered all the political analyses of sex he had ever read. "I'm a big blond Swede. He wanted to get fucked by me. These kids were dark skin, short, he wanted to fuck them. It's all political, racist shit." He was wringing his hands as he talked.

"Does that sound like Allen Chisle to you?" Alex asked.

"No. But, damn it, we've all internalized so much of that crap. Of course it could be true of him. So he acted one way with me, then he turned around and acted another way with these guys. What happened between us doesn't matter."

"What does matter," Alex said in a slow voice, "is what you thought of him. It matters whether or not you think he was capable of this kind of thing. You've been seeing him for a long time. You're bright, observant and sensitive. What do you think? Did Allen Chisle do what he's charged with?"

"No." That was a definite statement. "He just *couldn't* have."

"Then that's what we'll go on," Alex replied. "that he couldn't have done it. Then we have to find out who set him up and why they did it. What about that question? Do you have any clues?"

"Not a one," Mike answered. "I wish I did, but I can't think of a single damned reason why anyone who knew Allen would put him in this position."

"Listen, Mike. We need your help. There are too many things going on here. There are too many mysteries. I'm betting there's just a single answer to all of them. But it's going to take work to figure it out. Will you work with us?"

Any conflicts between the center's needs and those of Allen, between politics and helping the man he had been seeing for so long, had disappeared. *Then that's what we'll go on ... he couldn't have done it.* Those words produced a clarity to Mike's thoughts for the first time since this whole mess began. "Of course I'll help."

# XIV

When Danny woke up in their hotel room the next morning, Alex was already standing up, looking out the window. They were in one of the buildings in the IDS Center that was built around a huge glass-covered courtyard. The big king-sized bed was luxurious, but the room was so large that it wasn't too big for the scale of the space.

Danny got out of bed, stretched and then went to stand by Alex. Both men were naked. Danny snaked an arm around Alex's waist and followed his partner's gaze down to the floor of the courtyard. There were fast-moving crowds there, all of them rushing to work, to appointments, to the big department stores that were nearby.

"Why do they have this enclosed?" Danny asked.

"The weather. Minneapolis is too frigid in the winter for a lot of people to tolerate. In the summer it's nearly as bad. The temperature and the humidity go way, way up. So they have spaces like this. Over there," Alex pointed through the glass courtyard to the street where they could see corridors built over the streets, "they have a whole series of passages they call skyways connecting all the buildings. They're for the same thing – protecting people from the weather."

"Is that what you're thinking about?" Danny asked.

"The weather? No. I'm just thinking about all those people. I'm wondering how many of them are gay, how many

75

of them are going to be caught up in all this shit that's going on. I need to do that, Danny, when I'm out here. When I'm going to have to face down an enemy as violent and horrible as this one, I have to remember why I'm doing it, and who I'm doing it for.

"Look at them. They're just going about their business. Innocent people. A lot of them are gay. All they want is a decent job, a house or an apartment, a lover or at least some decent boyfriends. They want a little pleasure and they want some good times. That's all most people in this world want.

"Instead they're getting ..." Alex's voice trailed off. He knew he didn't have to finish his sentences.

Danny squeezed a little then let go of his lover. He saw that Alex had already had coffee delivered. He went over and poured himself a cup. There was a paper on the table by the service. Alex had already opened it.

Danny sat down and drank his coffee while he read the front page. He put the paper down after a few minutes. "This is why you're looking out there now, isn't it?"

Alex nodded slightly.

Danny went back to the paper and finished the lead article. The headline said it all: Gay Murderer Lurks Hennepin Avenue Bars.

"Let's shower and get dressed, Alex. We're going to have to go find Mike Anderson. This is getting even worse."

• • •

A television station mobile unit was parked outside the apartment building that Mike had given them as his address. Alex and Danny moved through the crowds and up the stairs to the third floor. Mike was at the door talking to a reporter in an agitated voice.

"No, you can't come in. No, I have no comment. I don't know any more about the murders than you do. I don't want to appear on television to defend the gay community against the charges. There are no charges yet. What's with you people? A month ago you wouldn't have bought this line. You wouldn't be acting like a bunch of rednecks sniffing out some gay corruption. A month ago …"

"Things were a lot different a month ago," Muriel Stang said. Danny recognized her face from a television broadcast last night.

"Well, this hasn't changed. I have no comment. You cannot come in and set up your cameras. There is no interview."

"We'll remember that, Mike," Muriel said with an acid smile. "We'll remember that the next time you want us to edit the coverage on a gay pride parade."

"We never asked you to edit your coverage. We just wanted you to show something besides the fringes, something other than the cross-dressers and the …"

"Don't bother, Mike," the journalist said, "the way things are going, you won't be having a gay pride parade this year."

The imperious broadcaster turned on her heel and marched down the stairs with her obedient camera crew in tow. No one bothered to pay any attention to Alex and Danny as they passed the pair of men in the hallway.

Mike Anderson slumped his big body against the door frame. He was dressed in a pair of jeans and a pullover shirt. Alex noted what a large man he was, more of a football player than political activist. He was healthy looking; a slight layer of spongy flesh didn't hide a well-developed physique. This was not a guy that a man interested in boys would go after.

"You might as well come on in." Mike turned and Danny and Alex followed him into his small apartment. Mike closed the door. The phone began ringing immediately. Mike went over, picked it up, immediately depressed the switch to cut the connection and then left the receiver off the hook. "It's been going like crazy.

"I remember when we used to beg them to give us coverage of anything. I used to plead for them to interview anyone in the community who could give a positive image or an intelligent answer to their questions. It was like pulling teeth. But now they want daily quotes and running commentary."

Alex was looking around the small studio apartment The walls were covered with posters announcing political rallies and denouncing every "ism" in the book. There were cases full of the expected volumes on gay liberation. The bed was a simple mattress on the floor. The galley kitchen was piled with soiled dishes and pans. There wasn't much on the open shelves in the way of food; Mike obviously lived, ate and breathed his political convictions. Alex knew that no one could be interested in him who didn't have some kind of interest in the same issues. Dr. Allen Chisle was looking more and more like an interesting person to Kane.

"You've seen the papers?" Mike asked.

Danny answered, "Yes, that's why we're here. What's going on?"

Mike sat down on the mattress. There were only two wooden-back chairs at a tiny table for his visitors to sit on. They took their seats and waited for a response.

"I just don't know. After the immigration scandals and the bars getting busted for breaking all the health and safety codes ..." His voice trailed off. "How can you fight that? How can you fight it when the city closes businesses that are obviously endangering the community's well being? Or when men are supposedly kidnapping and blackmailing innocent children ..."

"How do you fight murderers?" Alex asked.

Mike just shook his head. "Look, there have been three reported in the last two nights. They are clearly killings of gay men by gay men. All three victims were seen cruising in bars. They all were seen picking someone up. We have to assume it was their tricks. It was our own attacking our own."

"Was it?" Alex's question had a sharp tone to it. He'd seen this kind of thing before.

"What's going to happen now?" Danny picked up his own line of questioning.

"The police are combing the city. They're talking to – and scaring the shit out of – everyone who knew the three men. They're going to send undercover agents into the bars.

They're taking photographs of patrons on the sly, beginning tonight. They've announced all this over the media. It's produced something just short of total panic around town. There are just too many people who are terrified of being identified as bar patrons. That, and a whole lot of people are terrified of the danger that the bars seem to represent these days."

Mike went to his refrigerator, took out a bottle of orange juice and poured himself a glass. He offered his visitors some, but they declined. "Then there's Representative Marston."

"I read about him in the paper," Alex said. "Who is he? What's he doing in all this?"

"He used to be the very best friend of every good cause in the city. Our man at the state capitol." Mike said the sentence with a sarcastic voice. "I never trusted the guy. He had the right viewpoints, but none of them were ever put into action. I mean, he was all for women's rights, but no matter how often he talked about the ERA he always treated women like second-class citizens, second-class citizens he wanted to get into bed. He'd say he was for gay rights, but he was always uncomfortable around me, that's for sure. It seemed more acceptable if a gay guy was in drag, somehow that made more sense to him. But anyone my size and my appearance made him feel funny.

"I don't know, I can't prove it, but that's my impression of the guy.

"In any event, he's made this big turn-around. Now he's appealing to people in the political center to come out against gays. He's been saying that the experiment in gay rights – that's his term: "experiment" – has failed. He wants people to rally around him in a new, supposedly still liberal, political coalition that would be economically aligned with the Democratic Party, but morally somewhere to the right of Genghis Khan."

"Is he succeeding?" Danny asked.

"Oh, sure he is. And you know where a lot of his success is coming from? Gay men. They're terrified of getting caught up in this net, either as victims of some strange and unknown criminal figures after them – you can't blame people for that – or else they're frightened that their good reputations are going to get smeared by the campaign."

Alex Kane showed no emotion on his face. There was just a calmness about him. It was neither sadness, nor was it resignation. Danny looked at him, he especially studied Alex's eyes. He could see the glint there, that brightness that came with Alex's fury.

# XV

Larry Lawson stood in the gay bar and studied the crowd. What an easy score this was going to be. He had a nice wad of bills in his pocket, a down payment from Sonny LeBec. Sonny was one hell of a guy to have given Larry such a cushy job. He provided too – sure as hell, Sonny LeBec provided. Larry had his return ticket to Vegas already in hand.

Larry usually only got hired for the tough jobs, the real tough jobs that come from the Nevada underworld. He was so used to the danger and risk involved in going after other hoods that the idea of just making it rough for a gay guy was a piece of cake.

Sonny had been very specific and very easy about his job order. Larry had to pick up some fruit in a bar. He had to take care of him. Sometime in the far distant past murder was something that must have bothered Larry. But now? Now it was something that came with the territory.

He looked around for a mark. That was another thing. Sonny wanted it done clean and easy. It had to be a guy who obviously belonged in the bar, one who knew what was going on. Sonny expected there'd be undercover cops out this time. They could be trouble. That's why the big guns like Larry had been brought in for the second round. Larry could smell a cop a mile away.

Like that one guy who was just wearing a tank top across

the bar from Larry and trying to give him the eye. He was too old for Larry's taste. Not that Larry really got into guys, you have to understand that. But if it was part of the job to pork a young butt, well, that could be done – if it was part of the job and Larry *had* to do it.

But not one as old as that. The guy didn't look bad – nice muscles, firm flesh. *He probably has a nice ass,* Larry thought. But the idea was a fleeting one. It just wouldn't be right to prong someone nearly your own age. Besides, something told Larry that man could be a cop. Just a suspicion, but it was enough.

Larry smiled as he thought how appropriate he was for the job. He figured a good-looking guy like himself with a big dork would go over real well in a gay bar. These flits sure should be turned on to him. He put his back to the bar and stretched out his arms, still holding his beer in one hand. His polyester pants must be showing off his crotch to good effect. There was one young guy over across the room who was giving him the eye.

This one was more like it.

He was so handsome that Larry could even imagine him as a girl. His lips were a deep red, his skin was smooth and his hair was dark and curly. Too bad the kid seemed to have too much chest hair. That wasn't so hot. Larry would have liked to combine this one's appearance with the hairlessness of the first man who'd been looking at him. But Sonny said to get it over with fast, so Larry would compromise.

He walked the few steps to the young man's perch on a ledge against the wall. "How ya doin'?" Larry asked.

"Just fine." The kid had a good voice. Nice and smooth. Larry reached out and put a hand on one of his thighs. Whew, those were nice legs, good strong legs. This kid could probably throw a mean fuck. Larry was getting hard thinking about that. Thinking about the way someone with this kind of build could just milk his cock.

They went through the motions. Larry hadn't ever had a hard time when he'd had to pick up a gay guy. Just the same kind of mindless chatter that you had to give a broad in a singles joint would do. All they ever had to have was enough encouragement to believe you were dealing with them as a *person.* Oh, how they hated to be treated like meat.

*Well, kid, let's make believe you're a person, just enough to let me taste the slabs of meat you got around my cock.*

It was easy as pie. Just easy. Larry was walking out of the bar in a couple minutes, this kid following him with all the willingness he'd expected. Sonny wanted it done quick? Larry delivered. He'd done it in less than ten minutes. He'd just walked into the bar and pulled out the best looking thing with no effort at all.

The kid had agreed to walk back to Sonny's hotel, a fleabag a few blocks down Hennepin in one of the few areas of the downtown that hadn't been rebuilt yet. No nosy room clerk at this time of night. Nothing to interfere with what Larry had to do. He checked his watch. It was so early he could still catch the red-eye back to Vegas tonight.

What a fucking easy score.

Once they were in the room, Larry turned the lock on the door. He turned around and stared at the kid. "What's your name?"

"Danny." Kid had a nice smile.

"Well, Danny, I'm going to show you a real good time. You take care of old Larry, and Larry'll take care of you." *And then I'll kill you.* "Let's see what you got kid."

The smile didn't leave the young guy's face. Larry had to admit this was one time he wouldn't mind giving a gay guy a tumble. Hell, a hole's a hole. He wasn't about to say that to the guys back in Vegas, but hell, look at that body.

"I think we have some talking to do first."

Larry's smile disappeared. "No we don't, kid. We got better things to do than talk." Larry hated talking with people when he was going to do them.

"I want to talk, Larry."

"Then why you smiling like that?" Was the kid trying to egg him on purposely?

"I always smile when I meet strangers from out of town."

"What makes you think I am? You don't know I'm not from here."

"Oh, but you're not. I asked a couple friends. They'd never seen you before. Where are you from, Larry?"

"Kid, I don't have time for a lot of conversation. Come on, now. You got me all hot and bothered. Let's get it on."

"I told you, Larry, we have to talk first."

The kid was crazy. Larry might have put up with this shit to get him out of a bar, but it wasn't going to be worth doing it if it meant all this work. Too bad, it would have been a great lay. Larry knew it.

"Now, Danny, don't be difficult." Larry moved across to his suitcase. He hadn't carried his gun on the streets. It was too bulky, especially with the silencer on its barrel. It was amazing how quiet an automatic pistol could be with a silencer. "Let me just get some poppers." Larry went into the bag that was sitting on the bureau and reach for his gun.

He heard Danny's movement before he could see it. It was just a very quick couple of steps barely audible on the carpeted floor. Then there was a *whoosh,* followed by an incredible pain in his arm. The fucking asshole was standing on his suitcase. The metal edges were digging into Larry's wrist.

"*I* don't like poppers, Larry." The kid was smiling.

Larry let out a scream. As soon as he did the door burst open with a loud crash. Larry was trapped, he couldn't move with the young guy standing on his arm that way. But the noise was so sudden and unexpected that he had to look to see what was going on.

It was the other guy from the bar. The strange looking one. He looked angry rather than surprised. "What the hell happened? How the hell did you get there?" The newcomer was screaming at Danny, not Larry.

"I'm a gymnast, remember? A simple double flip off the mattress." Then, as though to emphasize his point, Danny did a quick little jump. A jump so fast that Larry's hand couldn't escape from the grip of the suitcase's edge. There was a loud snap as his arm broke. Then Larry passed out from the pain.

# XVI

They were back in their room at their own hotel. It was late now. There was hardly any traffic down on the courtyard of the IDS Center. Danny was on the bed, his arms behind his head, as he seemed to be studying the ceiling. Alex sat in a chair, still dressed, staring into space.

"Is this the big break?" Danny asked.

"Maybe. Probably not. This guy, LeBec, is a big gay bar owner, that's what Mike Anderson said. He's shady, but he's not the really big time. Besides, a gay bar owner isn't the kind to scare his customers out of the bars. He certainly shouldn't be hiring paid guns to get rid of his customers."

"So you believe what he said?"

"People in that much pain usually don't have the ability to lie well, Danny. He was in a *lot* of pain."

"I didn't know if he was right-handed or left-handed." Danny's reply was very matter of fact.

"So you made sure neither one would ever work again." Alex didn't seem to be questioning Danny's decision.

"At least not on a gun trigger."

They were silent. The courtyard had an eerieness about it at this time of night. They only had a small lamp turned on in the room. It was dusk-like.

"Alex, is this what it always feels like?"

"How do you mean that?" Alex's voice seemed to carry

great hurt with it. It was as though he knew what the question really meant, but he was hoping he was wrong.

"When you fight someone like that, someone who would have killed a weaker person, one who didn't have my skills and couldn't have jumped like that. Is this what it always feels like?"

"I was outside. I would have saved you."

"If you could have, I know you would have. But there was a silencer. I could have believed him when he said he was just after poppers."

"But you didn't. I trusted you not to."

Danny thought longer. "You're not answering my real question, Alex."

"You tell me what you feel like, then I'll answer."

"Like I was making believe I was Sy. I was making believe that Sy had fought back, that he had the ability to fight back and save himself. Like I was going to bring him back if I succeeded. I did succeed. But Sy didn't come back."

Alex was silent.

"Do I have to feel this every time?"

"Yes."

Danny rolled over on the mattress and buried his head in his elbow. Alex came over to his lover and covered Danny's body with his own as though he thought he could offer some protection by doing it.

"We don't have to do this, Danny. We can go back to New Hampshire. We can stay on the lake this time. We don't have to ..."

"Yes we do." Alex was startled when Danny talked. He'd expected tears. There weren't any. "We have to do it so there aren't any more Sy's. We have to do it because we know how. You know how and you're going to teach me how. We have to do it because there could be a lot more pigs like that if we don't. And they could create a lot more Sy's. We had to do it."

Alex reached around Danny's body and held his lover tightly.

# XVII

Mike Anderson was knocking at their door the next morning. He was a little startled when Alex opened the door wearing only a pair of gym shorts. Behind him Danny was dressed the same way. There was the distinct odor of a locker room, as though the pair had been exercising for hours.

"Come on in. We're finished, I guess. We're going to have to shower. Why don't you call room service while we're doing it? Get us all some breakfast." Alex told the young activist what they would have and encouraged him to order anything he wanted.

It seemed to take the pair a long time to clean up, so long that Mike couldn't help wondering if they were … Sure they were. He smiled. They didn't come out of the bathroom until after the meal had been delivered and set up by a bellhop.

Danny and Alex were fully dressed when they came to the table. Mike couldn't help but be a little disappointed. He supposed it wasn't right to want to keep on looking at their bodies when there was business to do, but … well, he wouldn't have minded the distraction for a while.

He put down the paper as they took their seats. "We have a day's reprieve. Nothing here today."

He caught them exchanging a conspiratorial look. Danny reached over and leafed through the newspaper. "Nothing," he agreed. Mike was a little angry that he hadn't been believed. He just didn't realized that Danny wasn't looking for the same story.

The phone rang before he could make any comment. Just as well. He supposed these guys had to double-check everything.

Alex had stood up and answered the call. He spoke in sharp monotones to someone he evidently didn't like. Only occasionally would there be a complete sentence. "Just tell me, will you!" Mike looked at Danny with a worried expression after a couple of outbursts like that.

Danny was putting jam on his English muffin. "It's his family." That seemed to amuse the young man a lot.

Alex slammed the phone down and stalked over to rejoin them. "Chisle is out this morning. We have to finish up and go meet him."

"He couldn't be!" Mike insisted. "I mean, they refused him bail. One of the charges was kidnapping. It's a federal crime, a capital offense. There was no bail."

Danny looked over to the clock on their bedstand. "It's nearly ten in the morning, our time. Alex's just pissed off it took so long to arrange."

"You're sure?" Mike was incredulous.

"He's sure," Danny assured him.

•  •  •

An hour later they were back in the hotel room. This time Allen Chisle was with them. The dentist had passionately embraced his friend Mike as soon as the door had closed.

"You didn't have to wait that long, I was ready on the street."

"So was I," Allen insisted. "I was waiting to get inside for your sake."

"My sake? Allen, I'm the one who goes on television."

"Well, I do too now. So I guess that's one less problem we'll have to deal with."

Their arms clutched one another all over again.

Danny seemed to enjoy the sight. Alex Kane wasn't joining in on the festivities though; he was already pacing the floor in frustration.

Finally, Allen and Mike seemed to regain some control over themselves. "Who are you? How did you arrange that?"

Alex was curt. "It wasn't that big a problem. A few phone calls, that's all. Look, we've got to talk."

Allen looked to Mike with a silent question. "Just trust them. It doesn't look as though we have any choice."

The four were all finally seated. Alex continued. "I need to know everything about these kids and you. Don't leave out a single fact. The truth, all of it."

"I didn't do it. I mean, not like they said I did." Allen Chisle was a big man. His stomach was a little pudgy, and his hair was receding. But there was something so intrinsically good-natured about him that Alex and Danny could understand what had attracted Mike.

"I believe you. Forget their accusations. I don't need to hear your defense against those charges. But you have to understand, someone was able to make a case against you that looks awfully good. Now, there's got to be something in the story that contains at least a grain of that case. There's enough there to construct the fabrications around it in a way that makes sense when the story's retold."

"Yes, yes, of course there is. I mean, I did hire the boy who testified against me. He was from Haiti. At least that's what they told me ..."

"*They?* Who's that?"

"People I know. One of my patients is heavily involved in finding homes for orphans from abroad. They sponsor their entrance into the United States and then have to find them work. Paco was supposed to be eighteen. That's what he said. They told me he was gay. I wasn't interested in him sexually, but I knew he had to ... Look, you remember when they brought in all the gay guys from Cuba, in that boat flotilla? Well, I was even deeper in my closet then. I've always felt a little guilty that I hadn't helped those guys out.

"They're our kind, I figured, but I was so scared I didn't dare come forward. Sure, I sent an anonymous donation, but that was all. I learned later that lots of them had to spend extra time in the camps the government set up because there weren't homes for them. If I hadn't been so frightened of myself and my reputation, at least one of them could have been leading a different kind of life."

"Why didn't you tell me about this?" Mike insisted.

"Because I thought you'd think I was just doing it to be politically correct for your sake. I wasn't. I was doing it for *me.* I was just making up for a past mistake, a time I hadn't acted. I figured I'd get Manuel set up and then I'd introduce you. They told me the kid would have to back to Guatemala if I didn't take him. They'd found out his sexuality and he wasn't going to find another placement."

"I still want to know who *they* are," Alex Kane wasn't giving up the question.

"Oh, Mrs. Martello. Her husband, Martin Martello, is some kind of big exporter/importer. I've been taking care of their teeth for years. I trusted her."

"Do you know this woman?" Alex asked Mike.

"I've never heard of her before, or her husband."

"We have another name to check out," Alex said to Danny. "Martin Martello."

# XVIII

"Everything's on schedule." Andrew Marston was gloating as he presided over his advisory council once more. "It's just perfect."

"Not perfect," Sonny LeBec contradicted him. "My hit last night didn't work out. I haven't heard from him."

Marston refused to be concerned. "So one of your guns ran out on you with your money. One little detail isn't going to derail this operation now."

"You don't understand, it was Larry the Gun from Vegas. I'm talking about one of the most professional enforcers in the business."

"Larry?" Luther Angstrom recognized the name. "It sure isn't like Larry to mess an assignment."

"But he did this time. Big deal. You guys don't exactly deal with the most responsible element of society." Marston was being lordly over his advisors these days. It was as though he could sniff his victory and their eventual replacement. It was a mistake. Every man at the table was able to sense what he was thinking. A letter opener appeared in Angstrom's hand and he began to pick at his nails, an unmistakable sign.

Marston ignored him. The press had been perfect. No one – at least hardly anyone – dared to question his new moral revolution. He had had one disappointment: The feminists who were sponsoring the anti-pornography laws had come over to his side. It seemed they were the most willing members of the Minnesota political establishment when it came to believing the worst about gay men. That meant Marston was saddled with them again. He'd hoped he could dump the women's movement when the moral crusade began. But it didn't work that way. A lot of feminists might be horrified by his new pro-family approach, but a surprising number weren't at all upset by it.

He wasn't going to argue. Votes were votes. If the pseudo-dykes were willing to march with the Moral Majority that had recently come to understand the new personage that was Andrew Marston, then Andrew Marston wasn't going to scare them away.

"We have to move again. There has to be still more. More to justify the speech I'm giving in three days. It has to be spectacular." Marston was having a televised address at the convention center. His new coalition of his own personal crusade to save Minnesota morality was coming in from all over the state. They'd all be there to hear him, and all their friends would be at home glued to the television set.

This was the big jump-off point. Marston fully expected to pull off that most perfect political campaign, that one where to vote for him was to do the right thing; to oppose him was to do the wrong thing. Right and wrong; there would be no grey areas left by the time he was finished.

"More spectacular? Marston, are you crazy? We have implicated almost every rich closet-case fag in the Twin Cities for child molestation, sexual slavery, sadomasochism or something equally as *spectacular.* What more do you want?"

"I want more, I want much more. I want something that will dramatically underline the moral degradation that's taking over the country through the gay liberation movement. That kid, Anderson. I want him. And the dentist, Chisle, what's the deal? How the hell did he get out? I saw that on television."

"The federal attorney sprang him. The orders were from

way up. *Way* up, they say. He'll still get his. I know he's still up for state charges ..."

Marston stopped Sonny LeBec's report. "No, no, I don't think Chisle should get his. I think we should show the good people of this state just what happens when a gay criminal is shown any justice."

Luther Angstrom was still playing with his letter opener. He was looking up, though, studying Marston. He seemed to understand. "A shame, a real shame, that a nice gay leader like that kid should have to pay the price for the liberal society's leniency."

"You got it," Marston said.

# XIX

Martin Martello's cover was the Mar-Beth Importing Export-
ing Company. It had taken its name from his and his wife's
first names. Its offices were in a warehouse district in St. Paul,
just over the border from Minneapolis on the long straight
stretch of University Avenue that connected the two down-
towns. The avenue was lined with department stores and
shopping centers and small businesses like this one, housed
in a single-story building of its own. The traffic on the street
was dense, but now the cars and trucks were moving to and
from the line of commercial enterprises; it no longer carried
much of the inter-city traffic. I-95 did that nowadays.

His books looked awfully good. Getting those kids into
the country and teaching them the ins and outs hadn't been
cheap. But the pay-off was more than enough to justify the
cost, he figured. At least in the long run it would be a good in-
vestment. It had to be. He had to get the state Attorney General off his back before the guy drove him crazy. Once Marston
was in office ...

"Hi."

Martin looked up. Two men were standing in the entry
to his office. One of them scared him instantly. He was the
kind of guy that Martin's girls talked about, the kind with a
facial expression somewhere between insanity and rage.
They were the dangerous ones, the ones that could turn on a

girl with little notice if the wrong buttons were pushed.

His clothing was that kind of stuff that gay guys were always wearing. Button-fly jeans, black leather boots, a tight t-shirt. The shirt left his arms bare, bare enough that Martin knew the guy was strong. At first it didn't bother Martin; it was just like those gays to go and spend their spare time in a gym to build a body they'd never know how to use. All image and no substance. Why, if one of those guys ever came up against the hired hands that Martin had ...

"Wait a minute, how did you guys get in here?" Martello spent a lot of money on protection – a whole lot of money. The least that Martin could expect is that his own private office would be guarded by the goons he had on his payroll. But here were two gay guys who just walked in on him.

"Oh, we let your guards take a break. They're ... *resting.*" The other, younger guy seemed to think that was funny. He was chuckling as he spoke.

"I didn't tell those guys they could do that!"

"We sort of took the responsibility, Martello." The young guy was awfully good looking. Martin looked him over with an appraising eye. If he ever decided to move into guys, this is the kind he was sure would sell. Nice body – his chest seemed to be made in the shape of a V – and a good smile. Those little dimples were an extra attraction. Too bad his beard was so heavy. Even though the kid was clean shaven, there was the darkness of ... *Wait a minute!*

"What kind of business do you have here? I'm a busy man. I can't just spend my time with anyone who walks in off the street."

"You have plenty of time for us," the older guy said. "We want to talk about importing. You know about importing, that's what the sign says on your building. We've even heard a little about your successes. Seems you have some very fine merchandise that comes in from Guatemala. We want to talk about that."

*Merchandise from Guatemala ...?* Martin studied his intruders with a clearer eye. So they were interested in those kids that Martin had gotten for Marston's operation. The pair in front of him was obviously gay. There was no question now, Martello had put together the pieces of the puzzle. These guys were in the same business as himself, but they were doing it with the faggots. So they wanted some fresh Latin meat to peddle, did they? This could be interesting.

"Well, yes, let's talk about it." He swept a hand over the chairs that faced his desk. The men each took one and looked at him, obviously wanting him to take the lead.

"Well," Martin began, "it's not easy. After all, we're talking about shopping for the goods, getting the appropriate licenses, then a front organization that can deal with adoption papers and such here in this country; it all takes a great deal of money."

"Your wife comes in handy for all that, doesn't she?" Did that guy's eyes actually change color as he was talking?

"Hey, Beth is a pro. She can sniff out the best stuff and she has an uncanny way of knowing which is ... more easily packaged."

"You mean, which boys will be the least difficult to manage?" the guy asked.

"Packaging these goods is a highly sophisticated business," Martin admitted. "Beth is just great at it."

"Where's Paco Rodriguez?"

"Who the hell's he?" Martin answered the young guy.

"The one you sold to Dr. Chisle. The one you made the police think Dr. Chisle bought."

"Hey, those kids are all in protective custody until the trial. I've helped arrange for the organization that got this all together to house them until –"

Before Martin could finish his sentence the older guy had leapt across his desk and was dragging him to his feet with an iron grip on his necktie. *"I'm going to put you in protective custody of my own if you don't tell me where the fuck that kid is."*

Martin had gotten used to the guy's eyes, and he wasn't the sort of man to give in just because someone was yelling at him. But he somehow knew that this was not someone he wanted to fight with. The fact that these two had gotten past his guards flooded back into his mind. How had they done that? And what *was* it about this man …

"They're north of here, near St. Cloud. I'll draw you a map."

"You'll do better than that, asshole. You're going to give us a guided tour. Right now." With that Alex Kane began dragging Martin Martello out of his office and toward the building exit. "Burn the building, Danny. Light a fire. Fire's the only thing that can clean a place like this after vermin have taken over."

"A pleasure, Alex, a real pleasure."

Martin Martello was desperately trying to keep his consciousness as the guy dragged him out. But he did catch a look at Danny's face as the young man gathered together inflammable materials to begin the conflagration. There was something about his extraordinary anger that suddenly made Martin glad that Danny wasn't the one with the grip on his neck right now.

# XX

Paco Rodriguez was scared and humiliated.

It had sounded like such a good idea when Señora Beth had come to his village high in the mountains of Guatemala. The well-dressed American lady had promised his mother that there would be great wealth if Paco would only take a vacation to America. He could receive an education here in the United States much better than any he had ever dreamed of in Guatemala.

*Education!*

He was sitting outside the shack they were housing him in, him and the others from the various countries around the Caribbean. They had all gone through the same thing. They had been taught that they would pose as servants and, some of them, adopted children in the homes of men here in this strange northern place called Minnesota.

Then they would only have to tell a few exaggerations in a court room. Some would be returned to their families with huge amounts of money. Others would be able to stay and go to American schools. They would only have to tell small lies.

Paco felt horrible about this. Dr. Allen hadn't been a bad men. Yes, he was a *maricón.* Paco had known that for sure when he'd found the glossy magazines with all the pictures of men in them. But he hadn't ever done to Paco what these men ...

He squeezed his eyes shut to block out the memory. Dr. Allen had been good to him and he had paid him back with treachery. He had done a bad thing and he was going to have to repeat his lies again in another courtroom. All the man had done was ask Paco to work a little, then he'd taught the boy some English lessons and taken him to movies and bought him new clothes. All Paco had done in return was lie.

If he could regain his honor by telling the truth, he would gladly do it. Gladly. But he had no honor left to regain. He looked out over the area around the shack. There was nowhere to run. They had shown them that. Laughing, the guards had dared one boy, the black from Haiti, to try. He hadn't gotten more than a few hundred yards before the huge vicious dogs had caught him. Those beasts were always on patrol. They had told the boys that. If the guard hadn't blown his whistle when he had they all knew that the Haitian would be dead now.

*He might as well be dead.*

So might Paco. He had to endure, if only for his mother and his starving family in Guatemala. But what he had to do! What he had to do to stay alive and to keep the guards happy.

"Hey, spic-boy, come here."

Paco shuddered as he saw the worst of the guards standing nearby. Two of the big dogs knelt beside him. They were panting heavily, their ugly tongues hanging out and their saliva dripping down onto the ground.

Paco stood, shaking, and moved cautiously toward the guard. His name was Sam. Sam had a big belly, a huge stomach that hung out over the top of his belt. He wore dirty coveralls and had ugly teeth, teeth with big holes between them. He never seemed to have shaved. He always stank. He also always leered when he saw Paco.

He was groping his crotch long before the Guatemalan youth reached him. Paco could see the all too familiar outline of the man's erection through his pants. "You spic-boys got great mouths, you know that. Man, I never had no broad could give head like you kids. Come on, I need a piece just about now. Come on, get down and take care of this 'fore the rest of them get back. Wouldn't do for one of them to see old Sam getting done by a spic-boy."

Paco closed his eyes. He'd dared refuse an order like this once before. The beating he'd received hadn't been too hard to take. What had been horrible had been the lecture he'd received from Señora Beth. The American lady had shown up the next day with pictures of Paco's family. She'd delivered her unmistakable warning then. They would pay for Paco's disobedience.

He had no doubt about the power of these strange Americans. There was no choice but to give in to them. Praying for forgiveness from the Madonna, Paco dropped to his knees. To do this to a nice man like Dr. Allen wouldn't have been so horrible. He would just have been thanking him for all the good things he'd received. But this pig-man! Paco's eyes were cast down. He heard the zipper opening. He could smell the foul odor that came from the man's unwashed crotch. "Got me a big load for you, spic-boy."

"I have a big load for you, too."

Paco and Sam turned their heads together at the same time. There was a man neither of them had ever seen before. He was only wearing jeans and a t-shirt. He had a look of great fury to him – the kind of fury that avenging angels had in the painting of the church in Paco's hometown.

"Get 'im." Sam ordered the big dogs into action. Paco averted his look. He had seen more than enough of the dogs' ability. He heard them attack. Their growling sent shivers through his body. Then there were a couple whines ... and silence.

Paco was startled again. He turned to see what had happened. The dogs were still breathing, but they were sleeping at the man's feet, and the man's fury had not abated in the least.

The stranger moved toward Sam and Paco. He moved quickly. Sam tried to run, but he didn't have time. The man sank his fist into Sam's huge belly, his hand actually disappearing into the flabby mass. Sam's cheeks blew out from the impact of the blow. Another fist lashed out and smashed into Sam's face and Sam crumpled to the ground. His now flaccid penis was still hanging from his pants. Its tiny size looked ridiculous against the man's bulk.

"Stand up, son. You aren't spending any more time on your knees around here. Not ever again."

•  •  •

Paco had never seen the other boys so happy. The same man who had beaten up Sam, the one who called himself Alex Kane, had set a trap for the rest of the guards with the help of his friend, an American boy not much older than Paco. This youth, Danny, was friendly to them all. They all seemed to understand that Alex and Danny were both *maricónes,* but they didn't care now. They were free, or at least they soon would be.

There were a dozen of them. They were all sitting at a MacDonald's eating their first meal of hamburger and fries in weeks. The Americans had even bought them all large colas.

The one called Danny asked them questions. He was writing in a small booklet with a pen. He was always smiling and friendly. The boy from Haiti, the one the others had supposed had enjoyed his adventures with the American *maricónes,* seemed to be falling hopelessly in love with Danny as the black-haired young man wrote all the things that they said.

Paco seemed to be the only one to pay attention to a single detail. The hand that Danny used to grip the pen was white around the knuckles. He might be smiling at the boys, but inside, Paco knew, he was furious.

Paco sipped his cola and studied these two strange Americans. Somehow he knew they were going to salvage his honor. Somehow he knew.

# XXI

Allen Chisle had a comfortable house near Lake Harriet, one of the nicer areas of Minneapolis. He could look out his front window and see the park that surrounded the lake. It was always a pleasure, but this time the water looked even more beautiful than ever.

"You're sure?" he asked Mike.

"Stop it, Allen, yes I'm sure." Mike was walking back into the front room with a beer in his hand. "I'm just sorry it's taken me so long to figure it out."

"Well, so long as ..."

"Allen, stop being so calm and rational. Yes, I'm willing to move in with you. I love you. I want to stay with you. It's been difficult for me to deal with the age differences and the money issues. But I want to do it. I trust you totally now." Mike leaned over and kissed Chisle on the lips.

"I'll register at the University for this fall. There shouldn't be any problem. The social work people have been after me for a long time. I can at least start some courses and then move into the Master's program as soon as possible, as soon as the red tape allows.

"I need to move on. In a lot of ways. It's time to get some more academics going and it's time to get some more relationship going with you."

Allen was delirious with delight. After the nightmare

they'd been going through, now there was more hope. There was something beautiful about it all. He'd always wanted to have someone like this, someone who he'd love to love. Here was Mike. Here was his happiness.

The two men stood and embraced each other. Their lips meshed nicely. Their arms went around each other's chest. They were so happy they didn't hear the door open.

"Pretty picture."

They froze, then quickly broke their posture and turned to look toward the intruding voice. There were three men standing in the living room. All three had revolvers in their hands.

"Hey, Luther, let's make it prettier," one of them joked.

"We're going to make it a lot prettier," Luther smiled.

•  •  •

Luther Angstrom had enjoyed the gang war that had won him absolute control of the Upper Midwest drug trade. The bodies that littered rural Minnesota had been a kind of job to him. They had taken him back to some forgotten pleasures of his youth.

Luther had always been the kind of kid who loved to pull wings off of living butterflies. He had enjoyed putting out cigarettes on young kittens. When he's played doctor with the little girls in his neighborhood, he'd seldom been willing to stop with explorations. The girl didn't squirm enough if you only "explored." He was equally happy when he was playing cowboy and Indians with the other boys. Then there was an excuse to tie them up. He especially had liked playing cowboys since he had declared that the rules made it necessary for Indians to be whipped. Luther had demanded that the games be played with great authenticity.

Now the drug czar stood at the foot of Allen Chisle's big double bed. He was grinning at the new stimuli that were rekindling his favorite childhood thoughts. There, spread-eagled and bound to the four posts, was the naked squirming body of Mike Anderson. The kid had a nearly hairless body, typical of blonds and in itself boyish enough to fire Luther's thoughts.

He should be squirming. He was looking at the little arsenal of toys that Luther had brought along.

"Hey, Luther, can't we just off the guy? This is going to be messy this way."

"No," Luther answered curtly. "We have to do it right. We have to make it look like the other one, the dentist, did it. It's gotta look like the kid was enjoying himself and being enjoyed by the other guy. Remember how we did that? You just pump a load of lead into him and it's too simple a murder."

Luther sat down on a chair in the corner. This was going to take a while. Besides, sitting down, Luther could cross his legs and hide the erection he was popping. It wouldn't do any good to have the boys see the boss throwing a rod over a young guy.

Luther's right hand man, Frank, shrugged. Luther paid him a damn good salary. If Luther wanted it, Luther would have what he wanted. Frank took off his sports jacket and unbuttoned the sleeves of his shirt. He rolled them up his arms till they were over his elbows.

He looked at the mess of equipment that Luther had brought, then finally lifted up a lethal-looking cat of nine tails. The leather strands hung from a single grip. "This do the trick?"

"Sure," Luther said. "But start at the ends, his chest, his legs. It's gotta look like they did it for a long time."

"Let me show you what he means." Alex Kane had appeared out of nowhere. He stalked across the room before anyone could react. When Luther finally reached for the gun he had replaced in his shoulder holster he froze. A cold piece of metal was against his forehead.

"I don't think you want to reach in there," a voice said.

Very cautiously Luther looked up and saw a young guy standing there holding the gun. The kid had dimples, for Christ's sake! But with that gun right at Luther's head, the gangster wasn't going to hand out compliments on dimples right now.

Alex Kane had first retrieved the guns from Frank and the other hired hand. He threw them out the open window he had entered through. The two men moved back into the corner; whoever this guy was, they didn't want to tangle with him. Besides, there was the other one with a gun at their boss's head. They couldn't take any chances with the boss's life, or so they rationalized.

Next Alex picked up the horrible looking whip and brandished it about. He came over to Luther Angstrom and smiled. Then, with one quick movement that gave Luther no warning, he reached back and brought the whip slashing across the dope peddler's face. Bright tracks of blood glistened in the whip's trail.

"Isn't that how it works?" Alex Kane asked.

# XXII

Sonny LeBec loved to count his money. He knew that he should just let the accountants do it. But every once in a while he loved getting his own hands on his own cash. It didn't matter to him that the stuff was soaked with beer, faded from the constant handling in one of his gay bars. It was real money – real cash that showed just how great a success he was. He was a very real success according to the piles of dough that he had piled up in front of him.

*"Boss!"* his manager yelled. Sonny looked up; Bruno should know better than to interrupt him at this greatest of pleasures. "Boss, they got Luther. He talked. It was on the radio. He mentioned you. Martello too. They got him. He's spilling the beans about everything."

"Everything?" Sonny couldn't believe his ears.

"Everything about you. Nothing about Marston."

Sonny did some quick calculations. It would make sense. That's what he'd do. If they got him involved in all this shit he could have his ass in federal pens for the rest of his life. His one hope would be a friend like Marston in the governor's chair making some deals with Washington. Marston would have to do it, too. He'd *have* to.

But Sonny wasn't about to take any risk like that. What could ever have happened to make a hardass like Luther

Angstrom talk? That man was the kind that made everyone else quake, the way he played with his letter openers and the way ...

No, not now. Sonny looked at the pile of money on his desk. There were thousands in cold cash here. More thousands in the safe. There were the bank accounts in Vegas and bigger ones in Switzerland. Sonny had always planned on having his options kept open, just in case.

This was definitely sounding like a time to exercise those options. Definitely. "Come on, Bruno, we're going to have a little vacation in Vegas. It's getting hot around here."

"But, boss, Nevada's even hotter."

Sonny looked at the over-muscled goon and sighed. Bruno never was one for brains. "Let's just get packed up." Bruno followed orders as Sonny brought out traveling cases and explained how Bruno should pack them with the loose money.

They had cleaned out the counting room and were on their way to Sonny's car. *Jesus, what could make Luther Angstrom talk?* Sonny was hurrying down the alleyway. There would be a very early flight west, it was already approaching dawn now. They could take anything available, to LA, Reno, Denver, Sonny didn't care. It just sounded as though it was a good time to get out of Minnesota.

He was thinking so hard he ran right into the man, hitting his head against a shockingly hard chest. Sonny was stunned. "Get the fuck out of my way."

The man smiled, and when he did his eyes seemed to light up into an awesome green. "You heard the boss, move." Bruno loyally stepped forward and pushed an arm against the man. He didn't budge.

"Don't hurt my friend," a voice warned.

Bruno and Sonny looked over to see where the words came from. A young guy with dimples was standing there with his arms crossed over his front. Bruno and Sonny smiled. A kid telling a pro like Bruno what to do. "You gonna stop me?" Bruno was having a good time now. He reached out to shove the strange looking man once more.

The other one just shook his head, as though in some kind of mock disappointment. "I told you so." Sonny watched as the kid seemed to take his mark, like he was going to run a race or something, he was standing a way Sonny had seen before. Oh, yeah, in the Olympics, when those gymnastic guys were getting ready to do their tricks.

This kid was just like them. Then he began to move, and once he did Sonny had a hard time keeping his eyes on the kid's movements. He was racing across the alley one second and then, unbelievably, he was airborne, *just like the fucking Olympics.*

The kid did some kind of somersault in the air and it was just fucking beautiful to watch. For everyone but Bruno. Because when the kid came down from his leaping somersault – he must have twirled around three times up there! – his boots landed squarely on Bruno's jaw. The huge man collapsed into a heap – he was out cold.

Sonny was very impressed – so impressed that when the kid told him to put down his bags and follow them, Sonny did *not* have a moment's hesitation in complying with his request. Not one.

"How did you do that?" Sonny finally asked.

Danny smiled. "It's just something you learn." Then he put an arm around Alex Kane's waist.

# XXIII

Tim Ranson's doorbell rang. He didn't want to answer it. He hadn't had a shower in a couple days. His clothes were dirty. He was working on a bottle of Vodka and he didn't want any company except the welcome relief of the booze. But the bell kept going.

"Oh, shit." Tim gave up and walked over to answer it. "You." The last person in the world he wanted to see was Mike Ahern. "Go fuck yourself."

Tim slammed the door shut and went back to his drink. He toasted himself. He'd wanted to do that for a long time. A long, long time. The buzzer sounded again. "Fucker can't take a hint."

Tim unsteadily got up and walked over to the door again. "I don't want to talk to you," he screamed at Ahern. "I don't want anything to do with you."

Mike walked in and took the bottle out of Tim's hand. The pilot tried to grab it back, but he was too blasted. "Come on, Tim. You look in pretty bad shape. Let's stop this for a –"

"I don't know what the fuck you're doing, but I don't need any help from a fucking breeder right now. I'd like to be left alone."

Mike hesitated. He bit his lip. "I deserve that."

"You're fucking right you do. You fucking asshole. It's your fault and all the others. I don't want shit from you." He made another attempt to retrieve the bottle. Mike wasn't ready to give in.

"Let's talk."

"Talk? Talk about what? Faggots and cocksuckers? Gangsters and pimps? Is that what you want to talk about? Lives ruined and men going unpunished? Is that what you –"

Mike reared back and sent a harsh slap against Tim's face. It was a hard enough blow that Tim went sprawling over the carpet. "Shut up! We're going to get your act together before this goes any further."

Tim ran a hand across his mouth. He could taste his own blood. He wanted to stand up and get even, but Mike had moved too quickly. He was dragging Tim into the bathroom. "I'm not sure what's the biggest mess, you or this place," Mike scowled. Tim couldn't resist when Mike began undressing him after having started the shower running.

"I'll … I'll do it myself."

"Can you manage?" Mike demanded.

"Yes." Tim could – barely. He climbed into the shower after he'd undressed. The water felt good, warm and comforting. There hadn't been many things that had been warm and comforting lately. Not at all. Nothing had been. He let himself go, just enjoying the almost strange sensation of becoming clean.

It was a long shower. His skin was actually puckered by the time he was done. He was a little more sober now. He looked in the mirror and saw the devastation of the past few weeks. The least he could do was shave; he reached into the medicine cabinet and brought out an electric razor, then ran it over his face.

He left his dirty clothes on the floor when he was finished. He put a towel around his waist and went into the kitchen. Mike had been cleaning up. The old newspapers and the dirty dishes were already gone and he was scrubbing the sink with cleanser now.

"What the hell are you doing?"

"I'm helping out a friend here who obviously doesn't

know how to clean up after himself."

"Why you? Why here? Why now?"

Mike didn't stop cleaning. "I've heard the stories, Tim. All of them. I know what happened. I know how it happened."

"Yeah," Tim wasn't sure he wanted to go through this right now.

"Yeah. It was his closet, wasn't it?"

Tim nodded.

"They say that what happened was they went to him and told him that if he didn't put out they were going to go to his law firm, right?"

"Yes."

"So he thought they just wanted a piece of his ass. Was he that good looking?"

"Yes."

"So, rather than fight back or tell them to fuck themselves, he let them do what they wanted to?"

"They started with one of the bartenders that LeBec had under his control, so it looked sort of real. You know, it was guy who worked at a gay bar. He just told Ralph that he had to play along. They had pictures of us on vacation in Provincetown and they'd show them to –"

"So, Ralph gave in. Then the gangsters who were for real moved in, right? That Angstrom guy that's in all the papers?"

"Yes."

"That's what I heard." Mike had rinsed off the sink. He moved on to find a bucket under the cabinet. He filled it with detergent and water, then retrieved a mop and began to wash the tiles on the kitchen floor. "There's a lesson there. It's a hard one for you to even think about. But it's one I have to learn."

"What?"

"Closets kill."

Tim watched as his co-pilot kept scrubbing. There was sweat running down Ahern's forehead. But then Tim realized it wasn't just sweat, there were tears.

"Do you mean ..."

"I always thought I could keep it secret. It's why I bad-
gered you so much. Hell, I spent the whole time in that cockpit
furious with you. I knew about Ralph. Everyone at Farmdale
Industries knew about Ralph. It didn't make any difference to
anyone else. But it sure as hell made a difference to me. It was
something forbidden. Something I couldn't have. I thought I
couldn't have.

"I hated you and I hated the thought of him. I was making
do with a couple blowjobs in tea rooms and you were living
together. You had everything I wanted and thought I couldn't
get. I was so damned worried about my reputation and what
people would think. Every time I heard them make a joke
about you – didn't happen often, but it did happen – it was
like they were talking about me.

"I should have gotten pissed off, I suppose, but instead
I just moved in deeper. I didn't want them talking about me
that way. I didn't want people to ...

"When I heard about Ralph and you, I even thought that
was more reason. He died because of it. Then I realized I'd
died a long time ago. I hadn't had any life in years. All my
money and all my time was spent perfecting my façade.

"You know what I wanted all that time?"

"What?" Tim asked.

"I always wanted to know a man well enough to wash his
floors for him."

With that, Mike started mopping with renewed vigor and
a huge laugh.

•　•　•

When Tim woke up the next day his hangover was worse
than usual. He realized it was because he'd stopped drinking.
He had learned a secret earlier: that if you just drank constantly you didn't get hangovers, you were always too drunk
to have one.

He slowly got out of bed and reached for his robe. He
made his way into the living area of his new small apartment.

There was coffee perking; the odor was surprisingly seductive. He could hardly wait. He sprawled on a chair and took stock of things.

*Coffee already brewing!*

He suddenly came to full consciousness. His apartment was spotless, absolutely, perfectly clean. The windows were washed, the woodwork shined, the floors had been polished. Mike Ahern came out of the bathroom just then. "Slept on your couch, hope you don't mind."

The co-pilot walked over to the kitchen counter and saw that the coffee was nearly done. He got two mugs out and then poured them full of coffee. "Black?"

"Fine," Tim mumbled.

Ahern was clad only in his jockey shorts. Tim had never even thought of the guy as anything but an enemy before. He certainly hadn't thought of him sexually. But now, seeing Ahern in a state of near undress with only the clinging cotton fabric to cover him, Tim had to acknowledge that he was a pretty well-built man.

Tim took the coffee and sipped the scalding hot liquid. "Thanks."

Mike sat down with his legs spread. He had the masculinity of a jock. It hadn't been just Tim's misimpression that led him to think of Ahern as a straight man. Few gay men sat like that naturally, with their legs open and the clearly visible pouch of their jockey shorts open to ...

Tim did a quick double take of his emotions. *Oh, no.* "Look, Mike, I don't really know what's up here. But I gotta tell you that I'm not ready for it. I mean, just because you think that you want ..."

"There's nothing up. You're someone who should have been my friend a long time ago. I just want to help a bit. So I got compulsive about cleaning. I think best when I'm doing things like that. So, I slept on your couch. I did sleep on your *couch.* You need a friend, Tim, there's no way you can deny it. You need someone to keep you from this solitary misery of yours. I need a friend, too. I need a friend badly."

"It's not just you, it's the … the memory."

"I respect that memory. Honestly, I do. It's a hard time for both of us. I … I'm not in practice about this stuff, being a good friend and helping out emotionally. But if you'll let me, I'll sure as hell try, Tim. I mean that. I'll sure as hell try."

A friend sounded pretty good right now. Tim nodded.

"Hey, look, I don't have to work today. Want to go see the Twins? They're playing."

"The Twins? Mike, I am *not* going to go out and make believe I'm some straight guy going to a fucking ball game."

"Do you like baseball?"

"Yes, but …"

"So we'll do a little shopping first."

•  •  •

That afternoon two men, both in their thirties, walking with big smiles on their faces, climbed into box seats to watch the Minnesota Twins play baseball. If they heard any remarks about their t-shirts which had "Gay and Proud" across them in bold lettering, they didn't seem to notice.

•  •  •

Two weeks later they were back in Tim's apartment again. "Don't you think it's time you did something besides babysit me?" Tim asked.

"What do you mean?" As always, Mike Ahern was cleaning.

"Mike, you've spent nearly every day with me. What about your job? What about doing something on your own? I feel like …"

"You know perfectly well that Farmdale Industries gives all kinds of benefits. There are personal days, there are days you can save up from vacation, all that. I just took them. Actually, I think it's more important for you to go back to work. You're in good shape now, Tim. Come on, let's start flying again."

Tim looked at Ahern. Mike was right. Besides, the prospect of spending time at work with his co-pilot was full of utterly new possibilities now. Mike had grown a moustache. After studying photographs in *Mandate,* he'd gone and had a new, short clone-style haircut. He also had quickly accumulated an imposing collection of t-shirts.

"Yeah, it's time."

•   •   •

Farmdale Industries had subsidiaries all over the United States. The company's planes were often loaned out to various charities as well; the pilots who flew their private fleet could be sent anywhere. But since the old man lived in California and since New York was the center of the financial world, those two were the most usual destinations.

The first assignment Tim and Mike had was to ferry some equipment from Minneapolis to the San Francisco area. It was easy to arrange a stopover. Mike was particularly delighted. "Show me the spots, Tim, come on. Do you realize I've only been in two gay bars in my life and they were in Duluth and Fargo?"

Tim smiled. He figured he owed that much to Mike. They did Castro Street first. Mike acted as though he were in Disneyland. The gymnasium-perfect bodies paraded up and down the thoroughfare in various stages of undress, their owners' bodies and sexual possibilities clearly apparent.

It was a difficult thing to introduce Mike to everything at once. There were the handkerchiefs to explain and the leather icons as well. When they walked into an S&M bar Tim had a rush of sadness and discomfort. He didn't want to stay there, not after what had happened to Ralph. They moved on and ate dinner at a gay restaurant on Market Street.

"Does he really want me that badly?"

Tim laughed, "Yes, he wants you that badly." A cute waiter had all but thrown himself on Mike's lap.

"But I'm older than he is by ten years. He's the one with

the body."

"Well, the ten years is probably what he wants. It's a daddy trip."

"Daddy trip? Hell, I'd just want to wax his linoleum." They both laughed at that.

"And you have a perfectly fine body." Tim blushed as he said that. The thought had been going through his mind since the first time he'd seen Mike in his underwear that day. But he didn't ...

Mike seemed equally uncomfortable."Well, let's get our check cleared up and then get out of here. I want to go to some more bars."

"Oh, Mike, really?" There was a sharpness in Tim's voice. He immediately regretted it.

"No, we can go back to the room if you're tired. Or, if you wanted to just go on by yourself, well, I guess I've taken up a lot of your time. I mean, you're probably horny and want to go and get your rocks off. I guess I'm just not used to all these things yet and I should have –"

"*Stop it!*" Tim's command was quick and harsh. He took a deep breath. "That's not what I meant. Look, we're supposed to be honest, right? Okay. The reason I don't want to do bars any more is that I'm sick and tired of watching you and half the men of San Francisco cruising each other. Not because I don't like looking at you or them, but because ... I'm jealous. What I really want to do is take you back to the hotel room and fuck the brains out of you."

Mike sat back in chair, stunned. Tim thought he'd really blown the whole thing this time. *What a jerk I am.*

"Well ..." Mike stuttered, "that'd be great. If you leave enough grey cells so I can still fly a plane and wash a dish, that is."

•　•　•

*The first time.*

They were so tentative. They were a little frightened of

each other, not frightened of rejection or pain, but because they didn't know the secrets yet, the places that hurt, the places that gave great pleasure.

They were in the hotel room and began undressing. *We're going to do it.* They were both in awe of that fact. They were not just watching another man strip; they were watching the revelation of a gift they were going to receive. When their shoes, socks and shirts were removed, they moved close to one another. They embraced.

The little electric shock started when they felt chest hair against chest hair. They could each smell the other's odor as their arms were lifted, and the musky aroma goaded them on. Hands moved over backs, feeling muscle and prodding flesh. They could feel each other's hardness as two erections fought for escape from the confines of their pants.

But most of all, there were the kisses, the saliva moving together, the tongues rolling wetly off one another; those explorations were the symbol for all the intruding and all the submitting that was to follow.

It was Mike who couldn't wait. Mike who had been waiting for too long. Mike who pulled back and looked longingly into Tim's eyes. Then he fell to his knees. He wasn't just undoing a zipper when his hands moved against Tim's fly. He was beginning an adventure. One that, somehow, they both knew would go on and on and on ...

He finished, leaned forward and pressed his head against the bulge there, the restraining cotton of Tim's underwear acting as a tease to both of them. Mike opened his mouth and ran it along the hard shaft.

He kept at it until there was a moan too real from Tim's mouth over him. Only then did Mike reach in and release the hard cock. It sprang forward, a tiny hint of wetness at its tip.

*The first time.*

Mike looked at it with obvious delight and quickly took it all in. For the first time, he finally had that longed-for erection in his mouth. He worked it, moving up and down, sucking on it, desperate to give it as much pleasure as he was receiving himself.

Tim finally pushed him back, not willing to go over the edge into orgasm yet. Kneeling on the floor, looking up at this other man's face as his cheek was being caressed with tender care, Mike felt an overwhelming sensation. *This is what it's like when someone looks at you with love.*

They finished undressing and moved to the bed. For so many years Mike had been so closed, his secrets entrapping him in his guilt and his self-protection. Now, with the memory of Tim's expression, he wanted to shatter that whole series of buffers. "Fuck me, please. Fuck me." He whispered the words as he clung to Tim with a pressure that let his pilot know just how important this was.

Tim had a lubricant in his bag. He got it and greased himself. An oily finger moved into the private entrance to Mike's body. A groan came from the co-pilot. It was half surrender and half victory, both merged together. "Yes."

Tim moved on top of Mike, spreading the other man's legs apart and lifting them. He pressed: there was resistance, then there was none. There was nothing but the undeniable and total pleasure of feeling his cock encased in this man's ass.

The movements were slow, as though both men wanted to linger at this place for as long as possible. But the pent-up passion and frustration wouldn't allow it. Tim began to move faster and faster. Mike did nothing to slow him down, he gripped Tim's hips and pulled – sometimes savagely. He wanted these defenses destroyed, absolutely destroyed.

There was a sudden tightening of Tim's body. Spasms shook his whole being, a cry came from his throat, a guttural roar. Then he collapsed on Mike's body. The two men were panting. Their breath took a while to slow to a more manageable level. Only then did Tim realize that they were being glued together with a fluid beside their sweat.

"You came? That way?"

"Oh yeah."

They kissed. *The first time.* Without speaking they knew

this one was going to last.

•  •  •

It was a couple months later. They had moved again, this time to a larger place. A house, actually. Tim had always wanted to own his own house, but he and Ralph had decided that their schedules wouldn't allow them to keep one up.

Mike and Tim's schedules didn't really give them that kind of time either, but Tim could count on Mike's unending energy. The idea that there was a whole structure that belonged to them, themselves, was too much to allow him to sit still. Mike continually assured Tim that the workload he carried didn't have to be matched. "Just let me run free."

"Running free" meant: cleaning, washing, ironing, painting, scraping, polishing, refinishing, refurbishing, re…

"You make me tired just watching you," Tim finally complained. *"Please,* have a beer and let's just watch some television."

"I know, I know I'm boring about it all. Okay, I'll do that." Mike had on his Christopher Street t-shirt, a new purchase they'd made on a recent trip to New York. "Can we go to Fire Island next summer," he suggested as he sat down.

"We probably should. There or Provincetown."

"You agree then? I figure I need the exposure, you know, to that kind of summer gay life."

"I figure you need to go to a place where there's going to be a constant supply of sand being tracked around to keep you happy as you clean it up."

They laughed and kissed and Mike finally made himself put his feet up on the table as the news came on. "That's him, isn't it?"

Andrew Marston was being interviewed.

"Our next governor." Tim took an angry drink at his can of beer.

"How did it happen?" Mike asked. "How could a crook like that not only get away, but put himself on the road to the state mansion? I mean ...”

"It happened because the others won't talk. They got caught, they're in prison. They think this guy's going to become governor and then they'll get pardoned. All the squealing they did on one another was one thing. They just weren't going to get rid of their one shot at freedom.”

"But that guy Mike Anderson said that it *was* him.”

"It was. We know it. But no one's going to believe us. Besides, you've watched how he's side-stepped the issues. He made himself seem to be the one who brought about the capture of all those others. It was his moral crusade that set them up.”

"Who can believe that shit after what he had said about gays?”

"Anybody. Saying stupid things about gays isn't going to lose anyone any credibility. You should have learned that by now.”

"I can't believe it. Anderson told me about that pair of guys who took care of everyone. Why couldn't they have handled Marston, too?”

"Because, if they did anything to the leader of the moral crusade in Minnesota, it'd just fire up all the right wing crazies and we'd be in worse trouble. There's nothing to do.” Tim put down his can and sat back on the couch, his arms crossed against his chest in a sulk.

Mike wouldn't drop it. He knew he couldn't. The life he and Tim were putting together was a good one, a fine one. But it had a shadow, one that could blot them out. The memory of Ralph and what had been done to him was too painful, it was baggage that even a relationship as good as theirs couldn't handle.

"He should be punished,” Tim announced.

"It would have to be God or nature that interfered. Hell, if anyone laid a finger on his holy body we'd have a crusade going that wouldn't ever be stopped.”

*"He should be punished."* And I think I know how to do it.

•  •  •

Later that night, when Tim had already gone to bed, Mike decided to make a phone call. If he was right there was something that could be done.

He had had enough conversations with Mike Anderson about the events in Minnesota to understand that the two strangers had been involved in the clean up of the anti-gay forces in the Twin Cities. They had a lot to do with it.

You don't just have white slavers like Martin Martello who've lived off children give themselves up to the police. Drug dealers who have existed outside the law don't get caught with as much evidence as that Angstrom guy had had on him without someone pulling something. All of it, the dirty bar business, the pushers, the murder, all of it stopped all at once. Everyone had been sentenced to jail and the best lawyers in the city weren't going to get them out of it.

Mike had put together his conversations with Anderson and his own observations of things. There was certainly something that could be done about Marston. Mike figured he knew a way to handle it, and that way needed some help from a friend in California. He dialed the number and listened to the phone ring at the other end.

# XXIV

Paco and his Haitian friend, Jean-Luc, splashed happily in the New Hampshire lake. The four adult men watched from the shore.

"The kids sure are happy," Allen Chisle said. "It's great having them around."

"How is he adjusting to you and Mike? And you to him? I mean, I'm not sure I'd want a budding heterosexual like that living with me." Danny had heard all about Paco's precocious straight sexuality.

"Well, it's fine. Really it is. I guess I wouldn't have taken a straight kid normally, but we figured he had some responsibility. He was caught in the net with the rest of them." Allen Chisle sipped his cola.

"But Jean-Luc *is* gay. Is Paco giving him grief?"

"No, no," Mike Anderson assured Danny "They're like guys who've been through combat together. There's a bond that can't be broken. They're the best of friends, you should hear them brag to each other. They do fight, but it's only over who has the better looking friend. What sex that 'friend' is doesn't seem the issue."

"It's good having them. I think it's good that the whole community has all those kids. There were twenty-five of them in all. It was a raw deal. It would have been an even worse thing to send them all back to their home countries without any of the things they had been promised. Now they're getting their educations and their futures. It's taken a lot of work and fundraising, but all the kids that were lured up to the states are getting what was promised to them.

"It sure has changed gay Minneapolis, though," Allen continued. "I mean, everyone seems to have an adopted teenage son these days. We go to more kid parties than anything else."

"Like this," Mike indicated the kids who were still squealing with delight. "We really appreciate your inviting us. But we couldn't have come without them."

"No problem," Alex said. "None at all."

"I'm not sure about Mr. Farmdale though. Do you think he'll mind that we're bringing these two to dinner with us? He's so intimidating to me. I just don't see him enjoying dinner with a couple youngsters."

Alex Kane seemed to be delighted with the prospect. "No problem."

•  •  •

"This is one of the finest and most proper eating establishments in New England." Joseph Farmdale was literally glowering. "How could you bring those hellions here?"

They were in the lobby of the Red Crow Inn. Farmdale had lured Alex away from the table, but Alex stood his ground. "It's your own fault."

"My own fault! How could you say that?!"

"You're the one who pulled all the strings in Washington. If it weren't for you, they'd all be back in their home countries right now."

"In dire poverty, after having been misused by those filthy gangsters. Why, those gay men were desperate to make it up to the boys. After what they'd been through, the way they'd been blackmailed ..."

"Especially Jean-Luc; after all, he's gay. Black and beautiful and gay."

"Don't you *dare* throw that at me! You know perfectly

well that I do not condone any kind of racial prejudice. Now, this is one issue, but what's going on in that dining room is quite another issue. I mean, really, Alex. Those children ..."

"Are your guests."

"You told me there would be houseguests of yours. But ..."

"They are my houseguests. Now look, Farmdale. There's no way around it. You wanted to help. You did."

"But children would be best off in nurseries until they've learned their table manners. Those two ..."

•  •  •

"Yuck, look at all that stuff on the meat," Paco said. "What is it?"

"It is a perfectly accomplished sauce in the finest traditions of –" Farmdale paled as he watched Paco scrape the sauce off his New York steak.

"I don't like sauce."

"Me either." Jean-Luc peeled the skin off his chicken l'orange to remove the offending liquid.

"Without those sauces, this food becomes something that you could have been served ..."

"Why didn't we go to McDonald's? We love McDonald's."

"Don't whine, Paco. Mr. Farmdale's being very generous with you."

"*McDonald's!*" The sound that came from Joseph Farmdale's throat wasn't just a yell. It carried with it a great, intolerable pain, the pain of a man of tradition watching the emergence of modern day life at a closer view than he had ever been forced to witness it before. "*McDonald's.*" The second time he spoke the name, it sounded more like a cry of grief.

Alex Kane was enjoying himself immensely.

•  •  •

The next day it seemed as though Alex had understood that the night at the Red Crow had taken Farmdale too far. He called the inn and told the old man to come to the house for dinner. Only when he was promised that the boys would be restrained in some way did Farmdale accept.

The five men were sitting drinking some of Farmdale's favorite vintage St. Emilion. Off across the lawn Jean-Luc and Paco were happily eating hamburgers while, on the grill, the adults' venison steaks were grilling. There was a decent salad that Danny had already prepared to accompany the game, and potatoes baking in the grill's coals.

"This will do very well."

Farmdale was obviously pleased. Danny reached over and filled his glass with wine. "Yes, indeed, my doctors need never know about this."

"Is that why you've come all the way to New Hampshire?" Mike asked.

Danny was the one to express pleasure this time. "No, he comes pretty regularly now. To visit family."

"Oh, do you have relatives near by?" Mike was innocently pursuing this topic. He didn't understand why both Farmdale and Alex Kane looked away with such theatrical distaste.

"The closest," Danny beamed.

"Well, you and your family have certainly been most generous to us, Mr. Farmdale. I mean, the contribution you made to the gay adoption fund will certainly go a long way in helping us out. I can afford the extra expense of two kids, but some of the guys just wouldn't have made it without your help."

Farmdale seemed pained by Allen's exposure of his generosity. Alex Kane moved in for an attack. "Can't keep your hands out of other people's business, can you? You had to go and spread all your money around again, didn't you?"

"You will never know how much money I have spent on your latest adventure, and its repercussions. You will never know."

# XXV

Andrew Marston could not believe his good fortune. He'd made it! He had honestly and truly made it. He'd pulled off a change in his moral crusade after it had been a change of direction himself. The events in Minnesota had been a whirlwind of confusion and unbelievable contradictions.

But he'd ridden out the storm. He had proven his mettle in this baby, that's for sure.

All those assholes were in prison. They hadn't a shred of evidence to implicate him. It'd be a couple of years before they would realize they were never going to be pardoned. Angstrom, LeBec and the whole gang were gone. Sure, they'd make noise when they realized the extent of his double-cross. But he would have had time to bring together his resources and fill the vacuum. He'd be in charge of the above-board power of the state and also the underground power of crime.

He looked out his window and watched the Minnesota landscape racing by beneath him. His own state. The whole thing was going to be his.

He was deliciously pleased as he sipped his Scotch. He was thinking about the details. Another year and he could get a divorce. He'd be governor by then and it would give him and the electorate four years to forget that problem. He would marry any one of a number of women then. Women were always attracted to a powerful man. He could already see himself on the cover of *Time.* The television cameras followed him constantly. He was a celebrity.

Even his means of transportation proved it. Here he was in his private jet. Leased, granted, but it was his own. The deal had been great. So great he wondered about it until the salesman had explained that the company, a newly formed subsidiary of Farmdale Industries, needed the exposure of a star like himself to make it more credible in the marketplace. So they'd given Marston a deal.

That made sense. He's heard about all the women who got designer dresses and furs just so the creators would get the publicity that came with those well-known women wearing their clothes. This firm was just making a gamble, a gamble that made sense to Marston. They'd use his name in their advertising once they knew that Marston had won his election.

*Scratch my back, I'll scratch yours,* Marston smiled. There were lots of possibilities about being a governor of a state.

He looked up as the co-pilot came back into the executive lounge. Marston was the only passenger on this trip, a quick jaunt up to Thief River Falls. This two-man crew the company provided was a little weird. They seemed to always be studying Marston. They probably just had never been this close to someone as important as he before.

"Enjoying your journey?"

"Very much." Marston put on his best campaign smile.

"It's going to be a very important one for you."

"Yes, yes, any time I can get a chance to address a group of loyal Minnesota voters is very important." What a bunch of crap this guy was pulling.

Just then the pilot joined them. *Both of them...*

Then Marston saw the gun. "Don't bother moving." Mike held the pistol on Marston while Tim got the ropes.

The pilot secured Marston to his seat with quick and effective knots. "They don't have to be all that good. I made sure of his record. He can't fly. Not that it matters."

"What are you doing?"

Marston was panicking as he watched the two men put on parachutes. "We're climbing good now," the co-pilot said to the other. "This is more than high enough." They went toward the door.

"The plane's on automatic pilot. It'll keep in its path for quite a while, going directly toward Thief River Falls. No one will know the difference. It will climb, but not so much that you'll lose consciousness, we just wanted to get high enough to jump. You'll be wide awake when it happens. You'll hear first one engine sputter then the other. Then you'll feel the plane lose altitude. The plane's fall will accelerate quickly. Very quickly. You'll be able to feel that.

"We hope you enjoy this trip, Marston. You've got about an hour. An hour tops. You can think about it all. Think about the men you killed and the lives you ruined. We want you to do that.

"You can struggle if you want. Don't bother. Just in case you decided to play hero or got smart, I smashed the radio up. More insurance," Mike held up a handful of small electronic items. "The plane's not going anywhere we wouldn't want it to without these.

"Enjoy your hour, Marston. And think. Think a lot."

Then the two men opened the rear door, took each other's hand, and jumped.

Frantic, Marston turned until he could look out the window and see their parachutes loosen. They were drifting toward land. And he was drifting toward ...

# XXVI

The two figures were dressed in the traditional *gi*. Their martial arts costume seemed splendidly chosen for their flowing motions. They were practicing tai chi, the most graceful of the arts.

In liquid moves, their bodies moved in perfect synchrony. An arm mirrored an arm; leg a leg. The breeze of the early autumn in New Hampshire moved with them, complimenting them. Theirs was a ballet of physical perfection, a symbol of total companionship.

They kept at it for an hour as the dawning sun warmed the cool mountain air. They were unaware of any discomfort. They only were aware of one another and their two bodies.

When they finished, they gave the expected bow to one another. But then the taller, older of the two did the unexpected. He moved to his partner. First he removed his own *gi*. Then, reverently, he took off the other man's. When they were both naked, he fell to his knees. He placed both his hands under the testicles of the standing figure and seemed to cup them, as though they were a vessel of great value.

He leaned forward. His tongue came out and he ran it over the hair-covered surface, as though giving honor to the sweat that had come from their joint exertion. Only after he'd done his honor to all of that surface did he take in the swollen penis. His moves now were no faster than those earlier ones.

This was a quiet passion. It was the passion of a man who

knew that his lover was not going to leave him. Not for a long, long time.

When they both were spent, when each had taken the fluids of the other, they moved to the lake. Its waters were already chilled in preparation for winter. They dove in without hesitation.

When they came out their skin was ruffled with evidence of the cold. They embraced still again, as though they had cooled themselves so much only to be able to have the joy of giving each other more warmth.

Then, naked and pleased, they walked up to their log cabin home and went about making their meal.

•  •  •

That night, as they sat and read in front of the fire that roared with large dry logs, Alex Kane was aware of the peace of his lover and himself. "Danny," he softly interrupted the younger man's quiet. "We can just stay here."

Danny waved the objections away. "We've been through all that. We'll spend the time we can together here. And when we have to leave ..."

Alex went back to his novel. He was uncomfortable.

Danny's involvement made him look at his own so much. Was he addicted to all this? Was this something that he could do with another person? Could he lead this life with another man – who could suffer the consequences?

There was a knock on the door. It was nearly ten o'clock. It could only mean ...

Danny had gotten up and answered the summons. There was a messenger there. He handed Danny a package, then left. The two lovers looked at one another. They knew.

Danny went over to the fire and opened the parcel. He threw away the wrappings. But he kept the contents.

It was a book, a red leather book, bound in the finest old Spanish tradition.

# STOLEN MOMENTS

## by John Preston

# Author's Note

Its effectiveness hasn't always been perfect, its leadership has sometimes stumbled, its image could use some luster now and again, but when the need was strong, the National Gay Task Force has always been there to give testimony before Congress, do public education, keep track of the media and provide us with an absolutely necessary, on-going organization. It's a communal embarrassment that so few of us belong to this established and trustworthy organization. At time of writing, a general membership costs only $30.

National Gay Task Force
80 Fifth Avenue, Suite 1601
New York, New York 10011

Note: This organisation has morphed into the National LGBTQ Task Force and has relocated to Washington, DC.

National LGBTQ Task Force
1050 Connecticut Ave NW, Suite 65500
Washington, DC 20035

Alex Kane would be proud of your support.

# I

Hermano España looked out over the harbor of Santa Isabella. He tried to keep moving his binoculars enough that his fellow guards couldn't tell just how carefully he was studying those …

"Degenerate capitalists," sneered Ernesto Malca, standing next to Hermano. The tone of his voice sent shivers through Hermano's body. But at least the comment gave him an excuse to focus more clearly on the two men.

They were standing on the forward deck of a very large, long white boat. Each of them wore only a slight bathing suit, just as white as the paint on the private vessel's sides. *They were handsome!*

Hermano was quickly terrified that he had allowed the thought to enter his mind. He could never allow Ernesto or any of the others to know that about himself. If they did, he wouldn't stay a guard at the Revolutionary People's Prison much longer. He would be downstairs with *those* prisoners.

"Yes," Hermano agreed, "it's terrible that the government has to allow them to come here and display such ostentatious wealth. But we need the foreign exchange."

"Not that much!"

Hermano was shocked as he watched the activity that brought out the new spleen in his fellow guard's words. The smaller man in the boat, the one who had so much dark hair on his body in such contrast to that slight, white bathing suit, had moved up closer to the other and had wrapped his arms about the man's body. There was no question what that movement meant. The younger man was moving his hips, rotating so his crotch dug into his friend's buttocks.

But the friend didn't move. He allowed the suggestive activity to continue. He, his body as hairless as the other one was hirsute, simply stared ahead. Hermano suddenly wondered if the man wasn't looking right back at them, right at the prison. It couldn't be. No one would dare flaunt their degeneracy in that blatant manner. No real man in any event.

Hermano studied the nearly naked bodies on the boat's deck and felt an uncomfortable stirring in his pants. The bigger one, the one who had no hair, had a body that forced Hermano to react. It was so perfectly proportioned and its muscles were so wonderfully displayed that Hermano had to think: *He looks like one of those statues in the museum.*

Hermano put down his binoculars just in time. He was already finished staring at the men on the boat when Ernesto turned to him. "It's an insult to the people of the republic that those men are allowed to act that way."

"Yes," Hermano agreed, growing increasingly uncomfortable, "but they bring in the hard currency we need. They spend it foolishly in the restaurants, they buy crafts, they ..."

"It's counter-revolutionary."

Hermano had long ago learned that Ernesto was a hard-liner when it came to the morality of the revolution. To Ernesto everything was so simple. There were no grey areas, only the absolute blacks and whites of the revolution's slogans.

But Hermano had many questions about the new order. There were many mysteries. Hermano also knew that he himself was one of them. He had joined the freedom fighters. Not as early as the others, perhaps, but he had spent time in the jungle, he had been trained by the political cadres, he understood the importance of a new order for Santa Isabella. It made sense to him to be here, now a guard at the prison.

One of the mysteries was why it made sense for him and

not for Juan. He was both sad and nervous when the image of Juan came to his mind, as it so naturally did just now. After all, in the jungle, as members of the freedom fighters, he and Juan had acted just as those two men in the white bathing suits.

They had not been open about it. But Hermano knew that even some of the officers understood that Hermano and Juan slept close together at night and always went on patrol together. Everyone had known that Hermano and Juan did everything together. They used to, in any event.

Another mystery: Why had Juan *insisted* that people know those things about himself? Why had he talked about it so often? Everyone understood that the terroristic dictator had to be removed. No one doubted the need for a fair and equitable share of the land for the peasants. No one wanted to have the cruel wage scale of the city continued. They had been fighting for justice! For freedom! Why had Juan *demanded* that they include ...

And why had Hermano abandoned his lover?

All the rationalizations floated through Hermano's head as they had countless other times. For his family. For the revolution. For the sake of his manhood. For ... none of them worked. Not one salved the disgrace that he would feel all alone when the change of the guards came and Hermano had to walk through the prison yard. There, he would see Juan. He would have to see the disgust that his old lover felt for him. He would again get that feeling that somehow, in some way that had never been explained to him, his real manhood had been damaged by his own unwillingness to be as strong as Juan.

Why did he get that feeling? Juan was brave, he'd shown that in the jungle. But he was like a woman in so many ways. He had mannerisms that had often embarrassed Hermano when they had been in public. Hermano, on the other hand, was the one who got the first promotion. He was a sergeant now. He knew perfectly well that he had a bigger cock. So did Juan; after all, Juan had said so over and over again. He was the one in the proud uniform of the People's Republic. He was the one who was looked at by all the women as such a macho stud when he walked down the main street of the city.

But somehow, in some part of Hermano's mind, he knew that Juan was a better man than he and he knew it had something to do with that honesty that had consigned Juan to the prison yard and with something else that kept Hermano here, on the prison walls.

A siren blared. Time to change the guard. Hermano and Ernesto went through the motions of giving a report to the new shift and then, with the boredom that comes from constant repetition, they moved down off the walls. When they'd reached the bottom of the staircase they began to walk toward the gate.

Everything here was as it always was. There were the hardened criminals in one cluster. There were political prisoners, enemies of the revolution, in another, and in the third were the homosexuals. The People's Government had declared them to be a venom that had to be separated from the rest of the population. It was necessary, they had said, to remove the elements of bourgeois degeneracy from the society in order to allow the new order to arise with revolutionary purity.

*There he is,* Hermano said to himself.

Juan stood in the middle of the homosexuals. He stood with his legs spread defiantly, his arms crossed over his chest. His face was as handsome as ever. He had high cheek bones that displayed his *mestizo* heritage. He had always said that his long black hair was in honor of that, not something he had to appear to be a woman. Hermano remembered when he had believed that and how proud he had been that Juan would do something so impressive to declare himself honored by his race. They had all grown up to hate any part of themselves that wasn't white. So many of them had been taught to always insist that they were pureblood Spanish. It had been a lesson learned on the knees of their mothers and their fathers.

The revolution had said that was not correct. There should never be any division between the races, it had decreed. But while that one thing which they had been taught to hate about themselves was suddenly now honored, there was the other ...

Ernesto spit on the ground. "They should just kill those animals. At least they should give them their own prison so they don't infest the rest of the prisoners."

Hermano had heard that one, too. It only added to his mysteries. He could not understand why this one thing was so horrible that it was treated even worse than murder or theft, treason or other crimes. But it was an argument he was not about to have with Ernesto. "They are kept separate at night."

It was true. Hermano had plenty of reasons to know about it. There were nights when he was drawn back to the prison, when he had to see Juan. The homosexuals were kept in an old section of the building. It was slightly off to the side of the yard. There, more crowded than in the other sections and without any of the privacy that the newer cells gave to the inmates, the homosexuals were kept in a squalor that the prison officials said was only fitting.

Sometimes Juan wouldn't even acknowledge Hermano's presence. Those times usually came after one of their arguments about the revolution. Juan openly ridiculed Hermano's belief that it was necessary to allow the new order to develop. It must work for the good of the most people. "If your revolution doesn't include me, it can go to hell!"

Hermano often wondered why he dared to continue the clandestine meetings. They were dangerous. Hermano lived in constant dread that someone like Ernesto would notice how often he visited the homosexual cells.

*Why*, he thought as they were let out of the prison compound, *why do I continue to go there*? As soon as he thought that question he knew the answer. Because there were those moments, so rare but still they existed, when all the arguments would stop and all the anger would disappear and

Hermano and Juan would look at one another with that longing that told them that the times in the jungle had not been mistakes.

*This should only be for something base, for sex,* Hermano insisted to himself. But there was something wrong with that idea. He knew it. The torture that eroded his soul only grew in intensity. Each time Hermano demanded why Juan insisted on declaring his forbidden homosexuality, Juan would only stupidly reply, "Why are you on that side of the cell's bars?" Of course it was a stupid retort! But it always dug deep and caused great pain, because Hermano never could find the answer.

*But it was only for sex!* he insisted silently. Then why was the hurt not just in his groin? Why was it in his heart when he thought of Juan and that look of hatred?

He would put it aside. He wouldn't think of it. He'd go back to his family's house tonight and eat a good meal with them. He would attend a political class, maybe it could give him answers to these mysteries, though politics hadn't done that yet. Sometimes he would force himself to dream about women. He should marry. He should have children and bring them up to honor and respect the revolution. He had often thought that himself.

But the image of those two men in their white bathing suits was in his mind. The way they touched. Cheap! *Loving.* Degenerate! *Beautiful.* Disgusting! *Wonderful.*

Hermano thought of those two men and he knew that he would return to the prison very late, and he would have to see Juan and talk to him and find out ... something.

It was well after midnight when Hermano returned. He was no longer wearing his uniform, but the guards on duty knew him well enough that there was no problem allowing him to get in.

"So, back to kiss more ass," one of the men on duty said.

Hermano froze at that slight hint of sexual intent.

"Your kind are all the same, revolution or not."

Jesus! Who was overhearing this?

"Always after the promotions, always trying to make whoever's in power think you're indispensible."

Hermano was so relieved to finally understand what the man meant that he thought he might pass out. Instead, he somehow willed himself to just nod, just walk on by, and let the fool think whatever he wanted to about the nocturnal visits.

Then his spirits lifted. *That's what they think I'm doing!* All these late night sojourns to the prison and the rest of the guards only thought that he was pulling for another promotion. That improved his spirits immensely.

He made his way across the yard and into the offices where his and other prison guards' things were kept in lockers. There – near the officer of the day's desk – were the spare keys to the compound. None of the keys for the powerful outside gates were accessible, but there were keys to the library, the various internal compounds and to some of the common rooms. The security of the Santa Isabella prison was legendary. People simply did not escape from this fortress.

The structure had been originally built by the Spanish. In their days walls were constructed with incredible width and height. The outer defenses of the prison were solid rock and masonry. There was an internal wall as well. Over the years there had been a slow accumulation of modern technical devices. The dictator wasn't about to allow his political prisoners to escape easily.

While the revolutionary government had changed many, many things in Santa Isabella, the security of the prison was one thing they had been happy to acquire intact from the dictator.

With walls like these, impregnable walls that an army could never conquer, the internal security of the prison was lax. The clerk sitting by the keys barely took notice of Hermano's mission. "Going to the library," Hermano said. The clerk went back to his reading and didn't see that Hermano's hand had picked up a key that would never have worked on the library's lock.

It was simple to walk out of the room and into the yard, then make his way to the homosexuals' compound. He unlocked one of the doors that let him in. He knew where Juan always slept. There were lines of cots on the inside of the cells; there were at least twenty-five of the small, hard beds in each of the four rooms. Somehow Juan always got the one in the nearest corner. Hermano had never dared ask the reason, but he thought – he hoped – that it was the one thing that Juan did for him, no matter how angry they got with one another.

As Hermano made his way to that place he had a flashing thought about the men in the white bathing suits. He wondered, for some strange reason, if they had been alone. *Why do I care about that?* he asked himself. *What difference would it make!*

• • •

The two men were walking on the deck of their boat just as Hermano was thinking about them. But their clothing had changed. Black uniforms now covered their entire bodies. They were even wearing black knit caps to hide their hair. As though it were a part of their costume, they had smeared their faces and hands with black grease. There was no moon tonight. Only a very occasional light would reflect off the water and hint at their presence. They were like shadows in the dark.

They were not alone.

Their boat had appeared to be a pleasure craft, much larger than most of those that plied the waters of the Caribbean, but the size had made it even less likely that they would be searched by any questioning customs agents. The kind of money that people with these boats had was enough that even a revolutionary government wanted them to feel welcome.

If the customs agents had investigated the rear hold, only an unusually thorough search would have uncovered the real contents. The agents would have needed the architect's plans to realize that most of the walls were false.

But, if they had seen those architectural drawings, they would have understood that there was an extraordinary amount of space there. It was carefully camouflaged, or it had been. But as the two men who had worn white bathing suits looked on, four new men appeared. They quickly transformed the interior, removing false partitions and exposing two large amphibious vehicles.

The younger man, the one whose chest had been so luxuriantly coated with hair, smiled. It was not a pleasant smile. It was not a kind smile. It had a sense of the demonic about it. It was a smile of revenge.

The other man, the one whose body looked so like a statue, stared at the revelation of the landing craft with just as much emotion. One couldn't have seen it easily; there was no change in his facial muscles, no hint of anxiousness in his stance. But if you had been there, you couldn't help but notice the way his eyes seemed to light up. They seemed to sparkle. It was as though a small firestorm had begun inside his head. It made him seem to be a little insane. Maybe not a little, maybe a lot.

Silently, the four other men – all dressed in the same way – moved to their prearranged places. The amphibians were quickly and efficiently released from the stern of the boat, a stern which proved to be as false as some of the walls of the interior. It had all been a fake, in fact. Hermano might have noticed just how very long the boat was; so, too, might some of the customs agents. But they hadn't. The length had only appeared to be an added symbol of the ostentation of the capitalists. It wasn't. It was a sign of the determination of these two men.

They joined the four others. Even though they were all in black, one of them was dressed a little differently. His hat was also black, but it was the style of an American cowboy.

"We're all set, Alex," Luke McDavid said to the man with the iridescent green eyes. "What a job!"

Alex Kane just smiled.

The boats made their way across the harbor. In a matter of minutes they were beached on the sand just below the walls of the prison. The fore end of the amphibians opened onto the beach. With obvious planning, one of the men stayed with each of the vessels. The four others moved toward the prison wall.

They hesitated just at the bottom of the towering structure. They silently checked their four wristwatches with one another. Then, they immediately went to work.

The man named Luke McDavid and his partner began to scale the outer barrier. As though they were human spiders, they used suction cups on their hands and knees to climb the stone covering.

While they made their way upward, large packs bulging from their backs and a rifle slung over each one's shoulders, the man named Alex Kane and his own partner, the younger one, the one with the hairy chest and the demonic expression on his face, silently and carefully went about their business, emptying their own packs and placing things from them at very carefully calibrated points on the wall.

When they were done, Alex Kane looked at his watch. He slapped his friend hard on the shoulder and the two of them began to run – *fast.*

They could run, and they could run well. Even the difficult footing of the sand didn't seem to slow them down. They moved like black angels in the night, racing far from the place where only minutes ago they had been working. They had been able to go a long distance from that spot on the wall, almost as far away from it as the boats' anchorage.

Still, when the blast came, they were blown forward off their feet, sent spinning into the sand as if some force had reached out and slapped them down.

They were on their faces for a brief second. Then Alex Kane screamed. "Danny! Danny, are you all right?"

"Lousy calculations, Alex," the younger man responded. Then he stood. "Come on, don't stand around yakking. We have work to do."

As fast as they had run away, now they returned to the prison walls. There, where they had worked, was a gaping hole in the prison defenses. Just as they saw it they heard another series of explosions. They almost immediately saw evidence of the new blasts' effect as more stone and rubble was thrown through the wall onto the Santa Isabella beach.

• • •

Hermano had been trying to talk sense to Juan. But this was a night to argue, not one to talk. "You are going to let them kill us!" Juan had insisted. "They're going to execute us!"

"They would never do that. All they might do is reeducate you. Give in, Juan. We can find a way ..."

"Hiding and lying and deceiving and ... No. Never. If I wanted to do that I wouldn't have fought to end the dictatorship. What's the difference, though? If they are going to execute us ..."

"They won't." But as Hermano saw the honest belief that just such a tragedy would happen on Juan's face, he wondered. *Could this madness of the people's new order possibly go that far?*

The horrible idea was reeling inside Hermano's head just when the first blasts occurred. Their power shook the whole of the prison. He stood up and grabbed the bars that separated him from Juan. The crowded prison room came to life. The other inmates were frozen at first, but soon they began to yell and scream.

What was going on!

Before there was time to think of an answer, another wave *of* explosion ripped through the prison, just as loud and just as strong as the first. It seemed to knock Hermano back to full consciousness. He suddenly understood.

"The dictator's men," he said to Juan. "They've come to free their friends, the political prisoners. Pray they stay on that side of the compound. If they get in here, this could turn out to be a battleground."

Juan looked at Hermano and nodded silently and slowly. He understood. The dictator may have been disposed, but it was no secret that he still had many millions of dollars and much power and he had often threatened a counter-coup to regain control of Santa Isabella. It made sense. It certainly didn't make sense to Juan that anyone would attempt such a huge operation for any other reason. Unless it was an accident, the blast could have been ...

"Hiya, guys'" The man who was wearing a black cowboy hat and whose face was covered with black grime was smiling; you could just make out the white of his teeth. "Hope some of you can speak English."

"I can," Juan said automatically, and then was sure he had made a grave error.

"Well, you tell all your good buddies to stand back. I got one little thing to do and then we're all going to go for a boat ride. You guys got some disco to catch up on."

Juan was stock still for a few seconds. This was impossible! But something told him to move. He yelled quick instructions to the crowds in the four large cells that housed the homosexuals. Juan had early on taken a certain leadership role in their gatherings. His voice, deep and demanding, was instantly obeyed by the terrified inmates.

The man with the cowboy hat was working quickly and efficiently, pulling materials out of his pack. Juan recognized the plastic explosives. "First one ..." the man said, lighting the short fuse. The blast this time was very small, but sufficient to blow open the cell door. "Get your pals here running like hell out that door. Tell 'em to go to the left. There's a hole in the wall that's big enough to drive a Cadillac through it. They go straight out, towards the water. Tell 'em to yell like they were before. As soon as some of my friends hear that, there'll be some lights turned on and they'll see some boats. They're supposed to scoot onto those tubs as soon as they can. Hurry. Now. Get 'em *moving!*"

Juan translated the instructions to the people who were

in the same cell as he. They obeyed immediately. Even while they were still running through the cell opening, the man with the cowboy hat was working on the second load of plastic. "Give me some," Juan demanded. "I know how to use it."

"So do I. Give me the other." Juan turned to face Hermano. In his face were all the expressions of all the feelings he had for the man he had once loved ... and maybe still did.

"You." The word had contempt and respect, surprise and scorn in it all at once.

"Me." Hermano replied.

The man with the blackened face wasn't waiting for their fight to be resolved. He just put the small explosives in their hands, both of their hands, and went back to work, whistling some song they'd never heard.

Juan listened to the man with the cowboy hat and his song as he applied the explosives, and he did remember a song from the bars when he first went to them before the revolution. It had been American. Something like ... *We are family ...*

Three quick, popping explosions finished the remaining locks. Their doors fell open. *"Allll right!"* the man said triumphantly. "Get their cute little asses *running!"*

Juan screamed out instructions to the prisoners. They ran toward the open door. Luke McDavid slapped Juan and Hermano on their backs, one of his big hands on each of them. "Welcome to the home team, my men. Let's get out of here while we still got peckers."

The three moved to follow the crowd out the door. Another man, also dressed in black and also with his face camouflaged, guarded the entrance. A huge machine gun in his hands kept sweeping the space in front of the homosexual compound.

"Sammy, you still got your crown jewels? No one shot those off?" Luke asked his lover.

"Move your ass, McDavid. That is, if you ever want my crown jewels going up there again."

"That's what I call persuasion." Luke, still smiling, reached down and picked up his own rifle, as large as Sam's. The four of them ran through the hole in the walls.

Hermano was scared. Hermano was *terrified.* He didn't know what the hell he was doing! He was running with madmen and escaped convicts over the beaches of Santa Isabella. There were lights in front of them down by the water's edge. Why weren't they being pursued?

*Because they think they're after the politicos!* He immediately knew he was right. For the whole year they'd been on the alert for an attempt to rescue the men who once worked for the dictator. No one had ever thought that the homosexuals would be the target of a rescue attempt.

They were going to be free! But where were they going? Who were these men? What was going to happen after they got onto their boats?

He didn't have time to even think through his questions. He and Juan and the men in the black clothes ran up the ramp of the craft on the sand. Behind them came two more men, evidently a rear guard, dressed in the same ebony uniforms.

As soon as these last men were on board, they moved quickly to lift up the ramp and make it secure. They shouted something to the man at the controls. The engine roared, it pulled the craft off the land and moved it quickly out over the water. As soon as it could, the boat was turned around and its speed increased even more.

Behind them were sirens and random gun shots. The prison was coming to life. Hermano could see the powerful spotlights as they swept the grounds around the prison walls. As unexpected as the liberation of the homosexuals would have been, surely they'd soon discover exactly what had taken place. Then, they'd come after them.

Hermano would be one of *them.* He closed his eyes and wondered what he would do when they were recaptured. He could insist they had shanghied him to come along. He could insist that he was not one of the homosexuals. He could ... "I'm proud of you," Juan said softly into his ear.

A new emotion swept through Hermano. He turned and

saw how close Juan's face was. Their lips met very gently. For the first time in a year Hermano did feel proud. And happy. He felt all his machismo melt as they kissed. He would not lie. He would stop lying. Whatever happened to him?

The boats moved quickly across the harbor. Hermano and Juan stood and looked over the side to see their destination. *The white boat?* Hermano looked around wildly and wondered why that was the place they were going.

Then he saw the two men in black who hadn't spoken to them. They were standing on the fore platform of the craft. One was behind the other and had his arms snaked around his body. Hermano immediately knew they were the two men with the white bathing suits. They were smiling. Their smiles shone against the dark grease on their skin, and there was a weird glowing green in the eyes of the one who stood in front.

"Quick! Up the ladders." Juan was translating the orders the man called Luke McDavid had given him. The men in the two crafts scurried up the rope web that hung over the side as fast as they could. The operation was completed in a matter of minutes.

Hermano was now on the white ship he had been studying that morning. It was exquisite. The deck was made of shining mahogany. All the metalwork seemed to be gleaming brass. The boat was moving already. Maybe they would get away!

As the ship began moving out to sea, Hermano could watch the landing craft slowly sinking. They had been scuttled; obviously on purpose. Someone must have decided it was too dangerous to take the time to bring them along. That was fine with Hermano. He was in favor of anything that would save time.

A scream came from the mouths of some of the freed prisoners gathered on the deck. Planes screeched through air, as if headed directly for the ship. Hermano's spirits were deflated. There would be no escape. Those must be the new Russian jets that the revolutionary government had just received. They would sink the ship and they'd all drown.

But the planes, both of them, veered off. Hermano was puzzled. When the noise of the planes had subsided, and once he had gotten used to the sounds of the ship's engines, he was aware of more and more sounds coming from the mainland. They were the sirens for a full military alert. That meant the navy would be activated.

There! He knew it. Off to one side was one of the Santa Isabellan navy's destroyers. It was racing towards them. Even if this ship could outrace the destroyer, it couldn't evade its guns.

Suddenly the two jets had circled back. They were diving again, their engines screaming, their speed so great Hermano could barely follow their progress. They were diving! They would attack the ship!

But, again, they passed over. Now they were heading directly for the destroyer. Bright blasts flashed under their wings as their missiles were ignited. The deadly arms found their targets in almost an instant. There was one, then another explosion in the destroyer. A third hit the destroyer's fuel tank. A huge eruption sent blinding light into the night in the harbor. Then, almost as quickly, it was over. Only a few pieces of burning debris were left on the water's surface.

Jubilant yells went up from the crowded deck of the ship. They were going to make it! Hermano felt Juan's arm pull at his waist. They were going to make it.

• • •

The next morning Hermano awoke on deck. He and Juan had slept together on an air mattress with a blanket to protect against the sea's evening chill. Other bodies were similarly laid out, all still sleeping.

He immediately realized how strange it was that this shipload of refugees was scattered on the mahogany surfaces of such a luxurious ship. Last night they had been the most despised prisoners of the People's Republic of Santa Isabella. Now they were riding in style on a millionaire's boat.

As though some unseen force wanted to underline the contradiction, there was a sudden line of impeccably dressed crewmen carrying loads of tables and linen tablecloths. They quickly went about setting them up. There was even an elaborate candelabra that one man set down in the middle of the long table once it had been erected.

Then, while Hermano kept on watching, the men disappeared and quickly returned carrying trays of food, all carefully covered with metal. Others had the same kind of heating implements that Hermano had seen in the buffets of the old hotels that the rich people of the dictatorship used to eat at.

Then came stacks of plates, silverware, napkins, all the things that an aristocrat would use to entertain his most honored guests. The inescapable conclusion was that the banquet was for the prisoners.

Hermano stood up. He went over and watched the men at their work. They smiled at him, but didn't speak. One suddenly appeared holding a steaming cup of coffee out to him. Hermano took it, "Thank you," he said in his halting English. He'd learned the language well enough to speak to tourists, as had almost everyone in Santa Isabella.

The man who'd given him the coffee smiled and promised him it was no problem. Did he want cream or sugar? Hermano, not sure just what his own position was in this strange operation, quickly declined the added favors. Only when he started to sip his coffee did he realize two things both at once. First, the man had been dressed in a fashionable uniform, but he hadn't carried himself in the servile manner that waiters in Santa Isabella usually did during the dictatorship, the kind of manner that acknowledged the role of the other as master. He was a proud man, this server. He was willingly practicing a craft.

Hermano remembered some of the grand old men who used to be waiters in the most elegant restaurant in Santa Isabella. While some of them had been aloof and rude, most were pleased with their jobs and happy to have a well-paying and honorable profession. This server, who really must be a servant, had that same pride. He wasn't beaten down by his role. He was simply pleased with his job.

But much more impressive and even more noticeable, the man had let his eyes wander openly over Hermano's body. Hermano was clad only in a pair of pants and the server had certainly seemed to appreciate the thick chest that was so exposed. That already made Hermano happier. This man, too, must be a homosexual.

And one who appreciated a masculine man like Hermano.

Now, smiling broadly, Hermano felt more comfortable. He wandered over the rear deck where the tables had been set up and looked out over the stern of the ship. There was a trail of white churning water left by the boat's propeller. There was nothing on the horizon. They were far away from Santa Isabella and their past, headed for some new adventure.

"Well, got at least one of you up and about."

Hermano turned to look at the man who had talked to him. Even though his skin was now washed of the black grease, Hermano knew it was the one who had come into the jail cells last night and blown apart the cell doors.

He was dressed in that strange fashion that only gringo tourists would ever dare use. He had on a big-brimmed hat like the one he wore last night, but this time it was lightcolored. Underneath it he wore only a large, baggy pair of shorts made of a plaid fabric. He was barefoot, carrying his own cup of coffee.

"Just barely six o'clock," the man continued. "I always get up early. Figure the rest of your amigos will wake soon enough. The sun here gets fucking bright fucking early, if you ask me."

"And we all do." The other man from the escape, the younger one who had been guarding the entrance with a machine gun, came up to them now. He was wearing a little bathing suit like the other two had yesterday, but no hat. Hermano felt a little strange to realize he was staring at the pouch, appreciating that part of this man's anatomy as openly as the server had studied his chest.

"I'm Sam Manetti." The man stuck out his hand. Hermano shook it and then the man named Luke McDavid introduced himself. The little movements that these two made toward one another made it clear that they were lovers. They told him they were from someplace called Arizona. They were here only for what Luke called "a little excitement."

"Something to shake up things," Sam had smiled.

Hermano wanted to pursue that, he wanted to understand why these men had taken such risks. But the most pressing questions came first. "Those planes, where did they come from?"

"Oh, just some people, friends of Alex and Danny's. They come from Minnesota, seem to know a few things about airplanes," was all that Luke would say.

"Who is Alex?"

Just as Hermano asked his question, the two men from yesterday appeared on deck, once again only clad in those white bathing suits. They smiled, very gently, at the sight of all the bodies on the deck. Unlike everyone else, they went through the rows of bodies and carefully shook them, waking the sleeping refugees and pointing to the food. Hermano realized he was hungry, very hungry. He excused himself and went to wake Juan.

They walked through the line, piling their plates with all the meat, bread and eggs, pouring large glasses of juice. After all the horrible food in the prison, Juan, especially, was hungry for the feast. When they had taken as much as they dared, they started to walk to some empty seats. "No, this way," Hermano said.

He led Juan to the two men who he had been talking to. "May we join you?"

"'Course you can," Luke McDavid answered.

When the four of them were seated around a small table, and after Juan had been introduced to the others, Hermano, while picking at his food, asked the other questions that were so important. "Who are you? Why did you do this? Where are we going? What ...”

“Hold on, good buddy,” Luke said, holding up his hand as though he were a traffic cop. “Hold on! Let me think, what order should I tell you this? What comes first?” He looked to his friend Sammy as though he wanted help.

Sam looked down at his hands for a minute, then took a breath before he began to speak. “It seems as though the Council of the Revolution was going to start some new maneuvers with their new order. They were ...”

“They were going to execute us,” Juan said. His eyes were cold as he stared at the other man who was as young as he.

“There was some talk among some of the members,” Sam admitted.

“You sure as hell weren’t getting front row seats to the opera,” Luke said, disgust thick in his voice.

“Alex and Danny weren’t going to take the chance, that’s for sure,” Sam finished.

“So they planned it?” Hermano asked.

“Yes, seems they plan a lot of things. This time, though, the operation was a big one. They needed some help for a change, they called up the reserves,” Luke smiled again.

“That’s you? The reserves?”

“Well, see, they help lots of people do lots of things. Every once in a while, they ask if, maybe, those people wouldn’t like to return the favor for someone else’s sake.”

“Will they ask that of us? Will they expect us to be their army? Are they going to invade Santa Isabella?” Juan asked in a quick voice. Hermano couldn’t tell if Juan was concerned about those ideas or hopeful.

“No. No. No.” Luke put up his hand again. “They don’t work that way. I mean, they might ask, if they had the feeling that you would want to help on something. Just ask though. No obligation in this operation. That’s against all the rules. And so long as you guys got out, they could give a bear’s shit about Santa Isabella.

“No, these guys, see, they just work to make sure that little *solutions* like the ones the Revolutionary Council were thinking about never happen. Then they make sure you guys get settled somewhere in the United States, and then they go on. They always got something new to do."

"That's the truth," Sam's voice was the one full of disgust. "God knows there's enough to be changed just about everywhere. He looked up at the two Santa Isabellans. "Alex and Danny are a little ... fanatic. Somebody's got to be. They think it's their duty, the reason they were placed on earth, to keep fighting for gay people, whenever they're in trouble. They go almost non-stop. They go on forever."

"Why?" Hermano asked.

Luke wrinkled his brow before he answered. "Some people get hurt in some terrible ways, ways they never forget. Ways that never stop hurting. They get ... scarred. They have to work to make sure other people don't get hurt the same way. It becomes their lives. That's what happened to Danny and Alex. Things happened to them and they changed. "Their commitment is absolute. Let me tell you that those two would do just about anything to help out gay people. Got some gay guys in prison, then get 'em out! Need some planes? Get 'em. Need a boat? Get it. Just get 'em."

"They're heroes." Juan made the statement fervently.

"Oh, you can say that again," Luke smiled. "They sure are that."

"They are real heroes," Juan seemed to be growing more adamant as he spoke. It was the fervor that came from having seen other "heroes" – the heroes of the revolution – fail him.

"Now what?" Hermano asked.

"Well," Luke drawled out his reply. "You get a nice luxury cruise in the Caribbean. Then there's this little private island that a friend owns, close to the mainland. We get you there, pick up some ... *convenient* papers for you, some new clothes, and our friends the pilots fly you into some ... *convenient* airstrips we know of, or the boat drops you off at a port, carefully dressed as one of the crew, something like that.

"You'll all have new identities, a little money in your pocket, a couple phone numbers to call if you need help, a way to get a start in the United States. What you do with it? That's pretty much up to you. I got this ranch, out in Arizona. I know I need some help there. Decent pay, hard work, but good work ..."

"And if this Alex and this Danny need some men to work with them again, will you know about it? Will they come to you first?" Juan asked.

"They almost never need help, like I say ..."

"But if they did, would your ranch hands have time to train, to get their skills ready, to be in wait ..."

"Oh, could be worked into some spare time. A few things about demolitions, a couple lessons in ..."

"We would like to be your ranch hands. We'll work hard. We'll train hard." As though some enormous decision had been made, as though there was suddenly a clarity in his mind that removed an onerous weight, Juan began to eat quickly and with great relish.

Hermano studied him. It had been less than a day. Now he was no longer a soldier in the revolution. He was sitting talking to a pair of homosexuals with his own homosexual lover who had just announced that they were going to work on a homosexual ranch and still be soldiers.

Hermano closed his eyes and shook his head. These men, Alex and Danny, had great power. They could effect great change. The greatest change that Hermano knew about was inside him. He was neither sorry to be here, nor was he going to argue with Juan. They would do it. It was going to be strange. But he would do it.

He began to eat his own breakfast.

# II

"Is my yacht in one piece?" Joseph Farmdale asked the question while sipping a cocktail that was strictly forbidden by his doctors. At his age – he was past seventy – and with his heart, he was supposed to make do on carrot juice or something equally as repulsive. But a decent, civilized dinner called for a decent, civilized Scotch and soda and he was going to have it by god.

The other two at the table probably would sip their own drinks with some sense of obligation. Though it was seldom that Alex Kane did anything that he would acknowledge as an attempt to make Farmdale more comfortable. In fact, he loved making the old man damned uncomfortable.

"Your dinghy's okay." Alex enjoyed that one. Even if it was a little bit of an easy shot. It was an opening at least.

"My *dinghy*?" Farmdale almost choked on the word. That and the fact that he knew he'd played into one of Alex's verbal sorties.

"It's fine, Mr. Farmdale. We had to have a few repairs made ..."

"*Repairs*!" Danny Fortelli's casually presented announcement was a much more effective assault on Farmdale's peace of mind.

"Well," Danny said, "we fouled up the rear end ..."

"The stern, please, a yacht has a stern, not a rear end."

"Yeah," Danny said, "the stern. Anyway, we had to fix it up a little bit after the landing craft had been disengaged. Then, of course, the guys had a little bit of a party. Some of the dishes, the glasses ..."

"The Wedgewood, the Waterford," Farmdale raced through an inventory of the goods he kept on his boat.

"That stuff," Danny didn't seem to know just what he was dealing with here. "You know, they were young, most of them, they got a few drinks in them, a little pot ..."

"Marijuana on my yacht?!" Farmdale closed his eyes and with them still shut took a stiff draft of his Scotch.

"Only a little. We didn't have any."

*As though that made any difference,* Farmdale thought. *You two, with all your physical training and all your righteousness and all your crusading! I actually think it might be a good thing for you to go out and get drunk and full of marijuana. Break free. Live for yourselves!*

When Joseph Farmdale opened his eyes he realized that it would never happen. Certainly not to Alex Kane. He remembered once when it had occurred. After Joseph's own son had been murdered by a fellow American in Vietnam and Alex had taken revenge for that traitorous act, Alex had tried to break free as far as he could – all the way free. He had sunk to the bottom of the cesspools of San Francisco, drowning himself in alcohol and drugs, or trying to at any rate. Trying to and doing an awfully good job of it.

*Where would Alex be if I hadn't sent for him?*

Joseph had wondered that many times. Alex probably wouldn't have lived. If he had, then he would have been one of those faceless men who inhabit the cities of this country. He would have been another statistic of the homeless. The beauty that Alex had would have kept him going for a short while. That was undeniable, even though it meant nothing to Farmdale who didn't really find that much beautiful about people, male or female.

Perhaps he would have ended up in the mountains. Many other Vietnam veterans had done that, gone into seclusion, terrified of human company, ruined by the war and the inhumanity of it.

But, no. No, Farmdale couldn't take any credit for what had finally happened to Alex Kane. His son, James, had found Alex. That meant something. It meant that there was something so worthy about Kane that it would have finally allowed him to surface in some way. Though it might not have meant the destruction of the Farmdale family yacht.

"Alex, I have given you all the support possible, all the support conceivable, in your quest. I understand that it is all in James's honor, at least that was the original motivation. I understand that it is your enemy – this stupid hatred of anything homosexual – which led that insufferable person to kill my son. That's my own motivation for my part in this undertaking.

"But is it really necessary for you to ruin my yacht in the process? You already have me supporting you financially. I won't quibble about that. But only last month you wrecked my oldest and most prized Rolls-Royce ..."

"I did not!" Alex Kane stood straight up in his chair and stared at Farmdale.

"Oh, of course. How silly of me to accuse you! All you did was drive the innocent automobile across a silly white line. How foolish of them to expect you to stop for an international boundary. Those overanxious border guards! How impetuous of them."

"Well, I couldn't stop. They would have gotten those guys. Besides, the car isn't *ruined*."

"A few bullet holes, a dent the entire length of the right side, a bumper missing, you're right, simple details. I shouldn't be so picky."

"You're right, you shouldn't be." Alex Kane crossed his arms over his chest.

"Waiter! Another drink." When the glass had been taken from him, Farmdale took his handkerchief from his coat pocket and dabbed at the beads of sweat that were growing on his forehead. "Now, Danny, just what is this about landing craft and my yacht."

The Fortelli boy had been so much more sensible than Alex Kane. It had been too long, though. Perhaps their relationship had taken him over the limit into that strange world that Kane had inhabited alone for so long.

"Like I said, they got a little rambunctious. Some stuff got broken. But not much, don't worry." Farmdale tried to erase his firm knowledge of the retail prices for china and crystal at Tiffany's. "And, the boat's really okay, too. It's in a yard in New Orleans. The rear end … I mean, the *stern* got a little banged up. But it's all cosmetic, they said. They told us it'd be as good as gold in a couple weeks."

"It had better be," Farmdale replied as he took his new glass of Scotch from the waiter and immediately took a sip of it. "It cost as much as gold already, pound for pound at today's market value."

"You would care about that." Alex Kane spoke with open disdain.

"Yes, yes, I would care about that. My family's cared about *that* for all of recorded history. Which is why there was a yacht for you to abuse in the first place."

"Don't you care about the mission? Don't you want to know what happened?"

"I already do." Farmdale was glad to move on to more pleasant subjects than the expenditure of money. He took a newspaper from his briefcase and put it on the table.

### Rightists Escape From Communist Jail

"Rightists?" Danny said loudly, his face contorted with disgust.

"Don't quibble over that slight inaccuracy in reportage. It is making many things much easier. It's obvious that the Santa Isabella regime isn't willing to admit they were defeated by a group of homosexuals. Bad for the macho image so many of those Latins crave so very much. Therefore, they've blamed the entire incident on the deposed dictator.

"Since our current government seems to have lost all sense of decency and morality in the conduct of its foreign affairs, there are many people in Washington who claim that this is a blow for freedom struck by the forces of good."

"It was!" Alex insisted.

"I may agree, but they wouldn't have thought so if they had known the facts, gentlemen. If those yahoos in Washington knew that the freed prisoners were actually homosexuals they would have had the very heart attack my physicians warn me about. Rather, since they are convinced that the freed men were former compatriots of the dictator, they're giving out naturalization papers as though they were lollipops. Our operations aimed at getting your new friends into the United States have been greatly simplified. In fact, all we had to do was bring in the whole lot of them at once.

"It was only some very quick and persuasive convincing that the refugees would have to be assured anonymity – to protect them from reprisals – that kept that former actor who made his career putting bozo monkeys to bed from flying down to the Gulf Coast to personally welcome the whole batch of them."

"He should have," Kane said with his customary adamancy.

"Can't you just see it!" Danny started to giggle. "That President giving the oath to that bunch of guys? I mean, I love them, but most of them had been transvestites, some of them prostitutes ..."

"At least they could have given the First Lady some lessons in dressing well and acting graciously." Farmdale liked that one. He rewarded himself with another sip of Scotch.

"Shall we order?" Farmdale raised his hand to signal the desire for menus.

The food was chosen and appropriate wines discussed with the steward. Good food and decent dinner conversation were some of the joys of Farmdale's life. The overt sparring that he and Alex usually shared often seemed to be caustic, sometimes even cruel. But, beneath it all, the two men liked one another immensely. They certainly trusted and respected one another.

Their conflicts were covers, really. There was the difficulty each had in being so close to another person. That, and the shared memory of the younger Farmdale whose murder and revenge had brought them together. The memory hadn't been dimmed by the appearance of Danny Fortelli as Alex Kane's new lover and compatriot. Farmdale had no problem with the idea that Alex would finally turn to another man after so many years.

Farmdale had blatantly maneuvered to have it happen, in fact. When he saw Alex might finally have met a new mate, someone who could share life and also his work, he had become furious to see that Alex had withdrawn. Kane hadn't handled the opening of his affair with Danny well at all. But Farmdale's blundering insistence had forced the two to spend time together. His pushiness had helped them see that they were a perfect couple.

Indeed, they acted just that way during dinner. Danny gave reports on the latest addition to their mountain hideaway in New Hampshire. Alex went into a long discourse on the wonders of some new exercise regimen they were sharing – as though Farmdale could care less about the various methods with which they chose to torture their bodies. They were thinking about a new car. Danny was going to begin classes again in the fall. Their life appeared to be a special kind of perfection.

When he realized that, Farmdale again felt the onslaught of the greatest source of discomfort between himself and the two others. It wasn't caused by his not being used to intimacy with another; nor did it have anything to do with thoughts of his natural son. He certainly wasn't upset by the domestic conversation they were sharing.

What was making Farmdale feel a great sorrow was his own role in their operations. Here were two perfectly happy men, driven, perhaps; fanatically committed, obviously. But they were young and handsome and in love and they should be able to do nothing but enjoy that. They shouldn't know that there was a book in the briefcase Farmdale had brought with him, the same satchel from which he had taken the newspaper.

Farmdale suddenly became aware that the conversation had stopped. He looked up and saw that Alex and Danny were staring at him intently.

"You'd make a lousy secret agent," Danny said. There was a smile on his lips. Farmdale looked at them and, as he had often, appreciated Danny's face. It was a work of art. What Michelangelo could have done with that red on those lips, with the lines of his cheekbones. Why couldn't Danny give this up? He could move to New York and quickly become a fantastic model.

"You'd also play shitty poker," Alex said. Farmdale looked at him. What was he now? Thirty-two? His age didn't show in the usual ways. Farmdale thought that other people would actually think him younger. But there were those eyes, their strange green color, the way they lit up when certain emotions came over Alex Kane ...

"Yes, yes ..." Farmdale faltered while the waiters cleared the table. "Coffee and cognac for three," he said, anxious to have even a few more minutes before he brought up the new topic.

He didn't have the luxury of deciding just when it would happen. As soon as the waiters left, Danny reached down and picked up the briefcase. He opened it and brought out a book. It was the same one always. Bound in Spanish leather, it contained all the necessary information for their next mission.

In it, as always, would be the computer printouts. Farmdale owned one of the largest and most sophisticated computer operations in the world. It had originally been put together to oversee the various activities of Farmdale Industries, the family-run conglomerate. But it now traced patterns of crime and social abuse and personal abuse that went unseen by other observers.

There would also be sheets of background materials.

There would be biographies of involved people, both the perpetrators of acts aimed to hurt gay people and also the victims. There would be too much information. It would be information that everyone else in the world chose to over-look and avoid. It would be information that would point an undeniable finger towards an enemy.

Danny and Alex would be the ones who followed its path.

"You forgot a part of it, Danny." Farmdale reached over and picked up the newspaper whose headline they had all just been reading. It was the Houston *Clarion.*

# III

Frank Terkel was damned glad to get a job on a big city newspaper anywhere. So Houston had a lousy climate? It was a big, sprawling place. It was full of all kinds of action. There would eventually be something that could land him a big break and get him out of the rat race. He wasn't too old to think about that, only thirty-four. The past was past; he still had a future.

He could just take this job for what it was, a way he could continue to work on a large paper and pile up his clippings, get a shot at a big break and move on. If he succeeded here in Houston then no one would bother to study anything that had come before. Rhode Island was a lot of miles away. No one had to know about that.

Frank consistently gave himself those rationalizations. He needed them. He needed them badly. If he kept on thinking about the Houston *Clarion's* big circulation he might not have to acknowledge that it was really a sleazy tabloid. If he kept his mind on the big story that the wire services might pick up, he'd never have to pay attention to the nearly inane content of the actual newspaper he worked for.

If he kept his mind focused on leaving the past behind, he wouldn't have to notice that he was going nowhere new. He was, and he knew it deep inside, just repeating the same mistakes he'd made in Providence.

But it wasn't his fault. It was his wife and her stupid attempt to get some kind of adolescent revenge that had caused all his problems. Hell, he hadn't even been fired. He'd walked out of the office of that sanctimonious paper in Providence and told them that their Pulitzer Prizes didn't mean shit. He had his pride. He wasn't going to work in an office where he knew they'd all heard about Mindy washing his dirty laundry in public. Fuck them.

He was here in Houston, he was working for a bigger newspaper than the one before and he was going to be a success. Let her have the car, the house, all of it. The alimony check he had to send back to her every month was a small price to pay for the freedom it had bought him.

*That's right!* He slammed his fist on his desk.

"You all right, Frank?" asked the reporter who sat next to him.

"Fine. I'm fine. It's nothing." Frank waved his hand through the air as though he were dismissing some pesky flies that had been bothering him. The reporter raised his eyebrows and wondered just what was with this strange one they'd hired from back east. He had better be an awfully good reporter to make up for all his weirdness.

"Hey, Terkel! Come in here."

Frank jumped up at the sound of his boss's voice. Harvey Pearson wasn't someone you wanted to keep waiting when he called you that way. Frank walked right over to the glass-walled office of the *Clarion's* managing editor.

"Have a seat, Terkel." Harvey was already sitting. He lit one of his giant, cheap cigars and blew clouds of smoke into the tightly enclosed room. Frank thought he'd be asphyxiated if he had to sit here too long.

"Look, we got a new assignment for you. That stuff you've been doing on the freeway development issue's been great. All the kind of thing we need. But the boss has a new idea. A circulation booster. I need a hot gun on this one. I know you're our man."

"The boss" was Martin Banks, owner of the *Clarion* and a dozen other tabloids across the country. His word was law in all of them. His obsession was to boost the circulation of his "family-oriented" papers until he had the largest chain in the country. The *Clarion* was his newest. It was the first he'd started from scratch. This wasn't an acquisition. He'd decided that the already huge and constantly growing Houston market was the perfect place for him to begin his own first paper. He called the *Clarion* his virgin, though he'd raped it of its integrity with the first issue. Its headline had accused the governor of the state of adultery. The charge had been false, but the memory of it lingered. A front page accusation made a strong impression on the public mind; a two line, six point correction on page 59 could never hope to fully erase it.

"Anything," Frank replied. He always did. He wasn't about to rock the boat here.

"Seems we're in a bind. All the conservative stuff the boss likes to tout so much isn't going down too easy these days. There are too many environmentalists getting too much credibility to go after them. The feminists got too many friends, so no more stuff on them to goose up the circulation. Them and the spics got too much of a start in too many companies.

"It's a fine how-do-you-do to discover broads and spics sitting on corporate boards and making big company decisions, but there you have it. We keep up on some of the stuff we had going on the Mexs, and we're going to start getting some prime advertising pulled on us.

"Besides, the spics here got a lot more money to spend nowadays. Them and the women and the niggers are the ones walking around with the credit cards and going to Neiman-Marcus and god knows where else.

"Old days, when you wanted to get your circulation up and not upset your advertisers, you went after them. Now, hell, a man's left with no good way to get any attention. Those fucking limousine liberals at the other papers, the ones that look down their noses at us just cause we're tabloid, they've really fucked up what you can write about."

It was not Frank's position to suggest a more subtle analysis of the situation. Nor was he about to point out that the sheer frantic drive for increased circulation was hardly the stuff that made for good journalism.

"Well, what does the boss want?" Frank asked the only question that he thought was important.

Harvey smiled and started puffing at his cigar. "Fags. Lots and lots of fags."

Frank felt a cold freezing sensation sweep over his body. He felt a shiver move up and down his spine. He was sure that Harvey would notice, but the managing editor was apparently too much into his reverie about the new idea to pay attention.

"We're taking that black broad off of education. We're getting her going on homosexual child abuse. There's plenty of it that'll make great copy. Nothing like a dirty old man messing with a little boy to make them all stand up and pay attention.

"Then, the political desk is going to do an exposé on the political influence of fags in city hall, and in the state capital at Austin, too. Those guys are getting away with murder! They're hiring each other for real jobs and getting the pols to vote their way on everything.

"The whole thing is," Harvey spread his arms wide and gestured emphatically, "they've gotten out of hand. They're out of their closets, okay, but they didn't stay in the streets. They're in our schools, our churches, our government. They're trying to take the country over and the good citizens of Houston, Texas got a right to know who *they* are.

"That's where you come in. It's a top assignment, I don't bullshit you on that one. Your going to get front page bylines every day for weeks. We want a blockbuster."

Frank stared at the big man and started to say something, but the cigar smoke was too much. He began to cough. He was furious with himself. A real man should be able to tolerate another man's cigar smoke. He flashed on images of regular guys sitting around a barber shop smoking and talking and they didn't cough. He shouldn't either.

Finally, he got his words out, "What's the focus? I'm not

sure I understand ..."

"To understand," Harvey held his hand up dramatically, "you get to go to the very top. Seems as though the boss wants to have a little interview with you and a couple others. Go get your jacket and do up your tie, Frank. You and I are going upstairs. We get to meet Martin Banks himself."

•　　•　　•

Frank Terkel had met the boss only once. It had been one of those pro forma things for new employees where the proprietor made believe he knew your name and shook your hand. He gave you a glass of sherry in the executive dining room and made a little speech about the vision of a great newspaper. He told you all the good stuff and then sent you out to get all the bad stuff on everyone he didn't like.

Frank had been through it a hundred times all through his life. The Providence paper hadn't been like that, though. It had earned its Pulitzer Prizes, for one thing, with hard and diligent work. They hadn't gone in for that much bullshit there. But there had been other papers before it, some really small country sheets where Frank had earned his battlestripes after graduating from journalism school.

The fact that his one meeting with Banks had been so formal and in a large group that one other time, made this ride up the elevator even more ominous. Not that it wasn't already full of danger. The very topic that Frank was being assigned to cover was more than enough to convince him that he was in trouble.

He knew it was going to be even worse when he followed Harvey Pearson into the antechamber to Banks's office. This waiting area alone was larger than most other rooms in the skyscraper. Frank thought it was probably part of one of those business schemes you always heard about these days. Make the reception area large and forbidding, make the person waiting to see the executive aware of just how much power was involved in all this. Intimidate him. Frank knew he sure as hell was intimidated.

He was all the more nervous to see the other two reporters already there. The idea that he would have to have a conversation about homosexuality with a group of people he knew even slightly made Frank extremely upset.

He wondered what they'd think of this topic. There was Sandra Myers, the black woman who had been doing features on the local school systems. She was sharp, well-dressed and very good looking, with eyes that seemed to take in everything around her. That made Frank more nervous. He hoped that Sandra wasn't going to study him. He tried to calm himself by remembering the gossip about her. It seemed that Sandra had what had once been called "loose morals." She was rumored to have bedded a number of the better-looking men in the company. That, and, no matter what Frank thought of her observatory sense, most of the staffers of the *Clarion* dismissed Sandra's credentials. She was there, they insisted, only because of her gender and her race.

Sam Trident was another story. He was one of the old political hack writers. He'd bounced from job to job over his many years in the business. Now he must be nearing sixty. He was infamous for his drinking bouts and bragged about his ability to meet deadlines no matter how severe his hangover. Frank knew that the progression of jobs that Sam had held in the past twenty years was all downhill. He'd once been seriously considered for his own Pulitzer Prize while working for one of the big New York City papers. But the movement from there was from one paper to another, each smaller and less consequential than the one that preceded it.

Sam had the kind of bravado that a man like Harvey Pearson adored. Now they greeted each other with a loud blatantly masculine yell and over-exuberant handshake, as though they had been college classmates separated for years, not the co-workers who actually labored on the same floor of the building.

They were an appropriate pair in many other ways. Sam and Harvey were both beer-gutted. Their legs and arms were spindly; they probably hadn't been used for anything more than walking to an elevator and lifting steins of beer for years. They had pale skin, blotched with broken blood vessels. They never considered their poor physical appearance when they thought of themselves though. They were both convinced that they were lady killers. Who, they wondered, wouldn't be interested in men like them?

They let their attitude be known when they finally turned to Sandra. Harvey said an overly demonstrative hello to the black woman. Sandra sat still; she didn't move her head, only her eyes changed direction to let the men know she'd heard them. She was sitting forward in the chair, her legs crossed, her arms resting on her knees. She had a modified Afro hairstyle that accentuated the strikingly African features on her quite beautiful face. There was – Frank saw it immediately – nothing but contempt going between Sandra and the two men. They wanted to gloss over it with their hearty talk; she didn't intend to give them the time of day.

Frank sat down and continued to watch the antics of the other three players in this most uncomfortable melodrama. Really, he thought, if Harvey weren't bald and Sam weren't so obviously red-headed, it'd be difficult to tell them apart. They were twins, at least of the soul; they were two peas in a pod, and you didn't know which of them was the original and which the clone. *Clone!* Damn, the meeting was already getting to him if he was thinking words like that.

"Mr. Banks will see you now." A middle-aged woman made the announcement with all the formality of a member of a medieval court. She stood with her hair tightly done up in a bun. She looked more like a well-dressed prison matron than a secretary to a major businessman. That, too, Frank decided, was just another part of the charming tone that Banks wanted to have set when people came to his office.

The four of them moved into the huge corner suite that Banks occupied. There were four upholstered chairs carefully aligned in a semi-circle in front of the large desk. Standing with his back to them was Banks, hands clasped behind his back. He was staring out the floor-to-ceiling, wall-to-wall windows that oversaw downtown Houston. *He's examining his fiefdom,* Frank thought to himself.

Very few people had any doubt that Banks would gladly welcome the chance to consider this, the fastest growing major city in the United States, just that – his fiefdom. Frank couldn't see his face, nor had he ever really had a conversation with the owner of the *Clarion,* but he suddenly felt that Banks was caressing this view, and he was doing it with as much passion as he would ever fondle a lover's body.

Don't say lover, *he admonished himself.* Mistress is much better.

The silent internal conversation sent a new set of rivulets of sweat cascading down Frank's back, all of them gathering in the indentation of his spine. He hated being this nervous. It was the topic, and all these people who were going to ...

"Have a seat," the faceless body in front of them said, more as a command than an invitation. Frank overcame his own discomfort and was able to momentarily appreciate the foolishness of his boss's position. Harvey Pearson was trying very hard to walk a tightrope, acting authoritatively towards his employees – he had taken the role of directing each of them to specific chairs that he'd arbitrarily chosen – and at the same time he was clearly going to do anything possible to please his own superior.

"Mr. Banks, it's always an exciting possibility for us to have a chance to ..."

"Yes, yes." Now Banks turned around. He clearly didn't care what Harvey had to say. He was projecting an atmosphere of great severity. His hands stayed behind his back. His face was turned down, as though he were studying the carpeted floor. He moved slowly, theatrically. He walked towards his desk. It was slightly modern – teak, Frank thought, before he tried to tell himself to stop noticing things like furniture. People would think he was a god-damned interior decorator.

But it was teak. It was modern. It was enormous. The

surface was uncluttered. Only neat little piles of paper kept it from being bare, them and a few small objects. Frank recognized one of them as a letter opener that was given only to the most special guests at the White House.

The walls of the room were as sparsely decorated. There were a few photographs of Banks with heads of state and an occasional movie star. That was the limit of anything that could have been called art.

Frank was sure that all of this was just as planned as the rest. There were only a few things because everyone should know that Banks could have had many more if he had wanted to. The presence of anything really striking would have taken the spotlight away from the boss. It was clear he was the center attraction here. He wanted nothing to detract from himself.

He had finally taken his hands from behind his back. He put them, palm down, spread far apart, on the desktop. He was, Frank thought, a particularly unattractive man. He was short, barely five foot five. He wore the most expensive suits possible, but they couldn't hide his flabbiness. They only announced that the wrapping on any package could be more valuable than the contents.

Clothing couldn't do a thing for Banks's face. It was almost grotesquely shaped. There was a lilt to it, as though some unseen weight pulled down on the right side of his mouth. Frank knew from office talk, and from his one experience, that Banks had a strange habit, very disconcerting, of spitting while he spoke. His eyebrows nearly met over the bridge of his very prominent nose. On another man, his equally prominent jaw might have been attractive, but on Banks the proportions were totally off.

"We have a great vocation." Banks spoke as though he were a priest beginning a sermon whose weight needed to be foreshadowed for the congregation. His voice was nearly a whisper. It held all kinds of portentous doom in it. It reminded Frank of the Irish priests he'd grown up with. This was the way they spoke when they were talking to classes of adolescent boys and they were about to start one of their rampages against the sin of self-abuse. *You know you're guilty.*

"We have a great responsibility." The voice was picking up now. Banks had let his first statement hang in the air for a while to let its dire prewarning sink into their souls. *You know you'll burn in hell ...*

"The fine city of Houston is in danger! The moral fabric of this Christian metropolis is threatened!"

Frank caught a curl of a sardonic smile creep across Sandra's face. One of her earlier assignments had been to uncover a sex ring run by some of the city's school principals and including many of the high school's cheerleaders.

"It is the obligation of the *Clarion* to save Houston." That was a switch. All Frank had heard earlier was the need to boost circulation.

Banks, evidently thinking he could take a more comfortable perch after his opening pronouncements, sat in his chair. He was too short to fit. The back of the leather-covered seat rose high above his head as though he were too small to fit in a throne.

"All possible resources of this company are to be redirected to revealing the extent of corruption in Houston. We have got to uncover how much the sewers of this city have spilt over onto the day-to-day life of our town. We must show our readers just how impossibly torrid and repulsive this vermin is.

"For too long, we've ducked the real issues of homosexuality in Houston. Unwilling to take the raw details of that tortured lifestyle into American homes, we've left out the details of their existence. I want it all! I want every last, minute detail of it.

"We've entered into a conspiracy of silence with the perverted. We haven't named them. We haven't shown their pictures. We haven't talked about their activities.

*"I want it all!"*

They sat, stunned. There wasn't a lot of specific detail to go on, just a whole lot of intent. But Harvey Pearson knew when he'd heard his cue.

"Sandra. You got the story on the high school principals, the ones who liked those teenage girls. Well, that't the kind of thing we need here. There's got to be plenty of it. Coaches, teachers, doctors, you name it. If there's a single homosexual male in a position of authority who's doing a single damn thing with another male under the age of consent ..."

"Under the age of twenty-one!" Banks screamed.

"Right ... Right," Harvey tried to cover up his fluster, "anything under the age of twenty-one, we want it. It's first page stuff. I want features on every type of adult male. I want one on teachers. I want one on ministers. I want still another one on coaches ..."

"In the locker room!" Banks let fly one of his mouthfuls of spittle. It went *splat* onto the edge of his desk. "They allow those animals into the locker rooms where good, decent boys are naked, honestly taking athletic, masculine showers. They let those animals look on the bare bodies of those boys, their innocent buttocks becoming vile sexual objects ..." More spit flew through the air. Frank barely had time to duck as one hunk of it shot past his right ear.

"Mr. Banks, please, your blood pressure," Harvey said solicitously.

The publisher slumped back against his seat.

Harvey continued. "If there's a man on the Houston school system payroll who's ever done time for homosexual activity or about whom there's the slightest hint of scandal, we want it."

"Young lady," Banks leaned forward to talk to Sandra, "I don't want you to worry one little bit about erring on the side of protecting a clean society. This firm will back you all the way ..."

"Run loose with libel laws. Our lawyers will get you out of just about anything," Harvey translated.

Sandra seemed to be smiling when she nodded her head to indicate she understood perfectly what they wanted.

"Don't worry about the easy stuff. I'll reassign one of

the reporters from the city beat to cover things like the gay groups. They're just there for the picking. We'll start with an expose of just who their members are, how they're funded. We need your investigative talents on the more complex materials, the faculty and stuff like that," Pearson clarified.

"You." Banks pointed his finger at Sam Trident. "You already know Austin. You used to cover that den of inequity. I want you to get to know City Hall just as well. I want to know everything about the homosexuals they've hired. I want everything on their personal lives ..."

"Remember the beef they got going 'cause some legislators were hiring secretaries for big busts instead of big typing speeds? Get that on the queers. We're sure they're hiring their own boyfriends. Trace the employment circles. Who's signing the forms to get known homosexuals on the payroll? Is there a pattern to who's proposing homosexual laws? Why are married guys and women interested in getting gay rights? There are skeletons in closets there. Find them!"

Banks sat back on his seat, as though exhausted. But Frank, realizing he was watching a marvel in verbal manipulation, understood that the effect was purposeful. That kind of relaxation in the pulpit only meant one thing. A real lightning bolt was coming next.

As soon as he saw Banks's finger pointing straight at him, Frank knew he was going to be the target. "You have the most difficult job. The worst! The most distasteful, actually ... sickening."

Harvey seemed to gulp a little. "See, Frank, you're relatively new in town. You've never been on television, not even at a press conference asking questions. The assignments you've had were important to the paper and lots of people have read your byline, but you're clean in the public eye. You can go anywhere."

"Into the very bowels of hell!" Banks screamed.

"Yeah ... Well ..." Harvey seemed increasingly uneasy as Banks's pitch went up further. "Look, Frank, we want you to go undercover. You're young enough for gay guys nowadays.

You're good looking, not that I would notice, but the girls in the steno pool think so ..."

"He is," Sandra said, smirking. "He's a hot piece."

Harvey hurried on before Banks noticed just how sarcastic Sandra's voice had been. "Well, we want you to get the inside scoop. We want you to take a new apartment, we'll pay for the extra expense, of course. Get a place over near Westheimer, in the gay ghetto. Go to their spots ..."

"Combat duty, that's what it is," Banks broke in. "You'll be at the front, putting your soul and your body on the line."

"Go to the bars. We want reports on them. The ones with what they call back rooms. We want descriptions of what goes on there. And the bath houses ..."

"Orgy palaces," Banks spit right in Harvey's face. But the managing editor obviously wasn't going to be so unkind as to say anything. "Disgusting places where all kinds of activities are permitted, *encouraged!* It's where they're spawning that disease of theirs. It's where they're building it up in preparation. They're going to spread it through the whole community. We have to tell the world about the plague that they're going to bring on the innocent women and children!"

"Blow by blow, Frank, that's what we want."

Sandra broke up over that one. She tried to stifle her laugh with a hand, but she couldn't quite pull it off. Even when Banks looked at her with what he obviously thought was a violent glare, she kept on laughing. "Blow by blow" she tried to explain, but her laughter only increased.

Harvey tried to ignore her. "Descriptions, Frank. That's what we need. We need to show the world what a vile thing this queer stuff has become."

*"We need to warn the young boys!"* Banks was back in the conversation again. He was standing, his hands on the desk once more. "Think of the inculpable youth who are being lured into this heinous trap by the image of stylishness that these sick fiends have created for themselves!"

"You want him to pass!" Sandra had stopped her near hysterics. Now there was a sound of sheer amusement in her voice. "You want him to make believe he's a queer."

"Inside stuff! That's what we want! The real thing!" Harvey said, his chest puffing out.

"Combat duty is what it is. The front lines of morality and increased circulation! The unbeatable combination of free enterprise and Christian virtue! You'll get combat pay, young man! Combat!"

# IV

Frank couldn't quite believe his eyes when he picked up the next day's issue of the *Clarion*.

## These Men Teach Your Children

### Why Are They Spending Their Nights In Queer Bars?

"Pretty slick, huh?" Sandra said as she looked over Frank's shoulder. "They didn't actually say the guys were cocksuckers, but they got their message across."

"I thought we were the ones ..."

"We're the deep shit, honey. We're the ones that are going to get the big feature stories. What you see here is the newest comic strip for our fine example of American journalism. It's going to be in every single god-damned issue of the *Clarion*.

"They got the idea from the old McCarthy days, when they were all hunting pinko fag Jews. Some papers would take photographs of the swishes when they left their bars and put them in the paper. Ruined their lives. Turns out Banks can't understand why anyone would ever stop such a great service to the community.

"It looks big today, that's just 'cause it's the first one. It'll be inside, near the weather report from now on. Jesus, what a fucked up thing to do."

Frank wanted to talk to Sandra about all this. He wondered why she was allowing herself to be part of it. Why was she willing to do this dirty work?

"You," she started to laugh, "you better watch yourself with this new assignment of yours. You see that movie *Cruising*? You know what happened? This cop, he was assigned to a duty in the gay bars, just like you. But he *caught* it. The man became a queer. You better make sure you get plenty of those hetero vitamins in your body while you're pulling this shit. Make sure you stick your thing in some nice woman every once in a while, else you'll discover something besides motor oil where you dip it."

Sandra cracked up again, just the way she had at the meeting with Banks.

"Why do you think this is so funny? Why …?" Frank couldn't form the rest of his question.

The black woman looked at him. The humor disappeared from her face. Instead there was a sudden and quick anger, it was actually hatred. "You white guys deserve each other, you know that? What do *I* care if a bunch of white men want to make fools of themselves and destroy some other white guys' lives? It does make me laugh. I admit that. It is one of the funniest things in the world.

"It all makes me sick. Being some double token, having to take a job like this because there's so very much money for a black woman who has a journalism degree and I *need* that extra money. My brother's going to Baylor Medical School. It costs a fortune. But my brother is going to make it. I'm going to get him out of the trap you honkies put black men in. I'd do anything but sell my soul to see him through that school. And I might even do that if the Devil offered me enough of a deal.

"Besides, it makes me sick to see white guys laying their sexual trip on black men, too. Just sick, to see them lusting after their fantasy of some sambo slave left over from the old south.

"Why the hell should I care if you knock each other off? I don't give a shit about it. It's a damned sight more enjoyable to help you all than to cover school board meetings. You can bet your ass on one thing – before those leather guys get to it at least – you can bet your ass that Sandra Myers is going to play this one for all it's worth and she's not going to do anything about worrying except to think about how much interest she's going to start collecting on her fat new savings account."

Sandra picked up her shoulder bag and swung it over her neck. She struck a stylish pose. "This is the new black woman. One thing she knows, sucker, is she's just out for herself."

Frank watched Sandra walk down the aisle. Her smile was back as she waved to one after another of the reporters sitting at their desks here in the city room.

*Jesus.* Frank was deflated by the entire encounter. He suddenly realized that he was horribly, terribly disappointed. He had wanted something from Sandra. She not only wasn't going to give it to him, she was going to help make sure he never got it.

He rested his forehead in his palms, his elbows resting on his desk. His hands clutched, gripping his hair. Why did this have to happen to him? Why this job? Why this assignment? Why this ...

He remembered the humiliations in Providence and he remembered Sandra's outburst as he drove over to the Montrose neighborhood and started looking for his new apartment. If he was ever tempted by anything that went on in that part of the city, if anything tried to rekindle his old demons and seduced him into actions he'd been able to avoid for years, he would have to remember all these examples of what waited for him if he ever let down his guard again.

*If I really hate it, it means I have to do it.* That was Frank's sudden recognition. If something made him very, very uncomfortable, then it was what a gay man should do. That's how strong his defenses had become over the past many years.

Nothing had happened since he was in college. That had been the worst. That had been the real lesson. That goddamned fraternity and the god-damned ... It made him blush with frustrated fury just to remember back to those days.

He'd been a Big Man on Campus. He was getting ready to be editor-in-chief of the college newspaper his senior year. He was a member of Phi Delta, one of the best fraternities. He was already dating the woman who would become his wife. *She knew.*

That was the whole problem. And the fraternity caused it. He clenched his jaw with anger as the memory flooded in. It had been a toga party. His best friend, Randall Landtree, was there. They'd all drunk a goodly amount of beer and they were all as rowdy as usual. It had been a matter of pride for Phi Delta to give the wildest parties ever.

Frank had always known he was attracted to men. So long as he had lived in the small predominantly Roman Catholic town in Pennsylvania, it hadn't been a problem. He had hardly thought about it. Sometimes he and some of the other guys would get together and jerk off, but that was just kid's stuff. When the urge came on him after he'd gone away to the university, he just shrugged it off. The drive to be a regular guy, one of the team, a part of the in group was more important than an orgasm, he told himself.

He never knew just what it was that made that one night different. Sure, there was beer, but there had been beer lots of other nights. Maybe it was the moon, the fact that he and Randall had played tennis in just their shorts that afternoon and the sight of Randall's near naked body, and the sensation of his own, had been too much for him. Maybe it was the togas.

Even now, even when he desperately wanted to put that evening out of his mind, Frank could remember Randall's outfit. They had all made theirs from white sheets. Randall wasn't willing to sacrifice a whole sheet, he'd only cut up a pillow case.

The thing hung over one of his shoulders, barely reached his crotch. It was gathered at his waist by a leather belt, nothing strong enough to keep the side vents together. It kept falling apart, revealing his hips, covered only with his jockey shorts. The flaps in the front would often lift up to reveal the mound of the front pouch of the underwear.

The way the cloth fell, half of Randall's chest was naked. It seemed to Frank that as the night went on the one exposed nipple began to grow larger and larger, beckoning him closer and closer.

*Just how had it happened?* Even now, years later, Frank wasn't sure. But it had. There came a time when he and Randall were in one of the beds together. They were pawing each other. There was one detail that Frank always had a hard time remembering: *Randall was kissing him back!* Then, in a series of movements that seemed to be beautifully orchestrated, not the confused maneuverings of teenagers, but the first opening adult moves of men, Frank found himself licking that nipple that had been teasing him for so long. In a matter of minutes, he was further down, sucking on the beautiful cock that had been revealed so wonderfully in the shorts.

Then the lights had gone on and the dream had become a nightmare.

In contrast to the erotic moment of bliss, unlike any other that Frank had ever experienced, there came a prolonged scene of terror, of sexual aggression, of violation ...

There had been five other frat brothers. How they had found Frank and Randall, Frank never found out. But he found out what they thought of the scene of Frank sucking cock. They came at him like animals. They'd torn off his clothes, raped his ass, shoved their cocks down his throat, and finally, in some adolescent bravado, they had stood over him and pissed down on his weeping figure as he crouched on the floor, desperately trying to block out all that had happened. He'd kept on trying to erase it for the rest of his life.

He'd left the frat the next morning. He never talked to Randall again. He had no idea what had happened to him. He finally had to seek counseling. The therapist had told him that the only hope was to get the help of a woman. Frank, terrified but resolute, had gone to Mindy, his date from that night. Slowly, with great fear and great anxiety, they'd been able to make love to one another. It led, inevitably, to their marriage. That led, inevitably, to their recent divorce and all that had come with it when Mindy had taken the stand and expressed her grounds for ...

*Frank sighed. He shook his head to himself.* All that, and now I'm going to move into the Montrose and I'm going to make believe that I'm a faggot. I'm not! I am not! I will not be!

But even when he made that pledge, he couldn't forget the one other thing that so often came into his mind. *Randall Landtree had kissed him back that night!*

• • •

Frank was out looking for an apartment. Westheimer was a large avenue that snaked out from downtown. It was an area in transition; there were still a few single family houses that faced the boulevard, but not many. Commercial development had become more lucrative. There were many bars, stores, boutiques; a melange of enterprises bordered the street.

Frank had been here before. He had just moved to Houston and hadn't realized that this was the main street of the gay ghetto, the area they called the Montrose. He had discovered that oversight in his tourist guide soon enough. And when he did, he left and had never returned.

But this time was an assignment. He had a short list of gay places on a piece of paper one of the police reporters had gotten him from a member of the vice squad. What he needed now was to find one of the gay newspapers. He had to start looking for his new apartment.

One restaurant on his recommended list was open for lunch. Frank unwillingly decided that he might as well eat here. He was, after all, going to become a "regular" – a lot different kind of regular than he used to dream of being, but still one of the guys in a sense.

The place was called Daisy's Kitchen. It was a slight notch above the usual fast food places in Houston. The tables were formica, but there were ferns – real ferns – for decoration. *Typical faggot stuff,* he thought to himself.

It was just what he needed though, he could see that when he spotted piles of free periodicals stacked on top of the cigarette machine. He took four of them and walked to an empty table. He turned immediately to the classified section in the back of largest.

"Man, you don't need to be reading the personals," an insultingly effeminate voice announced. Frank bit his tongue to keep from responding. He looked up at the thin young man, his hair obviously bleached, who stood offering a menu.

On one side of the menu was a list of expected breakfast foods, southern style. There were eggs, ham, grits, sausage and so on. The opposite side, though, was a mix of omelettes and quiche. As soon as Frank saw the hated word, "quiche," he knew he had to order from that category. Whatever made him feel uncomfortable ...

He chose a broccoli and cheese and added orange juice and coffee to the order. Then, trying to ignore the waiter, he went back to the newspaper. But the hovering presence wouldn't leave.

"I told you, honey, a man like you shouldn't be letting his fingers do the walking through the pink pages. Tell me what you *want!* If I can't do it, and that's not a very likely chance, I sure as hell can find someone who will."

"I'm just looking for a place to live. I need a new apartment." Frank didn't look up.

"Like I said," the voice nearly sang, "just tell me what you want. There." The waiter put the eraser end of his pencil down on a display ad. "That is homo heaven. All newly renovated apartments in one wing, the other was done a year ago. Gives you the best of both worlds. You get a brand new place, but you got the stability and the track record of an ongoing concern. Gay owned, too. The guy who bought it and fixed it up is one big hunk. Hardly ever there nowadays, that's too bad. But there's this pool between the two main sections, is it *cruisy!* Some say you can do better in that place than in any bar in town. You'll save a fortune on gas and money on Saturday nights alone. Trust me."

With that, the waiter finally left. Frank went over the ad. He hated some of the gay touches; that was a good sign. They didn't have to include line drawings of men in such small bathing suits, for instance. No really natural men would ever wear stuff like that. The rents appeared reasonable, especially given the inflated prices that Frank knew were commonplace in the Montrose.

"The only problem," the waiter said as he returned with Frank's quiche, "is that I'm not there. But you'll survive, we all do." The waiter patted Frank's shoulder paternally and disappeared again. Well, if a flit like this waiter thought it was a good place to live, it might do. As soon as Frank finished eating, he drove there.

The place was called Magnolia Towers. There were no towers, of course, but Houston realtors made such claims regularly; no one expected anything different nowadays. It was actually three stories tall. There were two wings, at right angles to each other, joined by a single-story common entrance. In the V that they formed was a courtyard and in the middle of that, the swimming pool.

The building was older than a lot of others in the Montrose. It had probably been constructed in the thirties. It was of brick. While the interiors were obviously carefully renovated, much care had been taken not to disturb the flowering vines that had climbed up the exterior. Frank caught himself appreciating the touch too much.

"Well, what do you think?"

*I think you should stop looking at my ass that way,* Frank wanted to tell the manager who was giving him the grand tour. They were standing on the terrace of a third-story one-bedroom apartment that Frank had to admit was a good buy. The kitchen was well-equipped, the living/dining room, one bath and bedroom were all of good size. *And the manager makes me nervous.* "I'll take it."

The formalities were taken care of quickly. The *Clarion* had provided Frank with a completely fake background which could withstand any investigation that a real estate person would bother to pursue. Frank had the extra money in his account for the necessary deposits. "We're going to be very happy you decided to move into Magnolia Towers, Mr. Terkel. Of course, the law and the owner's ethics – you wouldn't believe what a stickler he is – demand that we take the first qualified offer, no discrimination here. But, well, we do prefer our own."

*I bet you do.*

Moving would be a bitch. It would take him all of today to make the necessary calls and appointments for services – electricity, phone, gas – and to arrange for a mover to bring enough of his stuff to this new place to make it believable that he was really moving in. He might as well start right now. He had a lot to do.

As he went about his errands, he thought about that remark. *Our own.* Frank would catch glimpses of himself in store windows as he moved through the city and he knew what the man was saying. Stripped of his carefully defensive covering, Frank looked like one of them, that was for sure. He certainly did in the outfit that he had so consciously put together this morning.

He was wearing the tightest pair of blue jeans he owned. They weren't as confining as many others he saw, but they didn't leave much to the imagination either. He had only a tight white t-shirt over them. He'd never given up his daily swim and he knew he was in good shape. But he would usually choose to wear baggy clothing on principle; he didn't want anyone to think that he was trying to show off his body. He only wore tennis shoes today.

He had always been terrified of the thought of having his hair "styled" and looking like a faggot. Therefore, he'd always had a very short, almost military cut. Now, as he walked through the boutiques and offices of the Montrose, Frank was startled to see that his look was as normal among the obviously gay men as he had once thought the razor cut should be.

He had never gotten over the idea that a moustache was

masculine. To him, real faggots were smooth-skinned wimps. But again, the moustaches seemed to be part of the uniform that the Montrose men were sporting now. Jesus, he looked like all the rest of them. They obviously liked that very look.

He felt himself stared at and evaluated at every turn he made that day. He began to be self-conscious of his buttocks. He eventually started to check them out in store minors as well. The jeans did make them stand out fairly prominently. And the shirt certainly accentuated his thick arms. He supposed that *if* he were going to look at a man, he would like what he saw in his reflection.

He wasn't young any more, but from the appearance of things that wasn't nearly as important here in the Montrose as he might have thought. He was in good shape. His clothes showed it off. He caught himself spouting the old college days cliché, "I wouldn't throw it out of bed for eating crackers." Then he stopped himself short. He would never have gotten a male into bed at all. That was not going to happen.

# V

Alex Kane knew something else that wasn't going to happen. It was later that night. He and Danny had just gotten into Houston and were getting their bearings on the city. They had studied Farmdale's report with their usual gathering anger. He could, he knew, just finish off the *Clarion*. He had images of the bombs that had been dropped in Santa Isabella.

It would be so easy sometimes to just do that kind of thing. Just take a bomb and just … But, no. Sometimes he did decide that the only proper way to respond to a situation was with that kind of drastic action. When any gay man, including himself, was actually threatened with violence, or if a gay man had been so horribly wronged and the other person had escaped any trial or justice, then he'd act.

But he had to set an example for Danny now. He couldn't just go off the edge and pop whenever he wanted to. He had seldom done that anyway. There had been the first time, when he had seen his first lover, James Farmdale, die in Vietnam. Then Alex, knowing who had murdered him, turned and performed his first righteous execution.

It had not been the only time he had acted that way. Nor would it be the last. But, now, with Danny …

He turned and looked at his lover standing beside him. He smiled when he did that. The simple action of smiling was enough to let him know that Danny had changed his life these past few years. After James Farmdale, a true love, that gift that you only expect to get once in your life, Alex had given up hoping for this kind of happiness. But he'd gotten it.

*I love Danny,* he thought. And what a person to love. In the noisy disco, there wasn't the peace and quiet to think about all of Danny's good points. The lights and the music were too distracting. Alex smiled to himself and decided he'd just take the physical ones for now. He'd be a raw sexual animal and do nothing more than evaluate his lover physically.

Danny was stripped to the waist. That pelt of hair on his chest was matted to his skin by the sweat he'd built up dancing just now. Alex could smell its clean, sweat odor. Danny's face was … it was just perfect. He had high cheekbones, a constant smile on his red lips, hair naturally and luxuriously curly. The skin never seemed to be pale. The Italian heritage left him with a rich olive tone to his flesh.

Alex let his eyes travel down a bit. As often as he had looked at Danny's body, as often as he'd touched it and made love to it, there was never a time when he didn't appreciate its sheer perfection. Danny had been the Massachusetts state gymnastics champion in college. All the evidence of that accomplishment was right there in front of Alex.

The pectoral muscles pushed out in two exaggerated slabs. The tiny nipples peeked out from the hair on his chest. Then his torso dove down to become a flat surface, truncated by the sharply etched abdominal muscles. Danny was moving with the music, letting his slight motions swing his arms and allowing Alex – and everyone else in the large room – to see his biceps, triceps and forearms in sharp relief.

*I love Danny.* What a good thought.

It was foolish for Alex to worry about Danny when another guy came up to him suddenly. He just wanted Fortelli to dance with him. But Alex sometimes felt as though he could never relax his guard whenever they left their retreat in New Hampshire. Alex was always the warrior on alert, the soldier ready to do battle, and the image of anyone approaching his lover always made him anxious.

It was especially foolish since Danny had become such an incredible fighter himself. If you didn't see the glint in his eye that was so hard, so acidic, so ready to attack, you would only pay attention to the dimples, the wonderful body, the youthfulness of it all. But that was a mistake, one that a lot of people had been making lately. Danny's fists had become lethal. So had a lot of other parts of his physique. He was especially dangerous with his legs and feet. He could jump and kick in a way that only an Olympic-quality track star could understand.

Danny looked at Alex quickly. It was a well-practiced move; it was a familiar question. He wanted to dance. Alex loathed it. The guy asking was safe enough. Alex nodded once to say, *Okay.*

The two younger men went toward the floor. Alex watched as they mounted the single stair and immediately began to dance. The other guy was black. His skin seemed to have a beautiful texture whenever Alex could see it under the revolving bright light. He was about Danny's own 5' 10"; shorter than Alex's six feet. He and Danny were both dripping with sweat within a few minutes of dancing. There was something especially erotic about seeing the two of them as their quick movement sent waves of perspiration flying into the air between them. They were good; they were both very good dancers.

They moved with a special synchrony. Though he knew they had only just met, Alex knew that they had found some similar chord in each other, something that let them know what the other was going to do. They played off each other. Danny would stand back and let the black youth take the imaginary spotlight for a while. He'd do a few things that showed his competency and then move back to give Danny the space to show his stuff.

It was a nice duet. Alex liked it; Alex hated it. He hated it because it made him think that he was responsible for Danny's missing so much in life. Danny's Olympic hopes were out the window. He would never get that big spotlight.

He would, of course, insist that this one was more than adequate. Alex often wondered about entering Danny into the Gay Games they had out in San Francisco, but he knew they couldn't do that. They were already too well known for their own good. Pictures in the newspapers wouldn't help at all when they had to go underground the next time. *And there always is a next time, isn't there,* he thought.

Danny should be acting like the young guy he was. He should be spending his weekend nights in nice gay bars like this one, having a little seduction on the dance floor, going to parties with people his own age. He shouldn't be committed to a crusade that was never ending, and so dangerous.

But, then, the people whose protection made the crusade so necessary shouldn't have to worry about the forces that acted against them, either. That black guy dancing with Danny now: He should just be going on with his life. He shouldn't have to live in a city like Houston when a pig like this Banks was on the rampage.

Alex was drinking his beer in a can. It wasn't even half empty, but as he thought about the stuff that Banks was pulling, the rage took over and before he knew it Alex felt his hand awash with beer seeping from the can he'd just crushed in his fist.

"Man, I know he's cute. But no one's worth that kind of anger," someone said nearby. Alex controlled himself and found the whole situation humorous. He wasn't jealous about Danny dancing with someone else. Maybe he should be, sometime. Danny was certainly attractive; he surely was young enough to want to roam ... No. Really, no. Alex knew that Danny didn't want to roam at all.

Danny and his new friend came off the floor when the set was over. It was time to go. Alex quickly took the offered introduction to the other man, Cecil, then he grabbed Danny around the waist and led him towards the doorway. The feeling of the sweat-streaked skin was strangely erotic, wonderfully sensual. All Alex could think of was getting back to their apartment and taking off their clothes, beginning that constant sexual duet that they were always practicing. Danny pulled the shirt out of his rear pocket and struggled to get it over his head and neck and then pushed it into his waistband, all while they were walking.

They went through the small lobby and out the final door. They were tired. They both just wanted to go home.

There was a sudden burst of light. They were blinded for a split second. When Alex had recovered, he found himself and Danny both in fighting stances, their hands extended, their bodies bent; they were ready.

They had assumed that it was some sort of physical attack. Instead, they discovered themselves confronting a wimpy looking man holding a large, professional camera. He was smiling at them. "If you're lucky, you'll catch yourself in the *Clarion* tomorrow. You can make life easy and tell me your name, or we'll just follow you to your car and check the registration in Austin. Wonderful things that computers can do nowadays."

The "we" obviously referred to the two large men who flanked the photographer. They were beefy guys whose appearance came right from central casting. They weren't just smiling in that contemptuous manner that the cameraman had, they were sneering.

So was Alex Kane.

"I don't think so," he said. He and Danny exchanged quick looks at one another. They were both happy to have this little diversion. One of the things they hated about their assignments was the amount of waiting they always had to do. It would often be weeks of walking, talking, investigating before they had a shot at an enemy that deserved their attention. Here it was the first night and they were already all set.

"Give me the film." Alex reached out an open palm and made his request with the most polite sounds possible.

"Fat chance, faggot," the wimpy photographer said.

"Give me your film, *please*." Alex repeated himself.

"No way, Jose. Your mug is going into the *Clarion*. If you got a mother, you better go and make peace with her. Or, do you think she'd be happy to see her son walking out of a joint like this?"

There was no need to say any more. Alex and Danny walked straight for the photographer. Alex was very proud of himself. He had given the man two chances. People were always saying he wasn't fair. Well, he had been this time. *Two* chances!

A man watched silently from the disco's doorway. He was ready to run in and phone the cops, that or get some of the others to come out and deal with this mess. There was something that overrode his panic. He couldn't explain it. But as he watched the two gay guys walking so casually towards the cameraman and his two guards, he really didn't think there was any danger. Something told him that he could just stand here and watch what was going on.

In only a couple seconds there was plenty to see.

The appearance of composure that the two gay men had was obviously put on. The two goons with the newspaper man fell for it. They each moved forward and were ready to deliver knock-out punches. They never did. In fact, the one witness wondered if they even knew what had happened.

The guy nearest the door, the one who was wearing an athletic t-shirt and who had that smooth, hairless skin, moved in some funny, quick way that denied his attacker a target. The goon had begun to throw his punch, and then its object wasn't there. He faltered forward, carried by his own momentum. He staggered for a bit, and when he did, the gay guy delivered a bone-crunching fist to his neck.

The big bully froze for a split second and then fell forward, hard onto the ground. He was obviously unconscious. He couldn't possibly have felt his nose break when it bounced off the concrete pavement. He was out for a long, long count.

The second one got taken with a lot more style. *Jeez, it was very pretty,* the witness thought. He, too, had thrown his punch, but this gay guy, the one with all the dark hair and with the flawless tan, *jumped over it!* The fist actually went underneath his curled up legs. The bigger man, also staggering from losing his balance, never did figure out why he was trying to belt thin air, because as soon as he understood that he was, the young guy guy was plummeting down from his hurdle. His feet landed squarely on the man's back.

When the two of them fell onto the ground, the kid showed his really pretty stuff. Somehow, he maintained his pose. This goon's head also pounded on the concrete. There was another sound of bones breaking when that happened. But somehow, the gay kid didn't fall, he didn't even waver. He was standing right on the man's back when all the action stopped. He was still perched there, as though he had been the victor in some Roman gladiator game, when his partner approached the photographer once more.

That sleazy smile was gone from the cameraman's face. Only raw fear and disbelief were left. He didn't even hear it when the sound of a single person's applause came from the doorway. "That's the way to go!" an unknown voice cheered.

"The film." Alex Kane didn't think he had to be at all polite any more. He was quickly handed the camera, ripped it open and broke the camera's case as he tore out the now exposed negatives. He threw the remains across the parking lot. "Now what the hell do you think you're doing and who told you to do it?"

# VI

*"What happened!!"* Martin Banks screamed.

Harvey Pearson was wiping his brow with a handkerchief. "They must have had inside information. There must have been an army of them. I've never seen such an extraordinary campaign in my life. The entire exposure project has to be cut off. Worse, we're totally dependent on AP and UPI for even the most mundane local photographs now. There isn't a single *Clarion* cameraman who'll go out on assignment – at least not after dark."

"But, how? What ..."

"They somehow found out just where our cameramen were stationed. They all had armed guards, but they did no good. There must have been an army of faggots. They not only destroyed all the cameras ..."

"Sacred private property!" Banks screamed.

"They ... they broke all the photographer's fingers. They can't touch a shutter." Pearson was sure there had to have been a whole organized group involved. The fact that the men involved who were willing to talk to him all described a very similar pair of assailants was obviously a coincidence. All the fairies dressed alike and had the same looks these days, that clone look they're always talking about. It was *impossible* that a single pair of men could have done all that damage.

Though it was suspicious that they had been so careful

about breaking all those fingers. One of the Emergency Room doctors had called it almost surgically perfect work. They were broken, but they weren't mutilated. They would eventually heal, though the ten men whose hands were now trapped in plaster casts didn't really find much solace in that.

There wasn't much to be happy about at all in the evening's activity, though the newspaper photographers really were lucky to have gotten off lighter than their guards, especially the couple who were apparently foolish enough to pull their pistols. Jesus, the hospital had looked like a battle scene when Pearson had finally gotten there in response to the frantic phone calls.

"They dare to defy the moral desires of the community. They *dare* it!" Banks was spitting again. There was a whole arc of mucus spraying out over his desk. "Then we'll simply have to mobilize the community against these new amoral forces. There must be new moves made, the danger must be made more important. And we must do it in such a manner that everyone in Houston will *have* to read the *Clarion* to understand the extent of the threat."

Harvey wasn't going to dare to suggest anything at this point. He was scared of the boss, he was just as frightened of that undetermined force that was doing battle with the boss's wishes outside.

•  •  •

The boss himself wrote the editorial for the next day's issue. Harvey read it and thought it was genius, pure genius. The doctor bills and the increased insurance payments weren't the kind of thing that would break Banks's checking account, but why should he have to pay even a penny extra for this crusade?

Martin Banks had been proud to tell all his employees an anecdote that he used to justify even the most nitpicking cost cutting at his newspapers. He told the story about Henry Ford walking up and down the huge mass assembly lines in his River Rouge plant when it had first opened. He discovered that there was a certain kind of oil drip at every work station. It was the kind of thing that had never amounted to anything of importance when the scale of manufacture had been small. But Ford was talking American industry in the Twentieth Century. He was envisioning a level of industrial output that was beyond the wildest imagination of even the most forward looking analysts.

To him, a drop of oil repeated thousands of times at every work station wasn't a simple drop of oil. It was drums of oil, hundreds of drums of oil. He had the defect repaired at every place he could find. The result was a savings of hundreds of thousands of dollars throughout all the divisions of his massive corporation.

You can't talk in terms of drips, Martin Banks had explained. You had to think in terms of all the drips repeated endless times in countless locations. The boss, who often dropped five hundred dollars on a business dinner for four, was adamant about the average time he expected a pencil to be utilized at every desk. That, he would explain if challenged, was why he could have those dinners and enjoy them. Though, of course, he was very seldom questioned on his policies.

In his editorial, Martin Banks suggested that the only way to fight the spread of homosexuality in the city of Houston was to isolate the disease before it – and the other deadly viruses that came with it – could spread any further in the city.

"Why should anyone complain about such a public policy?" Banks's editorial had asked. "The perverts have obviously expressed that very desire with their choice of habitats in the Montrose neighborhood. Why shouldn't the good citizens of Houston encourage them to continue their self-imposed exile from the Christian neighborhoods of which we are so proud?

"There's no reason that those of you who are so reckless with your lives that you are willing to go to perverted hairdressers couldn't travel to that area to let the disease-ridden *artistes* have their opportunity to infect you."

The editorial, which took up over half the front page, went on to describe the new policy of the *Clarion* in terms of disclosure of homosexuals. "The plan to publicly present the photographs of a few randomly selected sickos was obviously too narrow-minded," it said. "We are dealing with a massive conspiracy. The only way to fight it is to meet it at its own level.

"Therefore, to help the perverts find their own and their friends in order to aid them in their self-chosen exile into their ghetto, the *Clarion* will begin to publish a profile every day of a different business enterprise which caters to the perverts' whim. We will document all those companies whose employment practices do not prevent psychotic, disease-ridden people from working for them.

"You must remember that these are the places that openly say they will welcome homosexuals. Remember that they take homosexuals in as full employees and thereby subject you and your loved ones to exposure of physical *and* mental contamination."

The premier "profile" was on the first page of the business section. It was of the Fifth State Bank of Houston, one of the city's largest. With it was an unexpected bonus. Every profile would include a chart showing the risk factor to physical and mental disease. The Fifth State Bank, since it allowed homosexuals to handle money with their hands without washing every fifteen minutes, was given a disease risk factor of "High" and, since they allowed homosexuals to assume supervisory positions over "decent Americans," the mental defect rating was "Extreme." As the report stated, if a pervert were allowed to control a normal person's future advance in the firm, the person would be in a position to force his unwanted attentions on someone who would be pressured to give in for the sake of his job.

•   •   •

"Jesus Christ! Fifth State's stock has dropped ten points in one day."

"What've they got today? God, they can't get Mobil, can they? My father's entire retirement portfolio's in Mobil stock."

"No. It's Mid-American International Airlines, 'cause they allow gay stewards. A mental defect rating of only "Worrisome," but a disease risk factor of "Extreme." *Extreme!* Damn, this newspaper's sick. Just because the stewards handle food ..."

"Yeah, it's sick. What's really sick is that you bought it and we're all hanging on every word. Not only us, all of Texas. I bet you my life savings that every fucking airline that flies in and out of Houston will have a full page of ads of smiling *female* flight attendants in tomorrow's edition of the *Clarion.* It will be subtle, but they're all going to want to show just how heterosexual they are."

"Fuck, what a hell of a raw deal ..."

"You ain't seen nothing yet, honey. I bet you ain't seen nothing yet."

Frank Terkel listened to the conversation around the pool at the Magnolia Towers with his eyes shut against the sun. Even with his dark glasses, the sun was bright during the Texas summer and the humidity in Houston was murder. He was wearing one of those brief black racing suits that he thought gay guys liked to wear. It was just one more step in his transition into their world.

He had been surprised to see that so many of the gay men at the apartment complex wore very baggy surfer-style shorts to the swimming pool. He would have preferred them, but his discomfort factor increased whenever he thought of the racing briefs, so he stuck to his original choice.

He had listened to the conversation, hoping that this new strategy of Martin Banks would be so successful that his own part could be ended. But there hadn't been a phone call, and in hope of one that could tell him this torture could end, Frank had had an answering machine installed just in case.

He was going to have to start tonight. He had put it off as

long as he dared. The deadline was racing towards him and he'd have no good reason not to hand in some spicy copy in two days.

Banks had wanted the goods on the "sewers." It had been surprisingly easy to discover just what they were and where. He had become a regular at Daisy's kitchen and had even gone so far as to buy that bleached blond waiter a drink after he'd gotten off his shift one day. Frank had taken his advice and started easy.

The waiter had listened to Frank's made-up story about being new in town and also to the gay life. He'd always had a lover since high school, Frank had explained. That guy and he had lived together for years. They had never gone out while they were a couple. But work and other pressures had finally separated them and Frank just didn't know how to get started.

He had listened to himself talk about this made-up history and had been astonished by how easily it came. He had only thought of his old time fantasies in college before ... He used to have these plans for himself and Randall Landtree. All he had to do to sound convincing to the waiter was repeat those long-hidden dreams. Those sick, stupid fantasies.

"Poor baby, a virgin in this land of satyrs!" The waiter had thought Frank's plight touching. He had taken his pencil and written down a list of bars, baths and clubs. But he hadn't just randomly jotted them down. "Make believe you're starting your education. First, there's kindergarten. That's this group. Nice little piano bars, a couple decent restaurants, that kind of thing.

"Then you get to grade school. Okay? A few discos, not the high-pressured ones that seem like they were dropped on Houston from the middle of Manhattan, but the easy-going dance palaces we all love so much. Junior high school, well, you can go to some of the cowboy bars. They're butch enough that you don't have to worry about queens like me making you upset. But they're not so very butch that you have to worry about it. You know? No, you don't know. But, I'll explain that.

"So then," the waiter had drawn another line and begun another subsection, "you're ready for high school. That's the real discos and the real cruisy bars, the places where you walk in and half the men in attendance hold up cards with your ranking on a scale of one to ten, like you were some prize heifer at the feedlot.

"If you can get past them, it's time for college. I put the baths there. Now, you have to learn to watch yourself. This disease stuff is getting out of hand. Used to be ... Well, we won't talk about what used to be. But, you just have to take precautions in this day and age. So, you make sure you take one of the AIDS risk reduction pamphlets we got on the cigarette machine with you and *you study it,* hear?

"Then," he winked, "if you make it through that, you're ready for the real big time. Graduate school. That, without a doubt, means the leather bars. I'm not talking about some of the cruise bars where they dress up a bartender with a little leather. Oh, no, we're talking the hot spots. The hottest is Franny's. Right along with it is the Jock Strap. But you make sure you've done your homework before you take on those places. I mean it."

Frank could have cried at that moment as he was sitting by the pool. He hurriedly turned over without having opened his eyes. Just remembering the lewd descriptions the waiter had given him about the baths and those places, the leather bars, had given him a hard-on and *he didn't want it!* He especially didn't want to have any of the other men around the pool see it. But someone did.

"Honey, you need some help with that thing?"

Frank bit the inside of his mouth and refused to answer.

# VII

*"What happened!!"* Martin Banks screamed.

Cecil was standing in line outside the new disco, *Heaven!* It was supposed to be the hot place; from the number of people who'd been willing to wait to get past the doorman, it sure as hell should be. There were only muffled sounds of music coming from the building. The bass was so strong it seemed to shake the structure to its foundation.

At least the opening rush was over. The line was reasonable and moving quickly. He was near the very end and could expect to get inside in no more than fifteen minutes. He turned around to look at those behind him and there they were! Oh, man, there they were.

*Be cool,* Cecil thought, *just because they're the two most attractive male adults you've seen in your entire lifetime, there is no reason for you to make a TOTAL ass of yourself. Then he smiled, just a little ass of yourself is another story.*

Only a handful of people separated the pair from him. They signified only an extra ten minutes or so of waiting time. A realistic sacrifice, that was for sure. Cecil gave up his place and moved to the end of the line.

"Hi, we never got to really talk much the other night." The cute young one with the dimples smiled broadly, "Cecil, right?"

"Yeah." They shook hands.

"I'm Danny," the dimples reminded him, "and this is Alex."

Cecil smiled and hoped he didn't look like a fool. He would really have loved just taking them both in his arms and walking back to their place or his. This would be a sandwich to remember. He could just picture himself stuck between these two hunks. The hairy chest of the Italian kid rubbing against his own while that big muscular number with the green eyes went to work on the rear end. *Jesus!*

Who needed to go to a disco named *Heaven!* when the real thing was standing in front of him in the flesh?

They made small talk; the couple said they were from New Hampshire, just visiting Houston for a while. Like every other gay man in Houston, they discussed the shit that the *Clarion* was pulling. "Hell, those guys dig some of their graves themselves, the ones that are hiding so hard that their world falls in on them when the paper puts on the pressure. I'm not standing for that."

Cecil explained that, while, yeah, he had to admit he hadn't *really* dealt with shit with his family, still, he was out. He had even just been elected an officer in one of the gay groups at his school. He felt a little guilty, though, when he realized that he had ducked things and had never actually said what his school was. Hell, this coming out thing was a never-ending process.

They had moved right up to the door by now. They would be next. "Okay, three more," the bouncer announced. Cecil, full of joy that he had actually found Alex and Danny again in a city as large as Houston moved to enter. "Got some ID?" the bouncer said.

"Oh, *fuck!*" Cecil swore. He was so tired of this game. "Here's my driver's license."

"Got to have three pieces, at least two with pictures." The bouncer made his pronouncement with a bored drawl.

"I only have my driver's license." Danny's voice sounded calm at first, but Cecil caught another tone in there.

"Oh, you look old enough. I just need ..."

"I look younger than he does," Danny said. Whatever was

the thing that Cecil had heard before was right on the surface now. It was cold sounding.

"Look, kid, I'm going to let you in, this jig ..."

The bouncer never got to finish the sentence. Danny's arm had come out and grabbed hold of his shirt collar and pulled it roughly forward. The bouncer had been sitting on a high stool; now he staggered off it.

"My *friend,*" Danny said, "is older than I am and my *friend* is not to be called a *jig* by anyone like you." Then Danny let go and pushed backwards. The bouncer hit the wall and froze for a minute. All he saw was a cute, young, dimplefaced disco doll and he wasn't going to take anything from him.

The bouncer made the mistake of coming at Danny in a threatening manner. Cecil was frightened and was all for just leaving *Heaven!* No place was worth this kind of hassle, no matter how much he was offended by it.

Then, so quickly that Cecil couldn't really see it in detail, there was this flurry of movement. Somehow Danny's right leg came up and kicked, hard. His toe landed right on the bouncer's jaw. There was a sharp crack and Cecil knew that a bone had been broken. The bouncer began to slump forward, as though he would collapse, but now Danny's leg moved again and his foot, this time, landed in the man's stomach.

There was a *whoosh!* as the bouncer lost all the air that had been in his lungs. That, and he quickly lost his dinner, too. Not that it mattered. He was utterly unconscious when it happened. Cecil was stunned. He carefully made sure that the man's nostrils were free of his regurgitation; he didn't want him to drown in his own bile.

Then he wordlessly turned to Danny and expected to see something on his face. Surprise? No, not that. Danny was cool and calm and obviously hadn't wasted any energy thinking that anything would have happened except what did. Anger? Yes.

"As though we didn't have enough trouble, they have to bring that kind of foolishness into the gay world," Danny said with a trace of disgust. "Let's go dance."

*Somebody should say something about the fact that there had just been a major confrontation here,* Cecil thought. *But he only heard one more comment.*

"Sloppy work," Alex Kane said as he had to step over the vomit.

Cecil just plain decided not to even think about what had gone on. It would accomplish nothing. It would make no difference. That man at the door was *out.* He had still been breathing. He had not made a bit of difference to the night that Danny and Alex obviously intended to enjoy, and so why shouldn't Cecil just plain enjoy it himself?

He did. He and Danny danced together for hours. They were a top team on the floor. Both of them looked good; their flesh above their waist was bare almost from the beginning. Their movements were a physical form of poetry. There was no awkwardness, only pure art. Dancing! Cecil hadn't danced so much, so well with another man, in a long time.

The loud, loud sound the dj was putting out made any real conversation impossible between them. There were only the messages that they could send to one another with their bodies. He and Danny said lots. It was wonderful. And a little sad. Sad because Cecil knew in that indescribable way that he was Danny's for the night in *Heaven!,* but Danny wasn't going to be his afterwards.

At first he kept alive his hopes for a three-way. There would be nothing wrong with that, not in the least. But even that hope was crushed each time they took a break to go stand by Alex. Obviously, the two of them couldn't see another man in whatever way it was that they saw each other.

Alex was friendly and Danny was a great dancer and that was going to be the all of it. *Shit!* But then as he thought about it, Cecil realized that actually this was perfect.

While his body kept on moving and his eyes stayed on Danny, Cecil flashed back to his own self-evaluation. He was in a good place, working hard for a goal he wanted to achieve.

He would love to have a lover, but until questions got answered, this wasn't the time to fuck up someone else's life with infatuation games. He was a big man now, about to take on big responsibilities. He didn't know how another male could fit into his plans and until he worked that out, well, let things flow.

Good friends like Alex and Danny, decent men who'd like him and spend time with him and dance with him, this was what was going on in his life right now. That was *okay!* For the umpteenth time, he reminded himself, that was okay. *You do not need to have a lover to be happy.*

When some little grey cell in his brain finally sent back the signal, *Message Received,* it seemed as though the music got louder, the lights brighter and, if it was really possible, Cecil was happier.

Later, they all went to Daisy's for a cup of coffee and a piece of pie. They had silently agreed not to mention the incident at the door to *Heaven!* They weren't avoiding the issue of racial discrimination, but it seemed like an unnecessarily ugly topic to bring up among a trio of new friends who had much better things to talk about.

They just seemed to catch up on one another. Danny and Alex, for their part, were secretive, and Cecil had some things of his own to keep quiet for the time being. But that left them lots of leeway. They talked about Houston, dancing, the bars, lovers, being single, all of it ...

"You want to go to another disco tomorrow night?" Cecil asked.

"No, sorry. Alex and I are going to check out some other bar, Franny's, you heard of it?"

"Heard of it? I quake at the sound of its name. Are you two into that?"

Danny smiled, "Well, let's just say that Alex had a few ... encounters before we really got set with one another. We have reasons to want to go. Really, that's all. Want to come?"

*The two of them in leather! That hairy chest and those muscles and ...* "I've ... uh ... I've never been. I've always sort of been intrigued ..."

"Well, we'll play bodyguard for you again," Alex suggested.

"Only if you promise not to do too good a job at it. I mean, I might not want to get close to another cracker like that fool tonight, but there should be some numbers there that I might want to have get right to me."

"It's a deal."

Cecil didn't live too far from Daisy's. He got a ride in the car Alex was driving, obviously a rented job. Cecil was vaguely wondering what they were about, rented cars and secrets and all that. Well, he decided not to let it bother him. He had the feel and smell of his good-bye hug from Danny all over his body. He playfully thought that if he was finally going to go to a bar as kinky as Franny's tomorrow night, he might as well practice. Maybe he'd just jerk off holding the shirt soaked with Danny's sweat up to his nose.

He unlocked his door and closed it. He was tired. He had a long day tomorrow. A quick little session with his right palm would give him good dreams.

•  •  •

It had worked. Cecil had had the best dreams in the longest time. He woke up and stretched, feeling the crusted part of the sheets where he'd finally let himself cum after god knows how long he'd held back. It had been an Orgasm with a capital O.

Someday he'd have a lover, he supposed, but there sure were some awfully good times to be had without one until that moment came.

He was smiling to himself and vaguely wondering if he wanted to jerk off again when he heard a loud knocking on his door. *Who the hell wants me at this time of morning?* Well, whoever it was wasn't going to go away, that was for sure.

Cecil got up out of bed and pulled on his robe. He went to the door and opened it to find his landlady standing there with something in her hand. "What is it?" he asked. "What's the problem?"

"This is the problem," she announced, holding out the early edition of the *Clarion*. "I think you should find a new place. I think you should do it ... *soon.*"

# VIII

Harvey Pearson knew when he saw a winner. And he knew he was the winner in this race. Jesus, he was going to clean up on it. Leave all the moral crusading stuff to Martin Banks. Harvey couldn't care less about that. But, after all these years kissing ass and all this time being left in the running by the big time assholes in New York and Chicago, Harvey Pearson was a winner.

The managing editor of a daily newspaper whose circulation was going to climb through the ceiling was a hot property in anyone's book. After all the humiliations of being left out, never having his phone calls returned, his resumés always being sent back by return mail, Harvey was going to be in the driver's seat.

So what if the most liberal papers wouldn't like him. They'd tell him he had a taint to him. They wouldn't like this anti-gay crusade. But, by god, it was going to do the trick! It really was working. He looked at the new circulation figures that had been put on his desk and he could see that he was driving a winner.

Today's paper had opened a new front. It had been one of the easy ones. He had known that the gay students' groups were a sitting target. That young guy, the new one, had got 'em like ducks in the water. The headline alone was an unexpected bonus. Great angle.

"You like that?"

Harvey looked up and saw that Sandra Myers was standing in his doorway looking at him. He studied her for a minute. He wondered if it was okay to tell a spade that she looked pale. Sandra certainly did. Her face, usually covered with a smile, was drawn, gaunt. He thought she had seen a ghost – that or some other terrible thing.

Harvey smiled. "Hey! Good to see you, Sandra. Isn't this story great! Hell, when we get this shit you're working on about high school coaches and add it to this, the town's really going to be hopping."

"What do you see there, Pearson?"

This was the first time that Sandra had ever asked him a question in that kind of serious tone. He was puzzled. But he shrugged. He looked at the front page.

## The Clarion Wants to Know:

Are Gay Medical Students Spreading AIDS?

"I see a story that'll get 'em by the balls!" Harvey pronounced. "Look at it, pictures and everything. *Everything!* Well, you got to admit, these students are treating people in clinics all over the city. They joined that gay medical students' group all by themselves. Hell, they might as well have printed a formal announcement that they were putting the whole city at risk. Medical workers with AIDS? Hell, they shouldn't be allowed ..."

"They don't have AIDS! They're just gay."

"Sandra, you know damn well that the man in the street can't make that distinction. So far as he knows, so far as he cares, they all got AIDS. Probably just as well.

"But look, what's the problem? What do you see here? It's a great layout. Using these high school yearbook pictures is a nice touch, makes the disease carriers look as though they're innocent, it alerts the reader to know that you can't tell these fags ..."

"Shut up!" Sandra Myers wasn't getting any calmer and

she wasn't getting any healthier looking either. "I'm going to tell you what's on that page. It's the destruction of a human life! It's the end of a brilliant career! *And it's your fault!* All for a few more lousy subscribers!"

"What the hell's gotten into you, Sandra? Huh? Calm down. So, there are some casualties in a war, that's what the boss would say. No big deal. You got to ..."

Sandra slapped Pearson's face to stop his tirade. She slammed the newspaper down on his desk and pointed to one of the photographs that was illustrating the article. *"That's my brother!"*

"Sandra, Sandra, I'm sorry about that. We all got some black sheep in our families, you don't have to be worried. We won't hold it against you."

"Hold it against me," she hissed in reply. "That's the only reason I have for living. That boy is the only reason I've put up with the endless bullshit that comes with working here. I've saved my money and I've sacrificed everything – including my self-respect – to play your house nigger so that boy would never have to know what it's like to do without. And you ruin it all with one story in your fucked up newspaper."

"Sandra, that's enough." Harvey thought it was just about time to regain some control over this situation.

"You're damned right it is."

She reached into her purse and pulled something out. Before Harvey could say a word, she'd pointed the revolver directly at his head and pulled the trigger.

And then Harvey never, ever had to worry about the situation again.

# IX

"Mr. Banks, I was told to report directly to you." Frank Terkel had expected other people to be in the boss's office. He was surprised to find himself alone with Banks and felt he had to make some kind of apologetic excuse.

"Yes, yes," Martin Banks said, his eyes sparkling. There was a dead man, a trusted, high-ranking employee, on the coroner's slab and this guy's eyes were sparkling!

"Pearson, a tragedy, you know it's a tragedy."

*Then why do you seem to be so goddamned happy?*

"But we know that he was a pro. A pro to the end!" Frank barely escaped one of Bank's flying spit balls. "He would have wanted us to use him in the manner that would promote this newspaper, the journal he loved."

*I wonder if this guy is so looney that he actually believes this shit?* Frank thought.

"The *Clarion* was Harvey Pearson's life. His reason for being. He stood right behind all of its principles. Now, his tragic death will provide us with an opportunity to strike a blow for American values much sooner than I thought we would be able to.

"Those ... *liberals,*" Banks spoke the word with an unbelievable hatred, "in Washington think that one of the most important pillars of our Founding Fathers' thoughts is no longer applicable. But the martyrdom of Harvey Pearson has proven they're wrong. It's an opportunity that we won't mis-use.

"I want that story on the sewers of homosexual depravity in record time."

"I've nearly done it," Frank answered. "I did most of the research already. There's only one more place to check into, they tell me it's the worst of all."

"The worst of all!" There was a sound of awe in Banks's voice. "The idea that there would be something so horrible as to be the worst in that world is so astonishing that we have got to get the information to the people as soon as possible."

"I will. I'll have it for you in two days."

"Excellent. Harvey Pearson trusted you. He said you were just the person for this assignment. I believed him then. I will take his word for it now. Because it's time for you to take on the most important story of all. The story of the conspiracy."

*The conspiracy? What the hell ...*

"You can begin to introduce the subject in your article on the cesspools these people inhabit. Then, when it's done, you'll have to immediately move to disclose the hateful cabal that will stop at nothing until it's destroyed the very essence of what's made America great. You have to expose the alliance of homosexuals and blacks."

Frank was stunned into silence. He tried to find words to counter that horrible, perverted idea. Some finally came to him. "Mr. Banks, it appears to me that the gay world I've seen isn't really much different about racial subjects than any other part of the society ..."

"Subterfuge! It's all camouflage!" Martin Banks slammed at his desk; he didn't just spit now, a long line of mucus was falling out of the sunken right side of his mouth. "What hap-pened to Harvey Pearson downstairs was just the tip of the iceberg. Others may not have understood, but I could make the necessary connections.

"That woman murdered Pearson because the brilliant story about the medical students was about to expose the diabolical pact between negroes and homosexuals. She's admitted it."

"She told the police that it was the picture of her brother in the paper ..."

"The photograph that exposed a nigger queer. She was undoubtedly going to torpedo our campaign. Her job was to infiltrate our organization, to make it ineffectual the way they've castrated the spirit of the rest of the press in the United States."

*Jesus Christ, he was looney!*

"Anyone who's not with us is against us. If there is a moment's hesitation on the part of one staff member we know that he has tainted blood. He is a queer or he's a damned product of miscegenation. Our enemies will announce themselves."

*Me! He'll find out about me. Christ, I have to go along with this.*

"We are at war now." Banks turned his back on Frank and stared out his window at the Houston skyline. "We have flushed out the enemy. For once, they are there, in the open. I have to accept my role as the general in our battle plans. I will not shirk from that obligation."

Banks turned around again and faced Frank. That glint was still in his eye, his hands still clasped behind his back in an attempt at a military posture, but it was really something that appeared ludicrous. Banks was never going to be able to carry off a military presence. *Then again,* Frank thought, *they probably said the same thing about Hitler.*

"I am going to turn the *Clarion* Building into an armed fortress. I've hired every available security guard in the city. Security will be as tight as necessary to assure the safety of the rest of my staff against the threats of the racial/sexual alliance. The politicians be damned. It's time to talk honestly about the danger that blacks still hold in their hands to use against us."

"You're going to start a race war?" Frank asked incredulously.

Banks smiled now. "We'll begin with the homosexuals."

Frank stood there, unable to speak at all. Banks continued. "There was a reason for the pogroms of the old days in Europe. They kept undesirables in their places. They made the general population secure from those people who were supposed to stay in their ghettos. We'll use the correct language, but this afternoon's edition of the *Clarion* will announce the need for that kind of citizen action here in Houston. I've already written the editorial; it will appear on the front page, as my statements always do.

"We are standing at the threshold of a new time in Texas. It is time for new leadership and I intend to have this newspaper provide it."

•   •   •

Frank drove back to the Magnolia Towers apartment and tried to convince himself that the rationalizations that made sense of his life were still valid. Of course they were. They had to be. The racial stuff was … distasteful. But who was Frank to judge what Banks had said. Fuck, it was his paper, if he wanted to rant and rave against left-handed dwarfs, it was his right.

*Besides,* he reminded himself, *you just saw how disgusting the rest of it was – the homosexual part.*

Frank parked his car as soon as he got to the apartment building and went to his own place. He put on the air conditioner. As usual, it was hot and muggy in Houston on a summer day. He stripped off his clothes while the room was cooling off, anything to give himself some relief from this horrible climate.

He sprawled on his bed and ran through the things he had witnessed last night. He told himself at one level that he was getting his observations together for his article. At another, he was reliving the squalor he had seen to remind himself of how important it was that no one ever be tempted to go to those places.

Banks had called Pearson a martyr. Maybe that was just

Frank's own role. He tried to think of himself that way. He knew, all too well, that there were temptations offered him by the gay life. What he had to do, he went on thinking, was to document those temptations. Some were so insidious that you weren't even always aware of them. You had to be reminded of the price that would have to be paid if you gave into them.

The disease. There was always the disease. The way that gay men seemed to have such a wonderful, carefree time was a temptation, but to give in to it and to join their promiscuity was to invite the deadly disease. Remember that kind of thing.

What he had to do, he decided, was to ignore everything that had been interesting or fun or appealing in the baths he'd gone to last night and instead look at how loathsome it was. Forget how attractive some of the men were, forget the way they walked around with condoms in their hands, using them to show that they were taking the advice on sexual safety seriously. Forget that there were so many male couples who appeared to be so happy.

That wasn't important.

What was important was that nauseating scene that he'd witnessed where a man sat on his haunches and kept his mouth open, inviting infection, offering degradation to himself and to anyone else who offered it.

*Don't think about the shower room!* He couldn't bring that into the story. He couldn't mention that it had looked just like the one at his college gymnasium, that the men had looked so handsome standing there, naked, comfortably washing themselves and visually appreciating their neighbors.

*Don't talk about the television lounge!* No one was going to be interested in a little scenario like that. Just because the two men had been so overtly affectionate while they explored each other's bodies, there was no need to talk about it in a family newspaper story. What was important was their mixed races. Forget the image of the black skin, so richly ebony, as it rubbed against the untanned legs of the white man.

Frank looked down and saw that his cock had become totally erect. That was happening to innocent men all over the United States. They were all getting hard thinking of the temptations of the gay world. They had to be warned! They'd have to be warned or they'd get the same ugly hard-on, demanding, imploring them to give in and go to some horrible place like the baths.

*If you write about the other side of it, the erections will go away,* he told himself. *Your own and the others. They'll go away and the temptations will disappear. Write about the filth that makes these things happen to people.*

Frank lifted up his hard cock and stared at it as though it were a devil incarnate. *This thing has to go away!*

# X

Cecil heard the phone ringing just as he was about to leave his apartment to meet Danny and Alex. He stared at it for a moment. It was Sandra. He knew it would be. He wondered, for the first time, why she hadn't found out earlier. She worked at the paper. She should have seen it even before the landlady.

Well, he wasn't going to let his sister's bitching ruin his evening. He'd take care of the landlady, too. He was not going to be tossed out of his own home just because of a stupid, ignorant newspaper allegation.

He walked out and slammed the door behind him.

As he made his way toward Franny's by bus he thought over his situation with Sandra. It was going to be a hard time. He truly, honestly appreciated all the sacrifices that she'd gone through to make sure he'd had a decent upbringing, good schooling, everything he ever wanted.

She'd sacrificed too much. It made him feel guilty that she had refused so many dates because she had to tutor him for his finals or some other test all the time. Anything less than the top of the class was not good enough for her brother.

She could have gone to a top school herself, but she wouldn't do it. She said she couldn't stand the idea of Cecil staying with those hateful relatives who'd been their unwilling foster parents after their own mother and father had died. Instead, she enrolled in local state colleges and held down a full-time job while she studied journalism.

She had bet all her own hopes on his success. He was supposed to be the big black doctor. Once he'd finished medical school he'd be able to pay her back with all the prestige and all the money in the world.

He should have told her about being gay himself. He really should have. But he kept finding an excuse to put it off. He wanted to wait until everything was just perfect, then he'd be able to show her that the gay thing wasn't going to ruin her dreams.

He bet that someone like Danny Fortelli wouldn't ever understand that, the need to be perfect before you came out. Danny *was* perfect. He probably never had to hide things from anyone. In his fantasies of who Danny was, Cecil pictured him never having had any troubles. Whatever Danny's dreams had been, they must have come easy.

Cecil was in a little private world as he thought about how things would be. Well, now that the story was out, there would be no problem with Sandra any more. He was sure that they'd work it out. She'd be disappointed, but she'd come around eventually. Maybe he could introduce his friends Danny and Alex to Sandra.

Sandra lived in a world of make believe, insisting that the reason her brother had never brought home any pretty girls was simple. The demands of medical school were too great. No one who studied as hard as Cecil had time for silly things like dating.

He smiled at that. He did have to work awfully hard and he'd work even harder when he started his internship next fall. But he was such a diligent laborer and was able to discipline himself so well that he had been able to structure in careful allotments of play time. Tonight would be two trips to the bars in a row. That was unusual. But then, Alex and Danny were worth it, to say the least.

Cecil had felt funny walking through the lobby of the big luxury hotel. Not only were they mysterious about their backgrounds, they were rich, too. They had to be to stay in a place like this. Cecil felt foolish in this bar outfit. He'd tried to butch it up for the special occasion and was wearing a t-shirt that had the words "Under Construction" written across his chest. It was as close as he came to having something that might fit into a leather bar. He had also chosen his cowboy boots rather than his usual running shoes in another nod to the atmosphere he was going to enter.

The button fly jeans, he assumed, were universal. He certainly hoped so!

As nervous as he was about what to wear to Franny's, the ambience of this luxury hotel certainly wasn't appropriate to his clothing. He felt strangely on display here. The place wasn't one that made him feel at home in jeans, that was for sure. He felt everyone was staring at him, even though he knew they could care less about a black man walking through the lobby in casual clothes. They probably thought he was just one of the help who'd come in through the wrong entrance.

Well, they'd get over that when he'd finished his training and started to pull down a big doctor's salary, that was for sure. He stepped into the glassed-in cage that was the elevator. It was one of those that climbed up the outside of the wall, leaving the occupant a view of the high ceilinged lobby as it ascended. He'd bring Sandra back here one day; they'd both be dressed to the nines; they'd show them what real class was.

Cecil forgot his anger when he stepped off the elevator at the floor Danny had indicated. He walked down the corridors following the signs to their room. He knocked, hoping he wasn't much too early or late.

If Cecil had the slightest doubt about his attire, the appearance of Danny and Alex had erased it. If they could wear *those* get ups through the lobby of the hotel, then he could have worn ... *anything.*

He stuttered a bit when Danny had motioned him into the suite and then closed the door. He finally got out a greeting.

"We won't be long," Danny said.

Danny had obviously gone for the local western look. He had on a pair of fringed brown chaps, real cowboy stuff. Underneath was a pair of jeans that *forced* Cecil to stare at the crotch that was so tightly gathered up. Danny had on a matching vest. And nothing else. He smiled a welcome and offered Cecil a soft drink. When Cecil refused, Danny went on putting on his gear.

He had a new stetson, black with a black leather band around it. Black leather cowboy boots were next. "What do you think?" Danny asked, showing off his dimples again.

"Fine, just fine. No shirt?" Cecil hoped there wasn't, but would Danny just walk through the lobby with his chest bare? The lobby of *this* hotel?

"Nah. I like the natural thing, don't you?"

"Oh, uh … yeah. It looks great. But, what am I going to do? Look at me, I look like a drag queen next to you, not that I'm not …" Cecil tried to disarm the situation with his self-deprecation.

Danny studied him for a minute. "I've got a better shirt than that. And I have another vest. This is new. I usually wear just a regular black one to the bars. Come on, we'll fix you up."

Cecil thought he was going to gain back his composure with the help of the activity that he and Danny began. Work at anything was better than just sitting around and wondering, thinking … But then Alex Kane walked out of the bathroom, himself getting ready for the trip to Franny's.

"Jesus," Cecil whispered.

Danny looked over at Alex. "Yeah, he does that pretty well."

*That* was made up of a pair of tight, very tight, black leather chaps. The jeans underneath weren't the new and deep blue type that Danny wore. They were old and much used, so much so that parts of the area that showed front and back were not only nearly white in color, there were areas that were actually threadbare and they did *not* hide the fact that Alex was wearing a jock strap.

He didn't have on a shirt, either. Cecil was struck with the incredible musculature that Alex was displaying. You could make out every etched line in his abdomen, you could see the creases where his pectoral muscles melded into the rest of his torso. His arms were as clearly defined as in any anatomy text Cecil had ever studied.

*He has to wear at least a vest,* Cecil thought.

But, no, he wasn't going to. Instead he pulled on a heavy black leather jacket and didn't even zip up the bottom; he left the front flapping open. He then placed a biker's hat on his head. Alex took one quick look at the mirror. He nodded to no one, it was a simple statement that he was satisfied.

They were concentrating on Cecil now. He felt foolish pulling off his own shirt in front of them. His body seemed skinny and unappealing after what they had been displaying. But there was no choice. He took the plain black shirt that Danny handed him and put it on instead.

"Hmmm ..." Danny was obviously not satisfied with the result. His big chest had stretched out the fabric, which now just hung on Cecil. Then Danny's face lightened. "I know what to do." He went to his bag and got out a pair of scissors. He methodically went about cutting up the shirt until it was slit at least a dozen places. "Perfect."

Cecil went back to the mirror. The image was something close to punk. It no longer looked as though he were swimming in a too big shirt. Then Danny put the extra vest on him. This was getting *real.* It seemed to Cecil that he was transformed by the image. He felt ... butch.

"All right!" he said.

Alex stood up and walked over to him. He put one of those big beefy arms around Cecil's shoulders. "Look, just tell me one thing, how much trouble are you in?"

*Bummer!* "So you saw the *Clarion?*" Cecil responded.

"Yeah," Alex responded. "I just want to know what's going to happen to you?"

"I'll have some trouble with my sister. I can deal with it. But tomorrow, okay? I want to deal with it tomorrow. Tonight I just want to go to this place – Franny's – that *everyone* talks about all the time and I want to walk in on the arms of the two best looking hunks in the place. That's the limit. That's all I care about. Honest. Please?"

"Sure," Alex replied in a voice that didn't seem to indicate that he really meant it. "But if there's a problem with it, I want to know. We can help. These assholes, the way they use this disease! I could ..."

"Cool down," Danny said with all the efficient nature of an orderly nurse. He walked over to Alex and began to rub his neck. "He gets very upset when anyone says anything negative about AIDS. *Very* upset."

"Now you know I'm a medical student, I got to tell you, there's reason to get upset," Cecil replied.

"We know, we know," Danny had a blank expression on his face. Somehow it was more threatening than any other Cecil had seen there before, as though it were the cover for something with the intensity of molten lava. "We know how horrible it is, but that's not the same thing as using it as a tool against gay people."

"I should have done something earlier," Alex said to no one in particular. "I should have just stopped this."

"Shhh, shhhh." Danny tried to soothe his lover. He looked at Cecil again. "Alex gets very mad sometimes."

*He's crazy.* Cecil suddenly realized that there was a part of Alex Kane that was certifiably insane. It was some core that held the potential for actual violence he'd already seen happen. Yet, surprisingly, Cecil wasn't frightened.

*Why not?* he wondered. *How do I know that it's never going to turn on me!* But, he did know it wasn't going to.

Franny's was packed. It was a large bar, a series of rooms each with a slightly different decor. The men in it were, without doubt, the most masculine and the most muscular and the most intimidating that Cecil had ever seen all gathered at once place. "Jesus," he said.

"Like it?" Danny asked.

"I'm not sure," Cecil replied.

Alex walked away, saying he was going to get them some

beer.

"Are you very uncomfortable? We can leave," Danny offered. He was honestly concerned that Cecil wouldn't be able to relax here.

"It's so much. I mean, look at them. Big brawny guys ..."

"They're just the regular gay guys. For most of them it's just a show. There are just as many florists and interior decorators here as any other place. And just as many accountants and just as many auto mechanics."

"But this stuff, the leather, the chains ..." The bar was draped with an awesome display of hardware. The music wasn't anything anyone could dance with, but low, deep sounds that seemed to growl from the loud speakers. "These guys mean this?"

"It's a bunch of fantasies, Cecil. That's all. Believe it? I bet some do. To some extent."

"Danny, you got to understand that this is a very strange trip for a black man." It was always so damned difficult to bring up racial issues with whites, even the most friendly and the most intimate. "You have to realize that," he was about to say that he wasn't a separatist or anything like that, but stopped himself; he did not want to apologize for this. "Danny, a bunch of white guys playing at slave and master may seem innocent, and maybe it is, but to a black man, it sure as hell looks a bit too real."

There, it was out.

"Alex has taught me a lot of things, Cecil." Danny at least seemed to understand what the medical student was trying to say. "I sure know that there are things here and in other parts of the gay world you can find that are ... well, at best, they can seem like possibly dangerous ideas.

"Now, you certainly have a right to feel those things. You don't have to stay here. Alex has some work, he's looking into things here, but we can leave. That's not a problem. You can walk out and I'll gladly go with you. Or, you can change things around in your head. You know, nothing says *you* have to be the slave in these men's fantasies. There's nothing that says you can't use the play in a different way. If you want."

"What, me lord it over one of these humpy white guys?" Cecil was incredulous.

"If you wanted to play with it, I doubt you'd have any trouble. You're a pretty hot looking man, you know? And there are certainly a lot of men who are here for reasons different than trying to recreate the old south."

"Danny, it's the same thing if they want a black man to be their master."

"Maybe, I'm not sure. But there are so many of them, Cecil! You got to believe that there are some who just want to have some hot sex. And they're not all white." Danny smiled as a group entered through the front door.

*Now,* thought Cecil, *this is getting too much. Now I can't just argue the thing through because almost all the men are white.*

The men were all black. They were all huge. They were all handsome. They were all so sexy that Cecil thought he'd never, ever recover.

They had on leather vests, and the same patch appeared on the back of each one. It read: THE BROTHERHOOD OF MAN.

Cecil didn't realize how overtly he was staring until one of them just walked up and started talking to him. "Hey, bro', how you doing? I haven't seen that hot bod of yours in here before."

Cecil gulped. The man was at least 6'4". He wore nothing underneath his vest; there was only pure, unhidden black masculinity in the flesh staring back at him. The muscles were ... enormous. They were much larger and bulkier than Alex's. They had clear and sharp definition. They were so wonderful that Cecil just could feel the heat coming from them.

*I am not going to be a wimp.* "I'm doing just fine. Cecil's the name. Yours?" Cecil put out his hand and took the big paw in return and shook.

"Jack. Just call me Jack."

Danny, happy to leave Cupid to his duty – even if he was in full leather tonight – slipped away.

• • •

Jack proved to be something beyond Cecil's imagination. He was … *nice.* He was obviously educated, obviously sensitive. They could talk. They talked about the bar. Cecil admitted he wasn't a regular, but he wasn't ready to go much further. He let Jack think that he knew exactly what was going on here. They talked about being black and gay – the double whammy.

Jack explained that the Brotherhood of Man was a bike club. Just some black gay guys that got together and rode their motorcycles and partied together. Nothing intense, and it certainly wasn't a sex club. "Not," he added with a big smile, "that any of us have anything against sex."

There was some special energy in the air with Jack. Cecil knew it had to do with all the leather and the bare skin and the place they were. He discovered little bits of his fantasy life, things he'd never really brought out and looked at carefully, coming to the surface. There were so many things that had seemed funny or foolish or politically incorrect that were now very real possibilities and very real turn-ons.

There wasn't any doubt about Jack's intentions as they talked. The bigger man would rub up against Cecil, remark on his "hot" outfit. Cecil let him think that pseudo-punk, pseudo-leather gear was natural to him. He could have Jack. More interesting, he could have Jack in ways that he had never dared to ask other guys to do it.

They had talked long enough. "I'd like to see the rest of the place."

"You want to go in the back?" Jack's smile lit up.

"Sure," Cecil said, maintaining his cool composure.

They walked through the crowd, stopping quickly while Jack bought them a couple more beers. Cecil hadn't overlooked the fact that this new man was always insistent on performing those functions – getting the beers, leading the way through the throng of sweaty, good-smelling men. Cecil thought he was picking up some clues.

They were suddenly outdoors. The yard in back of

Franny's was a fenced-in area. The fences were abnormally high. They were obviously built to block out any possible view of the activities that were going on. And Cecil immediately knew that it was a good thing. If Cecil was this unprepared for Franny's patrons' fun and games, god only knew what the neighbors would think of them.

Some were doing sexual acts that Cecil had only read about in his few literary excursions into *Drummer.* One man was tied to a wall, spread-eagle, being belted by another. There were some clusters of bodies, all at least stripped to the waist, where whatever was happening – and Cecil wasn't sure – he did know it would frighten the horses.

"Jeeez-*us!*" He muttered to himself.

He felt Jack's hand on his bare arm. He was being guided into one of the corners of the yard. They got to the wall and stopped, staring at one another. Cecil forced himself to speak calmly. "I don't know what your plans are, mister, but I hope you don't expect me to be doing some of the shit those guys are pulling."

"No, no. We don't have to get that heavy." Jack spoke with a quiet voice. His hand found Cecil's crotch. As much as some of the activity had shocked Cecil, there was plenty that had gotten him going. He was hard and ready.

While he debated just how far he was willing to let Jack go with the S&M stuff – *what would it be like to have a man give your bare butt a good whack?* – he suddenly realized that he had read the script all wrong. Very, very wrong.

Jack was whispering in his ear. "Look, you know, the disease stuff, please, don't come in my mouth. Okay?"

Cecil nodded. He didn't dare say a word. He was sure his voice would have squeaked. Then he watched the enormous torso in front of him as it sank down to its knees. He felt the hands playing with his button fly. He had the sudden sharp sensation of the evening air hitting his bare cock. Then, just as suddenly, there was indescribable warmth engulfing it.

*Oh, man!* He thought he'd shoot in a second. He looked down and saw Jack kneeling in front of him. But it wasn't just that. The man was telegraphing all kinds of signals to him in all kind of ways. Jack had his hands behind his own back. His knees were spread. Cecil saw the clump of keys on Jack's right hand belt loop. *What does that mean!* He desperately tried to remember. Then it came to him. He was the one in charge. He was the one …

In any other situation like this, Cecil would have bent over and mouthed some sweet words, little things about the good feelings he had. But now he was getting into it. So, when he did lean over, he said instead, "You don't seem to have much enthusiasm down there."

The response was electric. Jack grabbed hold of Cecil's hips and *forced* them forward, swallowing all of his hard cock down his throat. Cecil knew enough to be quiet. He knew enough to realize that he had probably just made a great conquest.

"There's a spare room in our suite if you want to carry on with this in a little more … privacy," Danny's voice whispered in Cecil's ear. He felt a room key being slipped into his hand.

Cecil's debut at Franny's was going to be some night.

# XI

Frank was sweating profusely. Even though he'd just taken a cold shower to wash the filth from his skin, he couldn't stop himself from shaking. *What he had seen!*

It was every one of his worst dreams. It was everything sick and disgusting that he had ever imagined in his night-mares. He stared at his typewriter. The sheet was blank. He had to write about it. He had to warn anyone who would ever make the mistake of going into that place.

The bodies, their naked skin streaked with sweat, the ugly leather they wore, the way they did all those things to one another in the courtyard, daring innocent people to walk out there and see their depravity! It was all meaningless!

No. It was not. It had meaning. That was all those crazed people had to look forward to. That was all that could ever come from their perverted search for their sick lust's fulfill-ment.

If he hadn't been so strong, Frank could have fallen into that very trap. Instead of being the good citizen, the journalist with integrity that he was, he could have caved into the most primal and bestial desires and ended up there. Like them.

He felt acid trying to come up and escape from his stomach. It was sickening. It was disgusting. The people of Houston had to be warned.

He began to write. He wrote with the white-hot speed of

someone who was driven, maniacally driven by what he had seen. At one and the same time he understood that he was mixing things together, they were becoming a blur, but they were also the most powerful words he had ever put to paper.

It all came out. The baths. And especially the pig pen they called Franny's. That place. That place where the men had touched him, the crowd forcing him to come in contact with the bare chests of the young men with armbands around their biceps. The place where he walked out into the courtyard and saw white men with black cocks in their mouths. Black men with their big erections spearing the air.

It wasn't just the sex. It wasn't just the honor of men doing those things to men. It was the races doing it to one another. It was as though everything that was *necessary* to keep America good, clean, moral was being destroyed by those scenes in the back of Franny's.

They had to be destroyed. Frank now knew that everything Martin Banks had said was true. They had to be destroyed. They had to be driven back into their closets, at least. No. That wasn't going to do any good any more. There was something here that was beyond redemption.

He knew it because of his own cock. His own erection. He had spent every night and every day of his life since that encounter in college making the god-damned thing stay down. But there, in Franny's, it had been hard as rock. It had wanted to be touched. It had wanted to feel one of those mouths wrapped around it. It had wanted to enter a steamy, oozy asshole. It, it, *IT...*

•   •   •

Frank woke up hours later. He was on his bed. Sweat was still soaking his sheets. But the manuscript was there. His masterpiece. The thing that would make him famous. He had been right all along. Houston was his salvation, his redemption. He had been brought to Houston by a force greater than himself just to write this one piece.

It made up for Harvey Pearson's death. It made up for everything. He didn't have to worry about anything any more.

He felt himself. He now knew what was driving all the homosexuals. This *thing.* He would finish up his task here in Houston. He had more to write. About restaurant workers who were consciously spitting on the food in their kitchens to spread AIDS. About gangs of men who were roaming the streets looking for young boys to rape. About ... About it all. Then he wouldn't need this *thing* any more. He would get a knife and he would remove it. He would remove it and all the pain it had caused him all his life. Then he could finally be free.

There was a knock on the door. Frank went and opened it, dazed by his sleepiness. It was Sam Trident. "Frank, what the hell's happened to you? Everyone down at the paper's in a panic about deadline. You missed tomorrow's ..."

"It's all right. I'm sorry. I just got into my next story. But it's done. It's beautiful. It's going to save Houston."

"Yeah?" There was a sarcastic tone to Sam's voice. "What's left of it. Look, give me the next piece. Lucky I had mine ready to go so Banks could keep up his pace. We just substituted mine in the schedule. Your article goes in tomorrow. Fucker, you probably did it on purpose to get in the Saturday edition. You knew what had happened and you wanted to fire 'em up for the weekend, steal my thunder."

Sam was angry. He obviously felt that Frank had wronged him in some manner that Frank didn't understand. But Frank was too woozy to argue. "What do you mean?" he asked. "Fire who up?"

"Haven't you seen the evening paper? Haven't you watched the news?"

"No, no ... I've been working. I wrote straight through the night, then I fell asleep."

"Frank, I think you better turn on the television set. It's almost time for the eleven o'clock news. If you worked and slept all day, then you got some catching up to do with current events."

Sam took Frank's sheets of typed paper and left.

Frank looked at the clock. The news would be on in fifteen minutes. He took a very fast shower to wake himself up and poured himself a drink. He got it all done just in time to listen to the headlines. The usual plastic commentator was on the air. But all her smiles and all her perfect hairdos weren't going to make this a happy broadcast.

"Mobs continued to rampage through downtown Houston and the nearby Montrose neighborhood, destroying known gay-owned businesses and attacking anyone the crowd thought was homosexual.

"The governor has ordered the mobilization of the National Guard. All available police units have been ..."

Her voice droned on and on. It was perfect. It was right. If the good people of Houston were already this angry, wait until tomorrow. Wait until they saw what he had written about tomorrow.

Suddenly, there was a knock on the door. Frank was angry. The news was just now reporting the fatalities. He wanted to know how many people had been wounded. He would need the statistics. But the knock was too insistent. He finally stood up and went to answer it. "Who's there?" he yelled through the wood.

"Landlord. Quick, you gotta open up. There's some trouble out here."

*I bet there is,* Frank smiled. He yanked open the door and immediately froze. Then, a minute later, he screamed. He screamed and screamed and screamed until there was no air in his lungs.

It couldn't be! It couldn't be! He wouldn't let it be! But there was a body holding on to him so light and the warmth was too much and the sounds of the voice ...

"Frank, Frank, oh my god, Frank, all these years. The mistakes. The things I did to you. The way I was. Frank, I'm so sorry."

And fourteen years too late Randall Landtree was holding Frank Terkel in his arms once more.

# XII

Martin Banks stood in front of his windows overlooking Houston and felt very good. He felt wonderful. This was the way to do it. He could see it now even more clearly since it had begun than he had when he had first thought of the possibility. This was the way.

Beneath him was the usual cityscape. But tonight there were occasionally bright lights sparking the horizon. They were the lights of the fires that the inflamed citizens of Houston had set while they took their vengeance on the queers.

There had been so much good work preceding this. It would have been impossible if there hadn't already been that voter referendum about gay rights. That had started it all. It had given credibility to the idea of hating faggots. There had been so many business people and religious leaders who had condemned the homosexuals that it was easy to take the common man one step further. It had been so easy.

But they were only one target for Martin Banks. Now he'd taught all these people the joys of hating. They would have tasted blood and they wouldn't have been told it was bad. He laughed out loud, even though he was alone in his office, remembering the editorial that one of the other newspapers had run.

There had been a few incidents the night before, barely enough to form a pattern, but there they were. Even that liberal newspaper, so concerned with its good image, had noticed them and the editors were caught in their own prejudice. They had said that the violence had to stop. But they had undercut their message with a longer passage about the responsibility the faggots had in provoking it. *If they had only worked in more civilized ways …*

Banks had enjoyed that. Even the "good" people at the "good" and intelligent newspaper couldn't take a stand in favor of gay rights.

So, now it had begun. He had carefully, so carefully intertwined it all with the foreshadowing of what would follow. The homosexual stories had all purposely implicated blacks. There were plenty of details about the interracial sex in the gay world. There were more than enough hints at the way that AIDS would be spread throughout Houston, the country, the world. First the queers, who deserved it, then they'd give it to the niggers, and then …

But there wouldn't be a *then.* Because the American people would have heard the warnings of Martin Banks. Now his other newspapers were picking up the story. They would repeat the whole thing in every city. By the time he was done, with the wonderful coincidences like that black bitch shooting the managing editor, then they would be finished. Then they would be able to start to make America a place worthy of pride.

Martin Banks wasn't the only one who thought that something was finished. "You *scum!*"

Banks turned at the unexpected and unwelcomed sound. "Who are you?" he demanded in his imperious voice. "Who let you in?"

The man waved away the questions and took one of the seats in front of Banks's desk. He put his face in his right hand for a moment. "There are hundreds of wounded people out there. Hundreds. It's a nightmare."

"It's a cleansing with fire!" Banks responded.

The man's hand uncovered his face. He looked at Banks who couldn't help but respond to the compelling green eyes that seemed to be sending a laser beam of anger right at him. "You really believe that, don't you?"

"Yes, I do."

"Little, sick, deformed men like you – the Napoleons, the Hitlers ..."

"The great men of history." Banks smiled. He turned his back on the intruder and went back to watching what he had come to think of as his own bonfires. "You had better leave. There are guards all over this building. They're armed. They'll ..."

"There are no guards left."

"What?!" Banks spun around to confront this strange man again. "What happened? How could they ..."

"A plane. A plane flies, you know? It carries people. There were some people in Arizona. They got on a plane. They flew. They got off in Houston. There are no more guards. Those people in the plane from Arizona made sure there were no more guards."

Banks was frantic as he picked up his phone and punched in the number of the front desk. He was astonished to hear the voice at the other end answer in Spanish. He couldn't understand the words. "What the hell does that mean in real English?" Banks screamed.

"Gay Liberation Front at your service," the voice replied.

Banks hung up. "You're all too late. You're all too, too late. The fires are burning and they will continue to burn. The hatred is loose. The hatred that will clean the blood of American ..."

"Shut up." The man stood and walked towards Banks. He stopped in front of the desk and now leaned across it. "I should have listened to my instincts about you. I should have listened when my soul told me to exterminate you a long time ago. But, no. I was worried about the example I was going to give to Danny. I mean, the stuff we have to do is very difficult, the decisions are very complex and Danny wasn't ready, I didn't think, to see me make that kind of judgment.

"So I waited. I waited and I tried to be sensible and I

thought maybe I could just get the guys here in Houston to-gether. I worked with some of the bike clubs and I talked to some of the leaders and I did it all the right way. I raised mon-ey and where there wasn't enough to be raised, I got it other ways.

"I was setting a good example. And my good example gave you time to wreak havoc in this city. Those guys hurt! The houses burnt down. The hatred exposed.

"If I had stopped you ...

"If I had known what you were going to do about AIDS ... Don't you understand that these guys have gone through their personal hells and they came out of it on the other side? They had started to build their good lives, they were trying to be good citizens, and then, to have a piece of slime like you use that against them ...?

"That's not a political tool. That's a tragedy. That's not a weapon. That's a horror ..."

"They deserve it. You all deserve it. It's nature's way of teaching you the lessons you need to learn. That you are an abomination ..."

"*You* are the *abomination!*"

Banks stood back. The man's eyes had seemed to change color, that green had become stronger, the way his face was curled up in hatred and anger, and ... the tears. The man was crying tears.

"To have you use AIDS as a political weapon is the most disgusting thing yet. Have you seen the wards? The lines of dying young men? The agony? The way they're treated by society?"

The man stood up. He wouldn't make a single move to wipe away those tears that were now disgusting Martin Banks. They were a sign of weakness and Banks hated weak-ness, he loathed weakness. But the man seemed to wear them as a sign of his honor. They were still there on his face when he began to move around the desk.

He began to talk again. Now he was looking at the sight of the fires that had been so alluring to Banks. "You set us all back a lot. I'm at fault. I was wrong. I shouldn't have given you enough time. But I did. It will take more time to make up the difference."

The man swept out his hand and it burst through the huge plate glass window. Banks knew that no one should be able to do that. No one. That glass was made to withstand ...

But the man interrupted his thoughts. He had grabbed hold of Banks. Strong winds were swirling through the office. He had taken hold of Banks and now he was dragging him towards the opening. He was screaming something at Banks. But the skyscraper was one of the tallest in Houston and it was one that stood in such a way that the winds at this altitude and at this angle were powerful.

Then Banks was hurtling through the air. He had been thrown out the window by a man who was so weak that he cried and then, only then, and only for a short period of time, he understood what the man had said. "I've done this before. I will have to do this again."

And then Martin Banks couldn't hear anything more. Ever.

# XIII

Randall Landtree sat impatiently in the waiting room. He hated hospitals. This one was the worst he had ever dreamt of. Oh, it was clean and modern and well constructed and had all the little signs of being top of the line – the real art, the good magazines, all that. It was the best mental hospital in the world, so they said. So they said.

"Mr. Landtree." The nurse/receptionist was standing in front of him.

"Yes."

"Dr. Hilton will see you now."

Randall stood up and followed the woman in the white, crisp uniform down a corridor. She opened a door, finally, and signaled him to enter. He did, and found himself staring at a kindly looking old man, perhaps in his late sixties. The man, wearing that white smock that identified the psychiatrists here, stood up and offered him a hand.

They went through the formalities and Landtree sat down in the chair he'd indicated. Then came that awkward silence that always seemed to happen when you're sitting in front of an authority figure. *Strange,* Randall thought, *I'm a thirty-five-year-old success in every way and here is a doctor who makes me feel like some kind of twerp.*

"I suppose you want me to begin," Randall finally said.

"It will have to happen eventually," Dr. Hilton smiled.

Randall couldn't help but relax. The doctor seemed to be honestly warm and trying to be comforting. "I think I should be here. Not him."

"He's had a great shock. More than that. Things must have placed him under great stress for quite some time. You know he's tried to kill himself."

"You don't have to be so easy going when you tell me that," Randall answered sarcastically.

"We haven't the time for being very nice, do we? He's done that and he's repeatedly attempted to castrate himself. A shock may have set this off, but there must have been something that came before it."

"I told you, I'm the one who's responsible."

"And just what did you do to make you feel that you had so very much power over this man?"

"I ... I denied him. Like in the Bible. The way the disciple turned away three times. We were young, in college. We were discovered ... having sex. I lied. I told them that I was just using him. I ... joined them."

"They hurt him?"

Randall sat up and looked Hilton in the eye. "They raped him, many times. Then they ... we urinated on him. I never spoke to him again."

Hilton nodded. "I have a feeling – from the way that you just spoke – that you have never told anyone else this story."

"No, never. I was always too ashamed."

"You've carried around a great burden, Mr. Landtree, for a number of years. It must have taken its toll, just as your friend has had his own problems with the weight he was carrying. But you are not the only person to blame. I won't sit here and give you any sort of pastoral blessing. I won't tell you your actions made no difference. But there had to have been other things in his life ..."

"I've talked to his wife. The other people – the ones I spoke to when I first brought him here, asked me to. She told me that he had been ... impotent was her word. That was her grounds for divorce. That, and she had known about what had happened. She gave it as testimony on the stand during their divorce trial."

Dr. Hilton shook his head as though he understood something more now.

"Mr. Landtree," he finally began again, "I'm not sure that your paying for this treatment here is going to do you much good. It will not take care of the guilt you feel, nor of the feelings you've not dealt with about this ... incident. I think it's important for you to realize that you can't use your money to recover whatever it is that you lost fourteen years ago."

"I know that." Randall looked away. "I know that. I'm in my own counseling now, Dr. Hilton. I knew I'd need to face something before he ... before he comes out."

"He may not. You have to understand that. He may not."

Landtree closed his eyes tightly. "If he comes out, I need to be well too. I need to have this behind me. I need a lot of things.

"It's not just the guilt, doctor. That's the thing you'll never understand. It's there, you're right, we should look it in the face. It can't be ignored any more. But there's something more.

"For fourteen years I not only have never forgotten Frank Terkel. For fourteen years I've remembered one moment we shared. For every second of hating myself for what I did, there was another one – every day of my life – when I remembered that he was the first man I'd ever loved. And I never got to tell him that.

"Is guilt my motivation for all this? Perhaps. But Frank and I have some things to do for one another, Dr. Hilton. We have time to make up for. We have ...

"I honestly think I've always been in love with him. From the beginning. Ever since the first day we met in college."

Randall's eyes were glistening. He felt some new kind of freedom. Having finally said those words relieved him of some burden.

Dr. Hilton studied him for a moment and then stood offering his hand. "We'll need a lot of help from you, Mr. Landtree.

We consider you a very important part of Frank Terkel's therapy."

Randall stood and accepted the handshake. "You mean that? You mean that I can become something good for him after all these years?" The tears were coming faster now.

"I mean that very much."

# XIV

Cecil Myers sat in his apartment blankly watching the television set. He wasn't even really sure what the movie was tonight. Just some "B" grade thing that was taking up the silence in the room.

He was still in some kind of state of shock. There had been so much that'd happened in such a short period of time. So much ...

He'd spent the day talking to the lawyers Danny and Alex had arranged for Sandra's defense. They seemed to think that there would be no problem. If there had ever been justification for using temporary insanity, this was it.

Sandra had lost herself in her brother. The sight of his photograph in the newspaper had been too much for her. It was *her* future that she had seen destroyed. The lawyers had told him something else. They didn't always enjoy the idea of using this defense, they had seen some awfully evil people go free because of it. This time, though, there was no hesitation on their part. This time the term "justifiable" had meaning for them.

Cecil wasn't really confident in the judicial system. He knew too well that blacks seldom got a fair shake. At least this one time this one black woman was going to have the most powerful trial lawyers in Houston on her side.

It was too bad that Danny and Alex couldn't fix up

Houston as easily as they had fixed up Sandra. The city was desperately in need of healing. The riots had been vicious, exposing a level of intolerance and hatred that no one had ever really understood before. Parts of the Montrose looked like pictures of Berlin after the Second World War.

There were crowded wards in all the hospitals inhabited by injured gay men who'd fallen victim to the storming mob that had invaded what gays had thought was a safe space, a place where homosexuals wouldn't have to worry about the prejudice of straights. But Cecil, who had grown up in the black ghetto, understood that when the man wanted to get you, he got you.

Now the gay men of Houston had learned that lesson.

They had also taught some lessons of their own. They had fought back. They had done everything they could to protect their homes and their loved ones and the unknown men that they were just beginning to learn how to call "brother."

Jack had done it. Cecil remembered standing beside the huge black man who had led the defense of one block of gay homes. Jack had been *awesome.* He had been simply awesome. It had been something else to watch a man who was both black and gay doing that, standing up for his own in whatever way he had to. Cecil had been ... proud. And he had caught himself falling a little bit in love.

But right now, Cecil just felt a whole lot alone. Sandra was going to have to stay in jail till her trial. An accused murderer couldn't get bail. Danny and Alex had disappeared. They had just *gone.* Deep down inside Cecil knew it had something to do with the strange death of Martin Banks.

Cecil snorted blankly at the television when he thought of the way that so many people had revised the little bit of history that had ended up in Houston's most hate-filled hour. They said, now, that Banks had been distraught by the violence he'd unleashed. He had, they said, committed suicide in grief and remorse.

No one did what Banks had done and felt badly about it afterwards. No one.

Cecil stood up and went to get a cola from the fridge. He idly popped the top and returned to his seat in front of the TV. It had to have been Danny and Alex. And they must have had something to do with the scene at the *Clarion* Building as well. No one ever again heard about the small army of militant gay Hispanics who'd stormed the skyscraper-turned-fortress.

All the film and videotape that had been taken of the incident had been destroyed. There was no way to identify just which people had done it. There were reports of some long-haired Hispanic leading the charge. Someone had told Cecil he'd screamed out, *"¡Viva la Revolución!"* when he'd begun the fight that had scared the shit out of the hired men that Banks had guarding the place.

Just what revolution was that guy talking about!

There were a lot more angry and out gays in the barrios of Houston nowadays, but none of them would own up to taking part in the charge on the *Clarion* headquarters.

*If there's anything strange that went on, you know deep down that Alex and Danny had something to do with it,* Cecil thought to himself.

There was one part of this loneliness that had nothing to do with anything strange. It was so fucking typical. It was so damned predictable. And he had no one to blame but his own self.

There was a slip of paper in his wallet. It had a phone number on it. All he had to do was call Jack. That was it. Simply pick up the phone and dial the number. But he wouldn't do it. There was medical school. There was his independence. There was his ...

Cecil had tried it with other men. It just didn't work. They didn't understand that he was medical student, for Christ's sake. He had plans, a future. There weren't that many men who would understand that his future was as a professional. Jack, big, black Jack, was probably one of them. He probably had some simple nine to five job and he probably wanted some nice guy who'd be there every night and watch the tube with him and fuck and that would be it.

Cecil couldn't call Jack and be cruel about it. The sex had been fabulous. The way that Jack had let him live out his fantasies and the touch of that proudly handsome black man had been just fucking wonderful. But, Cecil assumed, Jack shouldn't be enticed into believing that Cecil would be there in that way. The demands that his academics made on him ...

He put it out of his mind. No. He'd leave Jack alone. As though his thoughts were being telegraphed to the television set, Cecil swore he saw Jack's picture. He took a swallow of his cola and calmly noted that it was the same brand as the commercial. His mind was playing tricks. Jack on a commercial? He giggled at the thought. Then he looked back at the screen.

"Jack Jackson, star defenseman for the Seattle Seahawks, for Lone Star Cola ..."

*"WHAT!"* Cecil jumped up so quickly he spilled his can of soft drink on the rug. *"What!"* he repeated. He tore his wallet from his pants and opened it violently. He found the slip of paper. He dialed the number and listened to the phone ring on the other end.

"Hello."

"What the hell do you mean – Jack Jackson!!! What the hell is this? You're just some big black man standing in a gay bar and fighting cracker assholes on the street, and then you tell me you're Jack Jackson and you show your face on my television and ..."

"Cecil? Is that you, man? Cecil, calm down."

"Calm down! Get your black ass over here and explain this shit to me. Jack Jackson! I never watch football on television but I know that name. You're a fucking football star. You're ..."

"I'm yours is what I am," the voice said on the other end of the line, "and if what you want is my ass over there right now, it's on its way. I thought you'd never call."

# XV

"So, you got yourself a football player?" Danny thought the whole thing was amusing.

It was a month later and Cecil was sitting beside Danny on a dock jutting out into a lake in New Hampshire. They were both naked. No need for swim suits in this isolated location.

The air carried a harbinger of autumn. Now, the sun was bright and warm. Being naked outdoors was perfectly comfortable, but there was something that let Cecil know that the leaves here would be turning color and days of swimming were closing.

"Isn't it the end?" Cecil answered Danny. "I mean *damn!* I was thinking so many things, some of them I'm not proud of. Here I am, this proud Afro-American and I'm assuming that any black gay man in a bar was some kind of mindless idiot.

"Do you know Jack could have taken a Rhodes Scholarship instead of going into pro football? He says he's going to go back to graduate school later, though. After he's had fun and earned a bunch of cash from the sports.

"The whole thing was just too perfect, Danny. I mean, everything I was so worried about and so seriously concerned about ... *poof!* There I was convinced I'd never meet a black man who'd understand what my academics mean to me. I get a Phi Beta Kappa graduate of Berkeley. I worry about some man wanting to move in on me, take away my study time. Hell, I'm lucky if I get him a day a week with his practice and travel schedule. Or, maybe it was going to be a man who would want to get married. Huh, I'll never get that one to settle down."

"Oh, I don't know about that."

Cecil looked over at Danny and saw that he was gazing out over the lake with a smile on his face. Well, who did know about that, anyway? It wasn't a pressing point right now.

What was pressing was the closeness of Danny's body. They had just come in from a long swim. There were still beads of water on Danny's flesh. Some of them caught in his chest hair were reflecting the sunlight that was beating down on them. Then Danny stood up and stretched.

Cecil was still sitting. *Oh my god!* There it was, right at his eye level. That beautiful young cock just standing out there, the hair nearly obliterating his vision of the testicles underneath, and, *oh my god!*

Cecil felt his head whirling. His time with Jack had loosened up his head, let him think of things that had been unthinkable before. Right now the image in his mind was that Italian cock in his mouth. He could just ...

*No, no,* he told himself. He was sure Danny and Alex wouldn't do that. Nor had he and Jack done that either. Pure monogamous bliss. Wasn't it?

Then Cecil stood and the two of them walked up the path towards the wonderful cabin that Danny and Alex shared. Danny was totally nonchalant about being naked. Cecil tried to make believe he was just as comfortable. But Danny wasn't going to leave him in that peaceful state long. "You want to play?"

"Play?" Cecil said. He knew damn well what Danny meant. He just didn't believe it.

"Sure." Danny put an arm around Cecil's waist and drew him closer as they walked up to the house. "No pressure. I just like to ... play with my friends sometimes. Alex doesn't mind. Would Jack?"

"I ... um ... I don't know." That was the truth.

"Why don't you find out? If it's a problem ..."

"I'll find out." Cecil thought he'd better do it damned fast. The touch of Danny's skin, still cool from the water, was going to give his desires away with stunning physical demonstration if he didn't watch it.

They walked up the step onto the front porch that was built on the front of the wood frame house. Danny stopped, his smile grew more than a little bit. He had seen something through the window. "I don't think Jack minds," he laughed.

Cecil walked over and observed for himself. There were Jack and Alex on the floor. They were just as naked as the other two. They were slowly, wonderfully, working on one another, each had his head in the other's crotch.

It was a stunning sight. There was the fact that they were both such incredibly beautiful men, especially their bodies. The tension of their movements highlighted their big muscles. But there was another more powerful part of the image.

Alex, even at the end of the summer, was still very pale. There was so very little hair on his body that the white of his skin was strongly accentuated. Jack was a deeply ebony-skinned man. The contrast of their flesh was amazingly provocative and sensual. It was beautiful.

So much so that Cecil's earlier worry was becoming a rampant concern. He felt Danny's hand take hold of his erection. He turned and Danny was waiting for him. After all those times looking at those beautiful red lips, now they were touching his own. He could feel the tight hair on Danny's chest rub against him and he sensed the heat coming from Danny's own crotch.

They somehow made the maneuver onto the porch floor with a great deal of grace and there were no wrong moves and no awkwardness when they began to explore each other with hands and open mouths.

It was wonderful. Touching a friend, having sex with a buddy. It was tender and loving, easy and sexy. It was something of the moment that they shared.

When it was done, Cecil was sitting with his back against the porch wall. He was only barely catching his breath. Then Alex and Jack walked out. That mahogany skin against that whiteness was standing right beside him. "Pretty good vacation, huh?" Jack asked with a smirk on his face.

"Oh? Better than time at home?" Cecil wasn't quite clear about this multiple stuff yet.

Danny had walked over and wrapped himself around Alex. With his head buried in his lover's neck he said, "I don't know if it has anything to do with anything being better than anything else."

Jack reached down and picked up the much smaller Cecil in his arms. "We already got the most alternative lifestyle possible. Travel and study, little sex games ..."

"Little sex games. Shall I tell them about last night?"

"We heard," Alex said.

"Oh." Well, no need for details about *that.*

"Anyone ready for dinner?" Danny finally said.

"We're just going to be that comfortable? Two black guys and two whites. Walking around naked. Having sex with each other as though the fact we're different races and undressed and have lovers doesn't make a damn bit of difference? We're just going to do this and we're not going to be strange about it? We're not going to let the little guilt trips move in on us? This is unreal!"

"Not if you let it happen. If you don't see the barriers, then they don't exist. This society's got enough of them that are real to last you the rest of your life. No reason to keep the others in there too." Jack shrugged when he'd finished his speech.

"Hell," Cecil said, "you make it sound like there could be a happy ending."

"Don't see any reason not to make it happen."

It turned out to be a *very* good vacation.

**JOHN PRESTON**

Born in Portland, Maine, John Preston was an influential author of fiction and nonfiction, dealing mostly with issues in gay life. He was a pioneer in the early gay rights movement in Minneapolis. He helped found one of the earliest gay community centers in the United States, edited two newsletters devoted to sexual health, and served as editor of *The Advocate* in 1975.

He was the author or editor of nearly fifty books, including such erotic landmarks as *Mr. Benson* and *I Once Had a Master and Other Tales of Erotic Love*. Other works include *Franny, the Queen of Provincetown*, *The Big Gay Book: A Man's Survival Guide for the Nineties*, *Personal Dispatches: Writers Confront AIDS*, and *Hometowns: Gay Men Write About Where They Belong*.

Preston's writing was part of a movement in the 1970s and 1980s toward higher literary quality in gay erotic fiction. He was an outspoken advocate of the artistic and social worth of erotic writings, delivering a lecture at Harvard

University entitled "My Life as a Pornographer". His writings caused controversy when he was one of several gay and lesbian authors to have their books confiscated at the border by Canada Customs. Testimony regarding the literary merit of his novel *I Once Had a Master* helped a Vancouver LGBT bookstore, Little Sister's Book and Art Emporium, to partially win a case against Canada Customs in the Canadian Supreme Court in 2000.

Preston served as a journalist and essayist throughout his life. He penned a column for Lambda Book Report called "Preston on Publishing." His nonfiction anthologies, which collected essays by himself and others on everyday aspects of gay and lesbian life, won him the Lambda Literary Award and the American Library Association's Stonewall Book Award. He also wrote the "Alex Kane" adventure novels about gay characters. These books, which included *Sweet Dreams*, *Golden Years*, and *Deadly Lies*, combined action-story plots with an exploration of issues such as the problems facing gay youth.

Preston was among the first writers to popularize the genre of safe sex stories, editing a safe sex anthology entitled Hot Living in 1985. He helped to found the AIDS Project of Southern Maine. In the late 1980s, he discovered that he himself was HIV positive. He died of AIDS complications on April 28, 1994, aged 48, at his home in Portland.

# About ReQueered Tales

In the heady days of the late 1960s, when young people in many western countries were in the streets protesting for a new, more inclusive world, some of us were in libraries, coffee shops, communes, retreats, bedrooms and dens plotting something even more startling: literature – highbrow and pulp – for an explicitly gay audience. Specifically, we were craving to see our gay lives – in the closet, in the open, in bars, in dire straits and in love – reflected in mystery stories, sci-fi and mainstream fiction. Hercule Poirot, that engaging effete Belgian creation of Agatha Christie might have been gay ... Sherlock Holmes, to all intents and purposes, was one woman shy of gay ... but where were the genuine gay sleuths, where the reader need not read between the lines?

Beginning with Victor J Banis's "Man from C.A.M.P." pulps in the mid-60s – riotous romps spoofing the craze for James Bond spies – readers were suddenly being offered George Baxt's Pharoah Love, a black gay New York City detective, and a real turning point in Joseph Hansen's gay California insurance investigator, Dave Brandstetter, whose world weary Raymond Chandleresque adventures sold strongly and have never been out of print.

Over the next three decades, gay storytelling grew strongly in niche and mainstream publishing ventures. Even with the huge public crisis – as AIDS descended on the gay community beginning in the early 1980s – gay fiction flourished. Stonewall Inn, Alyson Publications, and others nurtured authors and readers ... until mainstream success seemed to come to a halt. While Lambda Literary Foundation had started to recognize work in annual awards about 1990, mainstream publishers began to have cold feet. And then, with the rise of e-books in the new millennium which enabled a new self-publishing industry ... there was both an avalanche of new talent coming to market and burying of print authors who did not cross the divide.

The result?

Perhaps forty years of gay fiction – and notably gay and lesbian mystery, detective and suspense fiction – has been teetering on the brink of obscurity. Orphaned works, orphaned authors, many living and some having passed away – with no one to make the case for their creations to be returned to print (and e-print!). General fiction and non-fiction works embracing gay lives, widely celebrated upon original release, also languished as mainstream publishers shifted their focus.

Until now. That is the mission of ReQueered Tales: to keep in circulation this treasure trove of fantastic fiction. In an era of ebooks, everything of value ought to be accessible. For a new generation of readers, these mystery tales, and works of general fiction, are full of insights into the gay world of the 1960s, '70s, '80s and '90s. For those of us who lived through the period, they are a delightful reminder of our youth and reflect some of our own struggles in growing up gay in those heady times.

We are honored, here at ReQueered Tales, to be custodians shepherding back into circulation some of the best gay and lesbian fiction writing and hope to bring many volumes to the public, in modestly priced, accessible editions, worldwide, over the coming years.

So please join us on this adventure of discovery and rediscovery of the rich talents of writers of recent years as the PIs, cops and amateur sleuths battle forces of evil with fierceness, humor and sometimes a pinch of love.

### The ReQueered Tales Team

*Justene Adamec • Alexander Inglis • Matt Lubbers-Moore*

# *Mysteries from* ReQueered Tales

### Sweet Dreams / Golden Years
*John Preston*

**The Alex Kane Missions, Books 1 & 2 –** Meet Alex Kane. In Vietnam, the only lover he had known had been killed by a homophobic coward. With his physical prowess and the financial backing of his former lover's family Kane's sorrow turned to action, and he is resolved to fight back against anyone, anywhere who dares to challenge the dreams of gay men.

In *Sweet Dreams*, someone was daring to mess with young gay men in Boston. Danny Fortelli, a high school senior and superb gymnast, gets caught up in a drugs-and-prostitution ring exploiting gay youth. Boston's South End had become the epicenter of violence driven by a corrupt elite. Enter Alex Kane to alter their plans forever.

In *Golden Years*, Joe Talbot, long retired and now widowed, dreams of an easier life in a gay retirement community that sounds too good to be true. But when his young friend Sam, left behind in New York, begins to suspect the "golden agers" are being mistreated, the news reaches Alex Kane's financier. Kane jumps into action, gaining the support of a local cowboy plucked right out of the Old West. These evil doers won't know what hit them when Alex Kane and his Cowboy ride into town!

A celebrated series of superhero adventure stories written for a general audience by bad boy John Preston whose journalism and fictional writings brought leather and bondage scene mainstream. This new edition includes a foreword by Philip Gambone (*As Far As I Can Tell: Finding My Father In World War II*).

"The first of what is to be a series on the adventures of gay avenger Alex Kane is both fun to read and uplifting. Any culture needs richness of mythos in order to grow. Preston's story is a step toward filling a deep need for gay dreams."
— *The Advocate*

## Let's Get Criminal
*Lev Raphael*

**A Nick Hoffman / Academic Mystery, Book 1** – Nick Hoffman has everything he has ever wanted: a good teaching job, a nice house, and a solid relationship with his lover, Stefan Borowski, a brilliant novelist at the State University of Michigan. But when Perry Cross shows up, Nick's peace of mind is shattered. Not only does he have to share his office with the nefarious Perry, who managed to weasel his way into a tenured position without the right qualifications, he also discovers that Perry played a destructive role in Stefan's past. When Perry turns up dead, Nick wonders if Stefan might be involved, while the campus police force is wondering the same about Nick.

> "*Let's Get Criminal* is a delightful romp in the wonderfully petty and backbiting world of academia. Well-drawn characters make up a delicious list of suspects and victims." — Faye Kellerman

> "Reading *Let's Get Criminal* is like sitting down for a good gossip with an old friend. Its instant intimacy and warmth provides clever and sheer fun." — Marissa Piesman

Originally published in 1996, the first book in the Nick Hoffman Academic Mystery series is now back in print. This edition contains a new foreword by the author.

## In the Game
*Nikki Baker*

**A Virginia Kelly Mystery, Book 1** – When businesswoman Virginia Kelly meets her old college chum Bev Johnson for drinks late one night, Bev confides that her lover, Kelsey, is seeing another woman. Ginny had picked up that gossip months ago, but she is shocked when the next morning's papers report that Kelsey was found murdered behind the very bar where Ginny and Bev had met. Worried that her friend could be implicated, Ginny decides to track down Kelsey's killer and contacts a lawyer, Susan Coogan. Susan takes an immediate, intense liking to Ginny, complicating Ginny's relationship with her live-in lover. Meanwhile Ginny's inquiries heat up when she learns the Feds suspected Kelsey of embezzling from her employer.

> "The auspicious debut of a black writer who brings us a sharp, funny and on-the-mark murder mystery."
> — *Northwest Gay & Lesbian Reader*

> "An entertaining assortment of female characters makes Baker's debut promising" — *Publishers Weekly*

> "It has adventure, romance, and some of the best internal dialogue anywhere." — Megan Casey

Nikki Baker is the first African-American author in the lesbian mystery genre and her protagonist, Virginia Kelly is the first African-American lesbian detective in the genre. Interwoven into the narrative are observations on the intersectionality of being a woman, an African-American, and a lesbian in a "man's" world of finance and life in general.

First published to acclaim in 1991, this new edition features a foreword by the author.

## The Always Anonymous Beast
*Lauren Wright Douglas*

**A Caitlin Reece Mystery, Book 1** – Val Frazier, Victoria's star TV anchorwoman, is Caitlin's newest client. She is the victim of a viciously homophobic blackmailer who has discovered her relationship with Tonia Konig. Tonia is a lesbian-feminist professor, an outspoken, passionately committed proponent of nonviolence. She is enraged by her own helplessness, she is outraged by Caitlin's challenge to her most fundamental beliefs, and by Caitlin herself, whom she considers "a thug".

As Caitlin stalks the blackmailer and his accomplices through the byways of the city of Victoria, she uncovers ever darker layers of danger surrounding Tonia. And she struggles against a new and altogether unwanted complication: she is increasingly attracted to the woman who despises her.

"A very accomplished first novel, which is distinguishable by an elegant flair for description and an obvious love of the language." — Karen Axness, *Feminist Bookstore News*

"Douglas' book is snappily written, peppered with wit and literary allusions, and filled with original characters."
— Sherri Paris, *The Women's Review of Books*

Douglas's debut novel in 1987 began a six part series for Caitlin Reece. This new edition includes an introduction by the author and a foreword by legendary Katherine V. Forrest.

And don't miss ...

**Ninth Life:** Caitlin is hired by a woman code-named Shrew, to pick up a package. Caitlin is sickened to the depths of her being by the contents of the package: a blind and maimed cat, and photographs of animal experimentation. And now Shrew is dead. As a member of the militant animal rights organization Ninth Life, she had infiltrated Living World, a cosmetics company. The other members of Ninth Life suspect she was betrayed by someone within their own ranks and murdered because of what she learned.

## A Body to Dye For
*Grant Michaels*

**A Stan Kraychik Mystery, Book 1** – Stan "Vannos" Kraychik isn't your everyday Boston hairdresser. Manager of Snips Salon, which is owned by best bud (and occasional nemesis) Nicole, Stan thought this day was an ordinary one. A delivery van backed into the salon's rear driveway and accidentally spilled gallons of conditioner, leaving Stan and hunky Roger) embracing in a gooey mess trying to staunch the flow, with little success as they slid and slipped with Nicole watching on with rolling eyes. Later Roger is found murdered.

Stan's client, Calvin Redding, who owns the apartment where Roger's body was found, can't explain why the body is dressed in little more than bowties. Enter Lieutenant Branco, dark, muscular, Italian, (straight) of Boston PD Homicide who immediately suspects everyone, especially Stan. In an attempt to clear his name, Stan travels to California, takes up mountain climbing, eavesdropping, spying, schmoozing, and a little bit of schtupping, all in an attempt to find the truth.

Grant Michaels' zany series of adventures starring Stan Kraychik garnered multiple Lambda Literary Awards including a 1991 nomination for Best Gay Men's Mystery. For this new edition, Carl Mesrobian reminisces about his brother Grant in an exclusive foreword, and Neil S. Plakcy provides an introduction of appreciation.


And don't miss ...

**Love You to Death**: Stan visits a chocolate factory after a patron drops dead at a chi-chi cocktail party

**Dead on Your Feet**: Stan's new boyfriend, choreographer Rafik, is accused of murder

**Mask for a Diva**: Stan nabs a gig as wig master to a summer opera festival but the final curtain for one star comes down early

**Time to Check Out**: Stan takes a holiday to Key West but a dead bodies turns up anyway

**Dead as a Doornail**: In the midst of renovating his new Boston brownstone, Stan becomes the (unintended?) murder target

## Sunday's Child
*Edward O. Phillips*

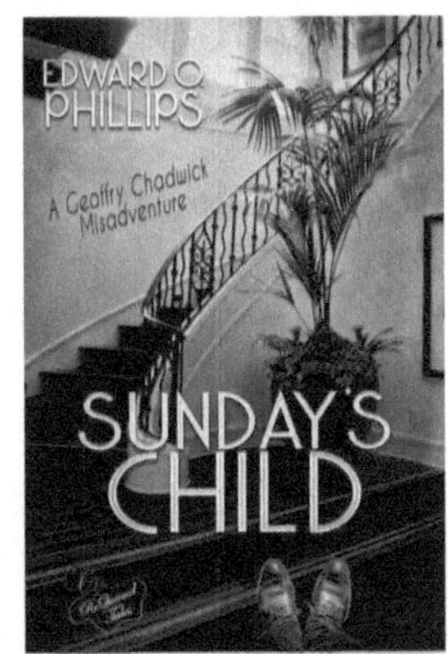

**A Geoffry Chadwick Misadventure, Book 1** – Lawyer Geoffry Chadwick is 50, Canadian, single, gay and, after a brief struggle with a hustler who tries to shake him down, a murderer. Herein lies the device for this macabre, funny, first novel. Although Geoffry must dispose of the body – which he does by dropping off sections of it around town at night – the trauma of the murder affords him the opportunity to reminisce and ruminate: on the recent termination of his affair with a history teacher; on the not-so-recent deaths of his wife and daughter; on the alcoholism of his mother; on growing old; on being gay. The visit of a nephew and the New Year's festivities only serve to intensify his thoughts. Although Chadwick is abrasively disdainful early on, he is fascinating when he loosens up. Phillips keeps the reader hopping with throwaway quotations from Donne and scatological references and puns.

First published in 1981, and a Books in Canada First Novel nominee, this new edition contains a foreword by Alexander Inglis.

And don't miss ...

**Buried on Sunday**: "One of the problems with weekends in the country" says Geoffry Chadwick's genial host in *Buried on Sunday,* "is that people feel free to drop in unannounced." And sometimes that includes criminals on the lam: forget the hors d'oeuvres, everyone is now hostage. Winner of the coveted Arthur Ellis Best Novel Award from the Crime Writers of Canada.

**Sunday Best**: Geoffry gets roped into planning a wedding for his niece Jennifer, but the groom has closet issues and a sexy latino chauffeur has a mixed agenda. Then there is widowed Montreal socialite Lois, mother to the groom, who casts her net for Geoffry ...

**Working on Sunday**: Geoffry Chadwick has a stalker. But between avoiding Christmas parties, gift shopping, moving his mother into a senior living facility, handling his recently widowed sister, and dealing with the loss of his long-term boyfriend Patrick, Geoffry Chadwick does not have time for a stalker.

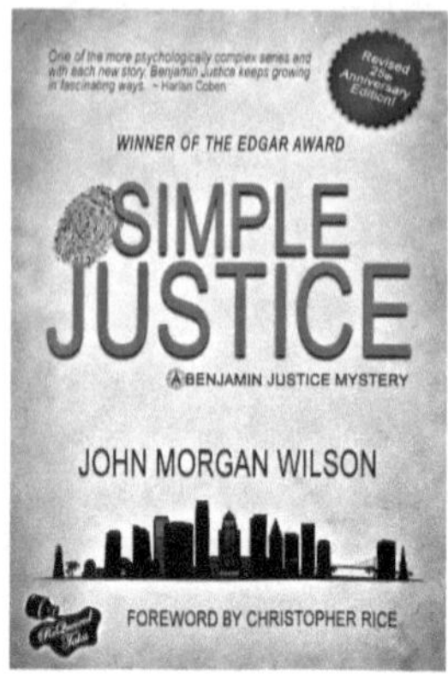


## Simple Justice
*John Morgan Wilson*

**A Benjamin Justice Mystery, Book 1** – It's 1994, an election year when violent crime is rampant, voters want action, and politicians smell blood. When a Latino teenager confesses to the murder of a pretty-boy cokehead outside a gay bar in L.A., the cops consider the case closed. But Benjamin Justice, a disgraced former reporter for the Los Angeles Times, sees something in the jailed boy others don't. His former editor, Harry Brofsky, now toiling at the rival Los Angeles Sun, surprises Justice from his alcoholic seclusion to help neophyte reporter Alexandra Templeton dig deeper into the story. But why would a seemingly decent kid confess to a brutal gang initiation killing if he wasn't guilty? And how can Benjamin Justice possibly be trusted, given his central role in the Pulitzer scandal that destroyed his career?

Snaking his way through shadowy neighborhoods and dubious suspects, he's increasingly haunted by memories of his lover Jacques, whose death from AIDS six years earlier precipitated his fall from grace. As he unravels emotionally, Templeton attempts to solve the riddle of his dark past and ward off another meltdown as they race against a critical deadline to uncover and publish the truth.

"Wilson keeps the emotional as well as forensic suspense up through the very last sentence. The final scene is not only a satisfying explanation of the crime, but a riveting study of the erotic cruelty of justice." — *The Harvard Gay and Lesbian Review*

Awarded an Edgar by Mystery Writers of America for Best First Novel on initial release, this 25th Anniversary edition has been revised by the author. A foreword for the 2020 edition by Christopher Rice (*Bone Music*) is included.

# *More from* ReQueered Tales

## Like People in History
*Felice Picano*

Solid, cautious Roger Sansarc and flamboyant, mercurial Alistair Dodge are second cousins who become lifelong friends when they first meet as nine-year-old boys in 1954. Their lives constantly intersect at crucial moments in their personal histories as each discovers his own unique – and uniquely gay – identity. Their complex, tumultuous, and madcap relationship endures against 40 years of history and their involvement with the handsome model, poet, and decorated Vietnam vet Matt Loguidice, whom they both love. Picano chronicles and celebrates gay life and subculture over the last half of the twentieth century: from the legendary 1969 gathering at Woodstock to the legendary parties at Fire Island Pines in the 1970s, from Malibu Beach in its palmiest surfer days to San Francisco during its gayest era, from the cities and jungles of South Vietnam during the war to Manhattan's Greenwich Village and Upper East Side during the 1990s AIDS war.

> "It's the heroic and funny saga of the last three decades by someone who saw everything and forgot nothing." — Edmund White

> "Harrowing and sad, and very funny, *Like People in History* manages to bridge the unnerving chasm between the queer present and the gay past." — Andrew Holleran

In a book that could have been written only by one who lived it and survived to tell, Picano weaves a powerful saga of four decades in the lives of two men and their lovers, relatives, friends, and enemies. Tragic, comic, sexy, and romantic, filled with varied and colorful characters, *Like People in History* is both extraordinarily moving and supremely entertaining.

Published to acclaim in 1995, winner of the Ferro-Grumley Award for Best Novel, this 25th Anniversary edition for 2020 features a new foreword by Richard Burnett and an afterword by the author.

## Second Son
*Robert Ferro*

Mark Valerian, the second son in the Valerian family, is ill, but determined to live life to the fullest – and live forever if he can. When he discovers Bill Mackey, a young theatrical designer who is also suffering from this disease neither wants to name, he also finds the lover of his dreams.

Together they develop an incredible plan to survive that will take them to Europe, to rustic Maine, and finally to the wonderful seaside summer mansion of the Valerian family, where father and son confront the painful ties of kinship ... and the joyous bonds of love.

"*Second Son* is transcendently beautiful; exquisitely written, exquisitely restrained. Its skillfully drawn characters come alive with an incandescent power as they struggle to preserve the romance, the passion, the tenderness that is vital to body and spirit. The accomplishment of *Second Son* reminds us of what literature has always been about – the deep examination of the soul. Rich, poignant, unforgettable, it leaves one with a rare feeling of having been in touch for a little while with the things that really matter." — Anne Rice

"I admired *The Family of Max Desir*. I love *Second Son*. The surprising story of the love between two men threatened by illness is full of fine authentic details and broader realizations about the human condition. Ferro's new work is entirely original, affecting, and yet strangely upbeat and heartening." — Doris Grumbach

Originally published in 1988, it was Ferro's final novel, completed in the months leading to his death from AIDS as he cared for his lover Michael Grumley. This new edition contains a foreword by Tom Cardamone (*Crashing Cathedrals: Edmund White by the Book*).

## Life Drawing
*Michael Grumley*

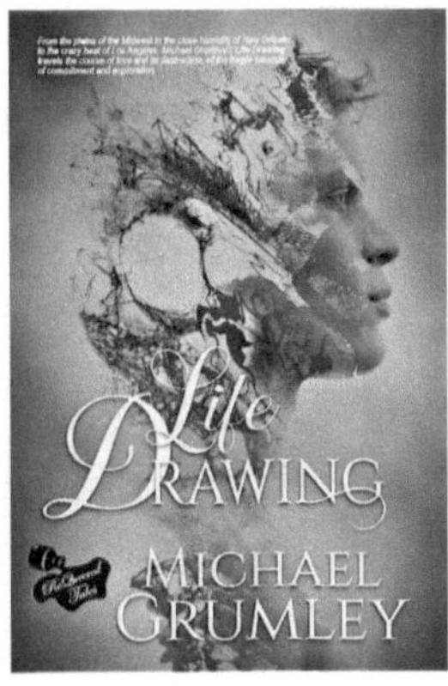

Born in Iowa to the sounds of Bob and Bing Crosby and the Dorsey brothers, Mickey grows up to the comforting images of his living room TV and the reassuring ruts of his parents' life. During the restless summer of his senior year in high school, drifting away from the girlfriend he could never quite love, Mickey spends a night with another boy, and his world will never be the same.

On a barge floating down the Mississippi, he falls in love with James, a black card player from New Orleans, and in time the two of them settle, bristling with sexual intensity, in the French Quarter – until a brief affair destroys James's trust and sends Mickey to the drugs and sordid life of Los Angeles.

"A simple, classic, engaging, and beautifully written tale of a boy who ran away from home, a man who didn't make it in the movies, an artist who found himself earlier than most and did it all west of the Mississippi, in places which, while very American, few Americans have ever been." — Andrew Holleran

"*Life Drawing* affirms the rich complexity of passion in the story of a small-town boy's difficult journey to manhood. Michael Grumley's crisp, direct language brings to life the demanding wonder of sexuality and the delicate tightrope of love between black men and white men." — Melvin Dixon

Originally published in 1991, it was Grumley's only novel, completed in the month's leading to his death from AIDS as he was cared for his lover Robert Ferro. This new edition contains the original foreword by Edmund White (*A Saint from Texas*) and afterword by George Stambolian (*Gay Men's Anthologies Men on Men*), close friends of the couple.

# JOHN PRESTON

## Murder and Mayhem
*Matt Lubbers-Moore*

**An Annotated Bibliography of Gay and Queer Males in Mystery, 1909-2018.**

Librarian and scholar Matt Lubbers-Moore collects and examines every mystery novel to include a gay or queer male in the English language starting with Arthur Conan Doyle's "The Man with the Watches". Authors, titles, dates published, publishers, book series, short blurbs, and a description of how involved the gay or queer male character is with the mystery are included for a full bibliographic background.

*Murder and Mayhem* will prove invaluable for mystery collectors, researchers, libraries, general readers, aficionados, bookstores, and devotees of LGBTQ studies. The bibliography is laid out in alphabetical order by author including the blurb and author notes, whether a hard boiled private eye, an amateur cozy, a suspenseful romance, or a police procedural. All subgenres within the mystery field are included: fantasy, science fiction, espionage, political intrigue, crime dramas, courtroom thrillers, and more with a definition guide of the subgenres for a better understanding of the genre as a whole.

A ReQueered Tales Original Publication.


## The Male Homosexual in Literature: A Bibliography *and* The Male Homosexual in Literature: Supplement (2020)
*Ian Young*

Ian Young's bibliography has served as a basic guide to English-language works of fiction, drama, poetry and autobiography concerned with male homosexuality or having male homosexual characters. Entries include titles published through 1980. Works are identified by author, title, place of publication, publisher, and date. For easy reference, entries are numbered and a title index is provided. Five highly acclaimed essays on gay literature by Ian Young, Graham Jackson and Dr. Rictor Norton, including essay on gay publishing, round out the listings. A title index of gay anthologies completes the work.

The present *Supplement* includes titles overlooked in the *Bibliography* Second Edition, plus works written before the 1981 cut-off date but published later, including works published for the first time in book form.

80

**If you enjoyed this book,
please help spread the word
by posting a short,
constructive review at
your favorite social media site
or book retailer.**

**We thank you, greatly,
for your support.**

**And don't be shy! Contact us!**

*For more information about current and future releases,
please contact us:*

E-mail: *requeeredtales@gmail.com*
Facebook (Like us!): www.facebook.com/ReQueeredTales
Twitter: @ReQueered
Instagram: www.instagram.com/requeered
Web: www.ReQueeredTales.com
Blog: www.ReQueeredTales.com/blog
Mailing list (Subscribe for latest news): https://bit.ly/RQTJoin

9 781951 092641